A seventy year old murder reaches across the years to tear apart the Crenshaws

Jim's sister stumbles upon an old boat; a boat that could be worth a fortune

A self-made man falls prey to his own hunger for women, money and influence. Only a miracle can save his marriage and his
business. Only a fortune can keep him from returning to the humble life he escaped so long ago.

Murder follows insanity as the pressure builds. The bankers want their money, and betrayal stalks Cole Prestcott's every move.

Jim Crenshaw faces his toughest test as a madman rips the family apart.

THE
COLLINGWOOD
LEGACY

THE COLLINGWOOD LEGACY

H J Gaudreau

Cover design by Margaret Schramke
www.moutainowlcreative.com

DEDICATION

For Eve – I've never had a better day in my life,

and tomorrow will be better.

Thomas – You're doing great pal, I miss you every day.

Mom – A gentlewoman too.

ACKNOWLEDGMENTS

Being an indie author is a lonely business. Unlike the big, and dying, publishing houses I don't have a host of people doing research, suggesting changes, correcting my spelling and editing my punctuation. But, I do have someone who believes in me, pushes me to be more creative, technically correct and, at the end of the day, take her out to dinner. While I may never be on the New York Times Best Seller List, I guarantee I'm on the Most Happy List. So, as they say in the school yard, "Na-na, my editor is better than yours."

Many, many thanks to Margaret Schramke.
Margaret is a creative guru and has a 'knack' for many things. Thanks so much for your help and advice. The music idea is a great one.

While in the Air Force, I deployed a lot of people to various hot spots around the world. Oddly, I believe it was harder on their families than on the members themselves. While none of the men and women, no...mostly kids....while none of my people were ever physically hurt, some were hurt in other ways. I love you all, each and every one of you.

Please Support:
The Wounded Warrior Project
www.woundedwarriorproject.org

THE

COLLINGWOOD

LEGACY

Chapter 1

Detroit, September 1931

Anna Lademan ran an iron along the length of a man's long sleeve shirt. Not satisfied with the result she sat the iron on its end and picked up a tall glass bottle with a yellow Vernor's Ginger Ale label and a cork sprinkler head. She gave the bottle a shake and scattered small droplets of water along the sleeve. Again taking up her iron she finished the sleeve, placed the shirt on a hanger, and hung it next to a dozen similar shirts. After a quick glance at the remaining baskets of laundry she placed her hands on her hips, bent backward, chin to the ceiling and sighed. At five cents a shirt she could not afford to rest, but she had earned a quick stretch.

Anna then took a woman's floral dress from her basket and began to spread it on her ironing board. She did this with a bit of nostalgia. Her wedding dress had been a pretty flowered dress like this one. They had met in late winter, 1916. Her husband Abell had been a big man, with a full head of red hair and a broad back. He was also a romantic; he loved flowers and the spring. He had insisted they marry when the earth was new, crops were in the ground, and flowers were blooming. So, in the spring of 1918, two weeks after Anna turned nineteen they married.

He died the next November. She always thought that ironic, so many people were celebrating the end of the Great War, and her husband, who had fought in it hadn't been there. Abell had gone off to war in January 1917. By the February of 1918 he was home, one leg left behind in France, but home. She had her man and they would be all right. Then came the Spanish flu. Abell left in the morning for his job at the post office, that night he came home with a cough, by evening he couldn't stand, and he died before morning. The speed of his death had always troubled Anna. She hadn't had time to tell him how much he meant to her, about their unborn child, to make plans. He hadn't seen his boy, didn't know how much his son looked like him; never tussled his hair. Anna's eyes began to tear.

In what seemed like the Almighty's ploy to drag her from the depths of depression a crash sounded from the small living room behind her. An instant later Anna's pride and joy, her son Ezra, exploded into the kitchen.

"David told me he needs help selling newspapers today," the boy announced.

There had been another murder; one of the Licavoli Squad had been gunned down by the Purple Gang. The Times had run an 'extra' edition.

"He said I'd get two cents for every paper I sell."

"How much does David get?" Anna asked with a knowing smile.

"He keeps three cents. He said it's because he's the official representative of the Times and he's responsible. Come on Ma, I can get us a half bushel of apples if I sell twenty-five papers."

Anna smiled a mother's smile and nodded at her boy. "Give me a kiss," she said and Ezra was out the door.

The fall of 1931 was cold and rainy. Today was no exception. David Puginwitz stood outside the Collingwood Manor apartment building and called to the pedestrians on

2

either side of the street. In the last hour he had sold only five newspapers, and the day was turning old. David pulled his collar up and shoved his hands deeper into his pockets. It worked for a moment but the strap of his newspaper bag slid off his small shoulder and the bag fell to the wet sidewalk.

Worried the newspapers would be ruined, David uttered a curse he'd learned from his father, removed his hands from his coat pockets and hiked the strap back to his shoulder. He then blew on his clenched fists and jammed them back into his pockets. If he hunched his shoulder the bag held its position. Sadly, and to David's never ending annoyance, the moment he relaxed his shoulder it fell to the sidewalk and the process was repeated.

As David pulled the newspaper bag to his shoulder for what seemed the fiftieth time he heard his friend Ezra's voice. The two boys greeted each other and immediately fell into a detailed discussion of their mutual obsession, the Detroit Tigers. David was a master of recalling the details of each of the summer's games. And, what he didn't remember he could invent. Ezra was a walking almanac of baseball statistics. Today, the conversation quickly turned to how bad this season had been and which players their team needed to replace. After a few minutes of baseball David pulled the newspaper bag from his shoulder and handed it to Ezra.

"I'm going inside to get warm. Don't let the bag get wet. I can't sell a wet newspaper."

David got all of two steps when Ezra suddenly exclaimed, "I almost forgot! Look what I've got!"

With that, Ezra pulled a tin from his coat pocket and opened it. Inside lay a small stack of baseball trading cards; several packs of cigarettes lay on top of the cards, and candy wrapped in foil lay scattered in one corner of the tin. Ezra put the newspaper bag on the sidewalk, causing David to grimace and handed one of the cigarette packs to David.

David examined the pack of Sweet Caporal cigarettes. "What do I want with these? I don't smoke. And I ain't startin' now. Ma says it makes your teeth fall out."

"Geeze, I know that. But, turn it over," Ezra said with a proud grin.

David did as he was told. To his delight on the back of the package was the prettiest Ty Cobb trading card he'd ever seen. "Holy smokes! This is great!" he explained. All thoughts of a warm stove disappeared.

Immediately David began offering combinations of his cards in trade for one of the new Ty Cobb cards. A brief argument over the value of various cards, new cards versus old cards, gum cards versus dry goods cards, a round of potential deals in which both boys tried to dump hated Yankee players on the other and soon a deal was struck. A few minutes later David was examining his new card when the possibility that Ezra had stolen the cigarettes crossed his mind.

"Where'd you get the cigarette packs Ezra?" David said with newly found suspicion. "If you lifted 'em and my Ma finds out..."

"I didn't steal nothin'!" Ezra then began to explain how Mr. Kacrozowski left two cartons of cigarettes and four shirts at his house. He was coming to the part about how a drunken Mr. Kaczorowski tried to grab his mother, and what she had called Mr. Kacrozowski when she hit him on the head with a frying pan, when a new, black four-door Chrysler coasted to a stop in front of the building. Instinctively, both boys ceased their chatter.

The front passenger door opened and a man with a

dark gray tweed overcoat stepped to the curb. He took a moment to study the street. His glance passed over the boys, then both sides of the street in each direction. Finally, he studied the windows of the nearby buildings. Satisfied, he nodded in the direction of the car. Two men climbed out of the back seat. One reflexively skimmed his hand over his hip and said, "I didn't bring my gun."

The other glanced at him, "I told ya, ya don't bring guns to a meeting like this." Walking around to the trunk of the car he removed a brown briefcase. The three men gathered on the curb. The driver shut off the engine, got out and walked to the front of the car. As if on command the three men, in matching strides, approached the steps to the building. Their shoes making a rhythmic 'smack...smack...smack' on the wet concrete as they approached the boys. The driver hurried around the car and ran to catch up.

Ezra knew something about the street. These guys were going to take his baseball cards and maybe shake down David for his paper money. Realizing it was too late to slip the tin back in his pocket he pushed it to the bottom of the newspaper bag. Then he stepped behind David.

The three men swept past the two boys without looking at them. The driver, now only a step or two behind, turned and flipped a silver dollar in their direction. "You kids! Keep an eye on my car," he snarled. Ezra tried to catch the coin and missed. The man stopped. The coin rang off the step and rolled to the sidewalk.

"C'mon Sol!" one barked, and the men entered the apartment building.

Chapter 2

Harry Keywell stood silently at the window Collingwood Manor, apartment 211 and watched the street. After ten minutes he finally said, "They're here."

Irving Milberg and Ray Bernstein both joined Harry at the window. Harry Fleisher remained sitting on the couch.

"I don't have any argument with Sol," Irving said.

"I don't want a witness," Harry replied.

"Look, Sol's alright. We leave him alone," Ray announced.

Fleisher stood up, "You sure about that Ray? I hope Sol doesn't bite us on the ass."

A moment later Keywell answered the door. Joe Lebowitz, Hymie Paul and Izzy 'The Rat' Sutker walked in. An awkward silence filled the room. Finally Bernstein broke the tension. "Boys, take a seat," he said and pointed to an oversized couch and easy chair.

Ray's eyes focused on the briefcase. Maybe this would go alright. Harry turned on Izzy Sutker. "I think we all know what this is about," he said.

"Sure Harry, we know we owe you some money..."

"Not just some, you owe us a lot of money Izzy."

"You know we're good for it," Sutker continued.

"I've heard that before," Ray said from across the room. "You've promised, and you've promised. You came to us and asked for a loan and I gave it to you. It makes me look like a fool. But the worst thing is that you idiots went and tried to cut us out of the business. Then you guys had the moxie to ask for another loan..."

"And we damned well gave it to you," Milberg cut in.

Ray glanced at Milberg, then continued, "Now you're telling us you need more time. We already gave you more time. After all that, you tell us you can't pay."

"What is this?" Harry demanded.

Hymie Paul concentrated on Harry's every move.

He glanced at Milberg and Bernstein then his partners Izzy Sutker and Joe Lebowitz. Finally he said, "I think we can work something out." He patted the case. "I've got half of your money right here. It'll take us a little time, but we should have the rest of the money to you in three months."

Keywell erupted, "Half? You come here with half? What the hell do you think this is?"

Almost imperceptibly Ray shook his head no.

Fleisher put his hands out as if to pat the air. "Boys, lets all be calm. Look, let's not get worked up about this. I've got some cold beer in the basement. I'll go get us some and we'll work out some terms."

The decision had been made. Ray, Irv and Harry Keywell all looked at each other. A silent agreement was reached.

"Yeah, I think you're right," Ray said.

Fleisher walked out into the hall and headed for the street. The car would be idling in back in three minutes.

"We need it all," Irv said a moment later.

Harry Keywell moved to the next window, his hand slipped inside his jacket and gripped his pistol.

"Look, we ain't got that much, we're lucky to have this," Hymie's throat had tightened; his voice was almost a squeal.

Irv grinned, "I don't think you understand. We employ you, we give you a good territory, and you knock over our runs, you don't pay your debts, you steal from us!"

Irv's voice was getting louder, he took a breath then very slowly he said, "We...need...our...money...NOW." His fist slammed onto the table.

Lebowitz glanced at his two partners. "Look, Irv, I understand. We'll get you the rest. But it will take time, we'll need a month."

Milberg looked at Keywell and shrugged, "Seems like an awful long time don't you think?"

Keywell pulled his gun from his pocket. "Times up."

David stooped to pick up the silver dollar. Ezra had failed to catch it when Sol had tossed the coin. "Those guys look like gangsters, Ezra. We've got real life gangsters right here!"

Ezra was staring at the door where the men had disappeared. David sat down on the wet step, Ezra joined him. Still shaken neither boy said anything. After a few moments Ezra stood up and announced, "I'm going home."

"What! You can't leave. Neither can I. That guy gave us a dollar to watch his car. That's a lot of money. If we leave he'll come back and get us. We have to stay right here." David was older and so he must be smarter. Ezra sat back on the step.

"I think those guys were the Purple Gang," David said a few minutes later. "There was a story about them in the paper last week. I saw their picture. They're famous."

Suddenly a series of pops could be heard from a long distance away. Both boys jumped to their feet, eyes searching the street as they turned a slow circle. Another round of gunfire and this time the two friends could identify the location of the sound. A one they turned and looked to the second floor.

A moment later the building's front door burst open and the driver of the car ran out carrying a brown briefcase. Taking the stairs two at a time he collided with Ezra and David knocking the boys over and falling to the sidewalk. The case flew from his hand scattering several bundles of cash on the sidewalk. The case slid across the sidewalk and under the big car.

"What the...," David cried. Ezra rolled across the sidewalk and came to rest against the Chrysler.

"Gimme that," Sol Levine shouted at Ezra as he jumped to his feet. Sol grabbed the newspaper bag and pulled. The boy was jerked forward and fell to the sidewalk, landing on the side of his face with a yell. Sol dragged the bag from the boy's grasp. Then he scooped up the bundles of cash laying on the sidewalk and stuffed them into the bag. After a quick glance at the door of the building he ran to the Chrysler. In a moment the engine roared and the car was turning the corner onto Grand Boulevard.

Seconds later three men tumbled from the door of the apartment building, each man carrying a pistol. They ran down the stairs, past Ezra and David and into the center of the street. The three men turned in circles looking for the car. It was too late. One man spotted the briefcase laying on the curb. He picked it up, looked inside then threw it back on the street. "The little shit! He took it all'" the man yelled.

"Ray, I'm gonna kill that little S.O.B.," another whispered.

The three men then walked back into the building. It was as if David and Ezra were invisible. Ezra dabbed his bloody nose and began to cry.

9

Chapter 3

Detroit was an ethnic melting pot. Poles, Czechs, Germans, French, Italians, and Jews. Each had their own gang. But the meanest and easily the most feared was a gang founded by four Jewish Russian immigrants, the Bernstein brothers, Abe, Joe, Raymond and Izzy. The boys began their life of crime with simple street jobs; muggings, purse snatching and "smash and grab" robberies. They quickly progressed to shaking down local merchants. Legend had it that the gang got its name after hitting a meat market. "Those boys are rotten, purple like the color of rotten meat," the shopkeeper supposedly said. The name stuck.

The country should have seen the rise in violence the eighteenth amendment to the Constitution would bring. Michigan had instituted its own version of Prohibition, the Damon Act, a year earlier with disastrous results. With the Damon Act's implementation the manufacture and distribution of alcohol became illegal everywhere in the state. Within months "rum running" was the fastest growing profession in the Motor City. As one newspaper complained, "the average citizen can make a year's wages in one month by becoming a gangster or bootlegger."

After every arrest the rum runners invented an even more ingenious method for smuggling and distributing booze. The police tried to stop the flow of liquor to no avail. The money, the resources of the gangs, the corruption and the intimidation was too much. Liquor flowed from Windsor Canada across the Detroit River and into the nation's fourth largest city in quantities no one could imagine.

The Purples knew a golden opportunity when they saw one. Soon they were the most powerful and feared gang in Detroit. Seventy-five percent of the illegal liquor coming into the United States from Canada came through Detroit. Its twenty-eight mile long Detroit River was just a mile from Canada and dotted with thousands of coves, boat yards, nooks and crannies - it was a smuggler's dream.

At first, the Purples tried to keep the Detroit river front to themselves. It was an impossible task. There were too many rivals; the Purples couldn't kill them all. But, they could impose a territorial system. Nothing moved along the docks of Detroit without the permission of the Purples. If it did, a savage lesson was taught. The Purples employed the new Thompson submachine gun as their business card. The 'Chopper' could cut a man in half in the blink of an eye. It ensured their rivals knew who had done the shooting and it left an impression.

The Purples dominated the Detroit underworld for years. No one went to jail. No one talked. The Purple Gang simply owned the police and killed anyone who complained. Business was business. The Detroit underworld flourished; the East Side Gang, "Singing Sam" Catalanotte, Chester "Big Chet" La Mare and the rest were, for the moment, happy with the arrangement.

The Purple Gang's lock on the waterfront and bootlegging couldn't last. The fall of 1931 saw an unprecedented opportunity for the competition. The American Legion was having its national convention in Detroit and the demand for liquor would surpass even the Purple's capacity to supply it. Now rivals from all over the country were slipping into the city. Worse yet, some of the gang's own associates began to moonlight. This didn't go unnoticed by the Bernstein brothers.

Foremost among the moonlighters were three new members of the 'Third Avenue Navy'. The Navy was part of the smuggling operation of the Purple Gang. Equipped with some of the fastest boats produced on the Great Lakes and armed with Thompson submachine guns the Navy made the run across the Lake and stopped others from making the same trip. The Navy's running fights with the U.S. Coast Guard were big news and widely reported.

The Navy was a major part of the supply side of the Purple Gang's operation. It was highly paid work, members were lost as a result of the work and to arrest. New members were recruited continuously. With the coming convention the Navy had to increase its size. New recruits were brought in without proper vetting. Hymie Paul, Isadore "Izzy" Sutker, and Joe Lebowitz were three of those new recruits.

That summer, in a show of supreme stupidity the three began diverting portions of each run. The lightened loads were not unnoticed, but good fortune smiled on the three double-crossers. A negotiation was taking place with the North Side Gang of Chicago. The Gang was losing its power in Chicago and the Purples were exploring ways of moving in on Al Capone's Chicago Outfit. A partnership seemed possible. The Purples simply didn't have the time to devote to these relatively small losses.

Unable to stand prosperity the three made another incredibly bad decision. They decided to start 'making book'. They set the odds, took bets from all comers, including the opposition, and counted on the betters to lose. The scheme should have worked, but the boys were swimming with the sharks.

A great pastime of the day was motor boat racing.

Different categories of boats from sail to yacht, professional and amateur, were raced on the Detroit River to the delight of the populace. One of the more popular races was the "Gentleman's Motor Yacht" race, and the most famous of those racers was the "Volstead Act," a 34 foot locally built Chris-Craft.

Not knowing the monthly river races were fixed Sutker, Paul and Lebowitz bet big on the "Volstead Act." Unfortunately, they lost to members of Detroit's Italian East Side Gang. The East Side Gang, with its heavy New York connections and Sicilian pedigree was not in the habit of overlooking debts. To say that losing a bet to the East Side Gang was bad business was like saying Babe Ruth was just a ball player. It didn't come close to describing the reality.

Hymie and the boys knew of only one way out. Trading on their association with the rest of the Purple Gang they bought a hundred gallons of Canadian booze on credit. They then watered down the whiskey and sold it, undercutting the Purples' price for the same watered down booze. It didn't cover the debt, but the boys figured to make the rest up through their gambling operation.

The big score, and their only hope of salvation, was the boat races. Hymie and his friends only succeeded in proving that stupid really can strike the same spot twice.

They again set odds on a river race, again the race was fixed, and again they lost big to the East Side Gang.

Forgetting the "First Rule of Holes", the boys didn't stop digging. Since the scheme had worked before they again approached their associates in the Purple Gang and again made a deal. A hundred gallons of Canadian whiskey were purchased, all on credit. Again they diluted the stock and undersold the market. It was one time too many for the

Bernstein brothers. Hymie and the boys had forgotten they were cutting into the Purple's trade. To make matters worse, they didn't make enough money on the watered down booze. They couldn't pay back the Purples and they couldn't pay off the East Side Gang. They had succeeded in provoking not one, but two of the most powerful criminal organizations in the United States.

Paul, Sutker, and Lebowitz were already dead and had simply been waiting for the Purples to tell them.

Chapter 4

April – This Year

Herman James Crenshaw preferred to be called "Jim". It never became an issue, but this morning a new teller at the bank had insisted he show two forms of identification. Ordinarily this wouldn't bother Jim; in fact, he was a big believer of better safe than sorry, but in this instance the young man knew Jim personally. Not only that, but Jim was putting money into his checking account, not taking it out.

He knew everyone in town, they knew him. Jim had umpired the kid's Little League games and coached his pee-wee basketball team. He knew it was "procedure," but knowing everyone was why he'd returned to a small town and not retired in D.C. or Boston or some other big city.

Plus, the whole idea of showing two forms of identification to put money INTO his account struck him as absurd. Jim didn't care who put money into his account; he just didn't want anyone taking it out.

Leaving the building he shook his head, smiled and started his truck. He had two more stops on his morning errands. He needed to stop at the dollar store and pick up five packs of suckers, five packs of number 2 pencils and a pack of colored paper. Apparently, Eve's kids had earned a reward of a sucker and had also broken, stolen or sharpened to extinction the five packs of pencils he bought two weeks ago. Computers and the internet hadn't made pencils obsolete, at least in Eve's classroom. Next was a quick stop at the combination feed and seed store and grain elevator office to check on the price of fertilizer. Here he parked his truck in front of the building, rolled both the passenger and driver's windows up to the two-thirds position and got out. His dog Molly watched him walk away from the truck with sad eyes, gave one bark, then curled up in Jim's seat to wait for his return.

April was a wonderful time of year, the snow was gone, there was always the chance of a tee shirt and shorts day, opening day of baseball season proved the Union would last at least another year, and best of all those fields around the house just looked anxious to get to work. Jim had planted corn the last three years and was beginning to think this might be a year for soybeans. Crop rotation was something he should pay attention to he knew, but he hadn't owned the farm long enough for it to matter. Now, for some reason he couldn't explain, it mattered. Jim had retired from the Air Force just six years ago. He'd worked for a defense contractor for a little while, found that to be an experience similar to a root canal without Novocain and quit. Four years ago he and his wife Eve had purchased their little sixty-acre farm. They'd taken a year to build a cottage style home, a barn and equipment shed and then planted their first crop. Jim grimaced as he recalled that first year. He termed that year's crop a "learning experience." Eve called it a disaster. Since then Jim had learned about seed depth, acid balance, seed spacing, nitrogen requirements, soil types, nematodes, a multitude of bugs, various fungi, and a host of other things that he'd never thought of before. He loved it.

Returning to the farm Jim parked the pickup in front of the garage, opened the truck door and moved aside as Molly rushed to be the first to the house. Jim walked to the rear of the truck, grabbed an armful of bags and headed for the house. Placing the bags on the kitchen table he filled Molly's water bowl, stood, then noticed the light on the telephone answering machine. Pushing "Play" he heard the welcome voice of his sister, Sherrie.

Chapter 5

The light turned red and Sol Levine braked the car to a stop. He checked the rear-view mirror for what must have been the fiftieth time. He had just witnessed three men murdered. He was on the edge of panic. What had he been thinking? In the confusion of the murders he'd grabbed the briefcase and run. He'd taken money from the Purple Gang; it was a death sentence.

His forehead was covered with sweat. He took off his brown fedora and wiped the hatband with his handkerchief. His hands were shaking. Sol had to get out of Detroit, he knew that, he just didn't know how. He checked the rear-view mirror again.

Sol had circled Detroit twice trying to decide what to do. Evening had turned to night; night was becoming morning. No one was behind him…for now. There would be. He thought he spotted a familiar Packard. Frantically he pressed the accelerator. Sol came to Jefferson Avenue and smashed the brake, attempted to downshift and missed the gear. The transmission gave a loud clatter and rattled the shift lever in his hand. He found third gear and accelerated as he turned left on Jefferson to parallel the Detroit River. He had to calm down.

Sol took a deep breath. He passed Owens Park, then Memorial Park. Suddenly Sol was inspired. He'd worked for Izzy Sutker before. A couple of times he'd helped Izzy unload booze at a boathouse just down the street. Once, Izzy had taken him on a run to Canada. They'd crossed at night, loaded the booze on the boat and come back all in one night.

He'd made fifty bucks for one night's work. The more he thought about it the better Sol liked his idea. What better place to hide out than in the Purples own boathouse

He slowed when he came to the Detroit Water Works building. A little further and he'd found a small dirt path, more a driveway than a side street. The big Chrysler crept silently down the small two-lane path, coasting to a stop at the water's edge. Sol turned the lights of the car off and carefully studied his rear-view mirrors. Nothing moved. No one had followed him. Sol had never owned a gun, he wished he did now. This was not a totally safe place, but it was the only place he was sure they wouldn't be looking.

He stepped down from the car and allowed his eyes to adjust to the darkness. After a moment he was calm, well, as calm as he could be right now. Sol carefully examined his surroundings. He was alone. No, maybe not. Maybe they were waiting for him. He couldn't decide. He stood next to the open door, engine running. Again Sol checked his surroundings. No one was here. He was almost sure. He bent into the car to shut off the engine. If someone was going to grab him it was going to be now.

With a grimace Sol turned the key. The engine died. He listened to the night. A horn blared in the distance. Street noise filtered down between the warehouses and garages along Jefferson. Against Windsor's lights he could see a working boat making its way toward Lake Huron. Sol relaxed just a little.

Nervously Sol fingered the newspaper bag. He glanced left, then right, took a deep breath and sprinted across the parking lot to a small boathouse and slipped inside. Happy that he hadn't been gunned down before he reached the door Sol sat down on the floor and caught his breath. He started a nervous laugh. After a few minutes he stood up, cracked the door open, and peered into the night.

Nothing moved.

Sol turned and groped his way across the building. Eventually outstretched hands found a workbench. Reaching into his pocket he found a match box. Fishing one out he gripped it in his fist and flicked his thumbnail against the match head. It flared and Sole tried to get his bearings. Quickly the match burned down; he struck another. He fixed the layout of the building in his mind and began to work his way to the end of a long workbench. There, he searched the wall.

It took a minute, but soon Sol found what he was looking for. He struck another match, turned up the wick in an oil lantern and a quiet light illuminated the inside of the building. Across from the bench, resting peacefully at its moorings sat a beautiful Chris-Craft cruiser.

Sol didn't pause to admire the boat. Taking a small step stool from its hook Sol placed it on the edge of the dock. A moment later he was aboard the boat and opening the door to the small cabin below. There he slid into the cabin booth and emptied the newspaper bag on the table. Out fell a small tin, several newspapers and packs of money.

Sol was amazed. The sight of the money didn't erase stupid, but it did make Sol brave. He quickly counted the cash, twenty packs of hundreds. Twenty thousand dollars per pack, four hundred thousand dollars. He grinned. This was the big score. Sol would be sitting pretty the rest of his life, all he had to do was grab his girl and get out of town. He could easily get lost in Canada somewhere. He'd always heard that Toronto was a pretty town, maybe Montreal...the possibilities were nearly endless.

Sol picked up the tin. It was a Blue Bird caramel container. Opening the top he shook out the contents. A pile of baseball cards, a few coins, several packs of cigarettes and a handful of caramels. He grinned, unwrapped a caramel and stuffed it into his mouth; this was perfect. Sol pocketed the coins, some of the caramels and two packs of cigarettes. He scooped the rest back into the tin. Pressing the cover onto the can he shoved it into the bottom of the newspaper bag. Still this was serious business. He had to think.

Gradually the grin returned. Sol got up from the bench seat and made his way to the boat's forward cabin. Here he removed a board from the floor to expose a small compartment. This compartment extended forward three feet and was specifically built to hold five cases of Canadian whiskey. Sol had loaded this very compartment when he'd gone on the trip with Izzy. Normally, no one would find it. But Sol knew that his friends were also his enemies and they knew about the compartment as well as he did.

Leaving the boat and returning to the workbench Sol took a few moments to find the tools he needed. He tied on a carpenter's apron, shoved the tools he'd selected in the apron and hurried back to the cruiser. Feeling better about his chances by the moment Sol sprinted up the small foot stool and bounced onto the cruiser's deck. Moving into the cabin, he pushed the compartment cover out of his way and lay on the floor. Then, turning on his back Sol wedged himself into the whiskey compartment.

He lay there for a moment, head and shoulders in the compartment, heels on the deck. The edge of the compartment cutting into the small of his back.

Reaching with his right hand he grabbed the lantern and sat it on the floor of the compartment above his left shoulder. Now he had light. Removing a screwdriver from the carpenter's apron he reached above his head deep into the compartment and began removing the brass screws which held the end board.

After a few minutes he had all eight out and was able to pull the board away from its frame. Sol then took the canvas newspaper bag, wrapped it in newspapers, and wedged it into the bilge of the cruiser. Forty minutes later he had replaced the endboard and painted a fresh coat of shellac over the entire compartment. No one would find any evidence of his handiwork.

He crawled out of the hole, stood and rubbed his lower back. Then Sol took a bottle of Windsor Canadian from behind the captain's seat and sat down at the settee. A grin began to grow; Sol lifted the bottle, toasted the now dead "Captain" Izzy and took a long pull. He imagined his girl Dolly in the finest Chicago fashions; she'd look just like Gretta Garbo. He pictured her leaning on a long bar and whispering, "Give me a whiskey, ginger ale on the side, and don't be stingy, baby." Just like Garbo herself.

He'd get himself a new suit and look just like Cagney. He had it planned. The grin broaden to a smile, things were looking up. Sol killed the light and went to the front of the boathouse. A narrow walkway extended along the wall to the opening and around the side of the building. It allowed operation of a large, garage-like door into the boathouse. Sol could just squeeze around the wall without falling in the river.

Sol liked this, it allowed him to see the surrounding area from a place no one would suspect. He studied the shadows between the buildings, the light was low, the morning sun was just peeking over Windsor. Satisfied that no one was watching Sol jumped to the shore then sprinted to the Chrysler. Starting the car Sol grinned again. "Who knows? Maybe Dolly Eleanor Grongoski would even become an honest woman," he thought.

Chapter 6

Dolly Grongoski was not a shy wallflower. Raised on the poor, sandy soil of northern Michigan she was used to long days, hard work and hard people. Small, just five foot four inches tall and skinny, too skinny by her own standards, she had left the farm for a job in Detroit the day she turned eighteen. That was just under a year ago. She'd fallen in with hard people and lived a hard life, but she was proud of the fact that never, not once, had any of them been able to take advantage of her. She could out think them, and she wasn't afraid of a fight.

The one bright spot in the past year had been Sol. She didn't love him, he wasn't very smart and he could never make it on a farm back home, but he had a kind heart and he gave her lots of things and spent money on her when he had it. It was a good deal for both of them; she only worried about getting pregnant.

But Sol was not her dream. Dolly intended to be someone, she did not want to end up like her mother or cousins. Spending the rest of her life ironing someone else's shirts or feeding chickens was not her idea of a life. She would be a nurse or a school teacher or a secretary to some big executive.

To add color to the dream Dolly liked to take the bus all the way out to Ann Arbor on her days off. That's where she was this morning. She would walk across the University campus and pretend she was a student. She would sit on the benches, admire the clothes the girls wore, and dream about having something more than a tenth grade education.

At noon Dolly began to get hungry. She used the engineering building's archway to leave the campus and made her way south on University Avenue. Soon she came to the East Quadrangle dormitory. She waited until several students were entering the building and joined the crowd.

A blond haired boy politely held the door and Dolly was in. Carefully she explored the building. It only took a few minutes and she'd found what she had come for, the cafeteria line. The line moved steadily along and Dolly closely watched the process at the door. A student sitting on a stool fought off boredom while checking each person's University identification card. Several of the students claimed they had forgotten their ID card or had otherwise lost it. The ID checker then consulted a list, found the name, then passed the offending party into the land of food and ice cream. Satisfied, Dolly gave up her position in line.

A few minutes later she was again outside the building's main entrance. She waited until one of the school's few women students approached, then leaned against a light post and began to cry. The young woman immediately came to her aid.

"Hi...ahhhh....are you all right?" she asked.

"Nooooo." Dolly moaned. "I just broke up with my boyfriend, and I want to go home." She tucked her chin down to her chest and gave a few silent sobs.

"Oh honey, that's tough." The girl put a hand on Dolly's shoulder. "We've all been through it. Maybe you should go back to your room and lay down."

"No, I can't, I've got to go to class," Dolly sobbed.

"Well, you can't go to class crying like this. Come on, I'll walk you back to your room." The girl gently took Dolly's elbow.

"Thank you," Dolly said and let herself be led along. After a few steps, in her most pitiful voice, Dolly said, "What's your name?"

"I'm Mary Ellen Bennett. What's yours?"

"I'm Debbie Williams." A few steps later Dolly shook herself, stood to her maximum height and in her most confident voice announced. "Oh, I'm alright. I'm not going to let him ruin my life. I really should go to class, it'll be fine."

Mary Ellen smiled, "That's the spirit. You'll have another boyfriend in no time, you'll see."

Mary Ellen didn't take a great deal of convincing and soon she went on her way. Dolly waited until the girl was out of sight then slipped back into the dormitory and rejoined the line for the cafeteria.

It wasn't such a pleasant day for Sol. He was on a frantic search for her. Nervously watching his rearview mirror Sol visited the diner where Dolly worked, checked her apartment and searched her favorite stores. The afternoon was slipping away and, afraid to return to his own shabby room, Sol took up residence in a bar on Fort Street. There he began calling her boarding house phone every thirty minutes.

At six that evening Dolly was back in Detroit climbing the stairs to her flat when Mrs. Boardman, the boarding house owner, stopped her.

"Dolly, a man's been looking for you. Wouldn't say his name. I don't approve of men in the building miss. You know the rules."

Dolly thought a moment, decided it had to be Sol, then examined the exceedingly large woman. Using her most charming smile Dolly said, "He's my cousin, I'm sure this is about my mother. She's very sick you know." The woman eyed Dolly. "I'm sure,' she said, then slammed her door.

Shortly after Dolly had closed her apartment door the phone at the end of the hall rang. It was answered by one of the building's tenants. Seconds later the loud cry, "Dolly, ya got a lover on the line," careened through the house. A minute later Dolly was talking to Sol.

"Dolly, babe, where ya been?" he didn't wait for an answer. "Never mind, I've got some big news. We've hit the big time baby. I need to pick you up. I'll be there in ten minutes. Meet me in back of the building.' And, before Dolly could argue Sol had hung up.

They drove to Grosse Pointe just to get out of the city and let Sol explain what he had seen and done. Dolly at first panicked. She wanted out of the car and intended to run as far from Sol as she could. She was no fool and knew what happened to people who crossed the Purples.

It took a while, but eventually he convinced her to calm down. When he did, Dolly began to think the situation over very carefully. Sol said he had a lot of money, more than a lot. And he wasn't lying. He was too scared to be lying, she could tell. She asked a few questions and slowly it came to her. This was legit. Dolly was convinced; this was their chance for a big score and to get out of Detroit.

They ate an early dinner in Hamtramck, then headed to the river. Dolly insisted on stopping at her apartment for a change of clothes and to pick up some keepsakes she'd brought from home. Then they headed to Sol's apartment.

Chapter 7

Sol rented a room above a small meat market. Mr. Spadoff went home for the day at six, the market was closed, lights off. They circled the block twice. Sol was careful to keep his speed up and tried not to draw attention to the car. Nothing moved, no one sat in some dark car. It looked normal.

On the third trip past the store they slowed to a crawl and Dolly peered through the windows inside the market. A small red glow flared in the back behind the meat counter. Dolly spotted the cigarette just as Sol began to brake, intending to park next to the front door.

"GO, GO, GO!!" she yelled.

Sol stepped on the gas and the Chrysler lurched forward, caught its wind and sped off. The door of the meat market burst open and two men ran out. By the time they reached their car Sol and Dolly were ghosts in the night.

Thirty minutes later, certain they'd not been followed, Sol turned off Jefferson Avenue and coasted to a stop ten yards from the boathouse. Sol moved Dolly's two bags from the car to the Chris-Craft.

"We're all set doll. I just need one thing. Run up there to the market and get me a razor and some blades would ya? A man's gotta look presentable when we get to Canada."

"Where's the market?" Dolly asked.

Sol walked Dolly to the door and pointed. "Around that shed, up the hill, between those two warehouses and down the street to the corner." Dolly agreed and was on her way.

Sol watched Dolly as she rounded the small tool shed and walked to the alley leading to the street. When she passed from sight he headed into the boathouse. Sol boarded the Chris-Craft and quickly checked the forward liquor hole. No one had tampered with it; the money was safe. He jumped to the side of the boathouse and grabbed a hose connected to two fifty-five gallon drums. The drums were on an elevated stand and gravity fed the hose. It took twenty minutes to fill the fuel tanks.

When he had finished Sol checked his watch and muttered, "Damn, bet she got lost. Where the hell is she?" Unfortunately, it was a question that Sol would never have answered.

Chapter 8

The setting west sun blinded Ray Bernstein as he peered at the street from his fifth floor apartment. It had not been a good day. They had hunted Sol Levine, they'd hunted him like the dog he was, and the game bag was empty.

They had come close. Somehow he'd spotted Ray's men in the market. Ray wondered if Sol had been tipped off. He shook his head. No time to think about that now. The trail had gone cold after that. They'd gone to his girlfriend's rooming house. Nothing. Some of the girls played cute, but none could say where Dolly and Sol were. Like a wounded animal the two had gone to ground. It would be hard to find them. Ray pulled the blinds closed just as the phone rang.

"Who the hell is that?" he spat. No one in the room answered, they didn't know, how could they? Ray picked up the receiver, "Yeah," he growled. Slowly his face grew hard. He listened closely to the little man on the other end of the line.

"A friend." Ray knew there was no such thing; this mutt was looking for a reward. Word had already gotten out. "How the hell did that happen?" Ray wondered. He slurped his drink then nodded his head. "All right, if it's on the level then twenty-five hundred, not a dollar more." A moment later Ray hung the receiver on the hook. "Some small timer spotted Sol down on the river. He's in the boathouse."

Milberg and Keywell each rose without saying a word. Milberg picked up his shotgun. The damn thing was a ten-gauge, sawed off to fit under an overcoat. It could blow a man in half. It had come to think of it. Ray hated that smell.

Thirty minutes later Berstein's Cadillac coasted to a stop outside the Detroit River boathouse. The three men got out, checked their guns and quietly closed the door to the car. Silently they walked to the boathouse.

Darkness was spreading across the eastern sky. It didn't change anything, the city was never quiet. The sounds of distant boats, cars, trucks and factory whistles were part of the background like a cicada's song in the summer. The men reached the door. Milberg took his position on the left and leveled his shotgun at the handle. Ray stood on the right and did the same with his Tommy gun. Harry prepared to kick in the door.

"On the count of three." Harry whispered.

Chapter 9

Dolly gave the kid at the store a dollar and a quarter and told him to keep the change. She was feeling lucky tonight and in a few hours a dime wouldn't mean squat. She nearly sprinted down the store steps. Then she remembered there were men after her, if she wasn't careful she'd be dead in the time it took to pull the trigger. It would happen, right here, right now.

She stopped on the top step and carefully studied the few cars parked on the street. Nothing moved, no glow from a cigarette. Then she shifted her attention to the windows and doorways overlooking her route to the alley. Nothing.

Satisfied, but not comfortable, Dolly took a deep breath. She knew she should walk, blend in, be part of the background. She couldn't help herself, she stepped off the shop step and began to run. To Dolly it took hours, but finally she reached the dirt path between the two small warehouses. Slowing to a careful walk she edged down the path. Sol's little shortcut would save her at least five minutes. Down a small hill, behind another warehouse, around the tool shed and she would pop out just thirty yards from the boathouse.

She was nearly giddy as she rounded the warehouse. She was going to be rich. Sol had told her and she could tell he was on the level. He wasn't acting. She knew that. Sol had been so scared he could barely light a cigarette.

She reached the tool shed, rounded its corner and stopped. About ten yards in front of the shed were two stacks of railroad ties and wood planks. Darkness had covered the city, but lights from Windsor and boats on the river lit up the boathouse and the ground around it.

Crouching behind the two stacks of wood she could see four, no five policemen. "Where the hell had these guys come from?" She'd only been gone fifteen minutes. Dolly quickly ducked into the shed; panic grabbed her by the throat, and she started to shiver. "Buck fever, it's just buck fever," she muttered to herself. Standing in the dark she imagined the feel of bullets tearing into her body. "No, no, no…get ahold of yourself honey," she whispered.

She'd gone to the market, just for some razor blades, maybe a chocolate. Then they were going to Rondeau, Canada. From there Long Point, Buffalo and finally Toronto. Sol had it all planned, no one would stop the boat, it was too fast. He said there was money, plenty of money, and it was all loaded on the boat. But there were cop cars parked behind the warehouse; "Shit, shit, shit!" she screamed to herself. She thought about running, but surely the cops would hear her, better to wait them out here. The building was small, a bench on one side about six feet long. A window on the other side covered in dirt and cobwebs.

Dolly stared out of the window. She moved to her right and looked along the edge of the parking area, she could see two policemen there. She thought she saw another to the far right of the woodpiles. She shifted to her left and, SHIT! There was a cop right there! She could see his outline through the window. He was standing with his back to the shed and pissing on a weed. Instinctively Dolly ducked. He hadn't seen her. She wondered if he heard her open the door to the shed. Dolly was trapped.

Several minutes went by. Carefully she raised her head and peeked out of the window. The cop moved back to the woodpile. Steam rolled off the weed. After a few minutes Dolly spotted more cops on the other side of the parking lot. She was sure there were more out there, but night was closing in, she couldn't tell. She knelt on the shed floor. She had to think; cops everywhere, Solly in the boathouse. Maybe they already had him? No, why would they be surrounding the place if they had him? They were going to shoot him, that was it, they were just going to pump the building full of lead and be done with it.

She wanted to run. Escape, that was it, she needed to escape. She could open the door and run, she'd be up the alley and down the street before... That wouldn't work. Dolly mulled the word around in her mind 'escape'.

She could picture a rabbit, safe inside a pile of brush. Her father would climb on top of the pile and jump up and down and pretty soon that rabbit felt like it needed to escape. It would come flying out of the pile and never, ever, did the rabbit make it past Daddy's shotgun. Dolly found a stool and carefully, silently placed it in front of the window. Putting her chin on her hands she positioned her eyes just above the window frame. She settled in to see what was going to happen.

She watched the cops. And they watched the boathouse. Dolly sat there for ten minutes, then twenty. She couldn't figure out how to warn Sol. Movement to her left surprised her and her head snapped up. Through the moist, heavy air she could see the outline of a big car. Its headlights were off. She couldn't hear the engine and thought that strange. Then she realized, the ignition had been turned off, it had simply coasted down the little hill and ghosted to a stop in front of the boathouse.

Three men got out; they all had guns, one carried a

machine gun. It was Ray, Harry, and that other guy, Millsomething.

She could picture his face, mean, deeply cut features and eyes that never smiled. They started walking toward the boathouse. Dolly's mind raced. They were here for Sol, they had to be here to kill Sol.

The cops. Surely they would stop the three killers. Silently she begged the cops to stop them. The cops didn't move. They just watched. How could she warn Sol? She tried to figure out what to do. She could scream, but it was too late. The men kept walking.

They were nearly at the door. She didn't understand. Sol? Where was her Sol? Suddenly two of the cops to her left lifted a spotlight and flipped it on. An instant later a second light exploded from behind a stack of crates lighting the three men up like strippers on a vaudeville stage. Then, nearly in unison, a chorus of voices shouted, "HANDS UP."

Men wearing Detroit police coats rushed at Harry, Ray and the other one. Dolly watched as Ray began to raise his gun, but someone shouted, "DON'T DO IT RAY! You'll be dead before you get a shot off."

Ray stared into the light. She could see him clearly. Ray squinted, held his hand up to shade his eyes. He was trying to see past the spotlights, trying to decide. The wet night air suddenly turned silent. Even the trucks on Jefferson had stopped their distant noise. The sea gulls, "rats with wings" Solly called them, had stopped their squawks. Out there, behind the lights the only sound was of men with guns. She watched Ray slowly raise his left arm and toss his Tommy gun with his right. A rush of feet and the three killers were swarmed with police officers.

The three men were slammed against the wall of the

boathouse. One yelled a curse, but she couldn't tell exactly what he said. A big man wearing a plain long coat handcuffed one of the prisoners then slapped him hard on the back of the head. She wasn't sure, but she thought it was Harry. Several police had the Purples by the arms, others held onto their coats. The big man pushed between the officers and put handcuffs on the other two.

She used to be afraid of them. She hated it when Sol took her to their clubs. Someone always got beat up or backjacked or shot or just something. Now…hell, now they looked like schoolboys she thought.

A patty wagon arrived. The three were marched, pushed, and shoved to the back of the wagon. One tripped and fell to his knees. The big man kicked him then pushed him to the patty wagon doors and swung them open.

Another cop tossed a crate on the ground. "Step up, get in and shut up," a voice said. All three climbed inside.

The police picked up the guns laying on the ground; one pointed at the car and another quickly ran over and got in. In a moment the car was driving away. She hadn't seen her Sol; maybe they hadn't found him. She began to hope.

Then two men opened the door of the boathouse. Sol, his hands cuffed at his waist, stepped into the light of the spotlights. A policeman, his hand under Sol's right arm walked with him to the back of the wagon. They made Sol climb in.

She wanted to scream; she wanted to stop them. She wanted to be rich and it had been right there, just one more hour and they would have been in Canada.

The truck backed up a few feet, stopped then lurched forward up the long two track driveway to the street. Sol was gone.

Dolly couldn't believe what had happened. What was she going to do? Would the rest of the Purples come after her? She didn't know. They might think she helped Sol plan the job. They might think she knew where the money was. She peeked out of the tool shed window again. If the Purples found her she was dead, she knew that. The last of the cops were leaving.

Dolly sat down, she needed to think. They would come after her, she was sure of that. She made up her mind. She needed to leave. Not just this boatyard, she needed to leave the city. When the last of the police cars had rounded the corner Dolly slipped out of the tool shed and began to run. She didn't know where she was or where she was going, but she knew she couldn't stay here.

Chapter 10

The Collingwood Manor murder trial was big news. All of the Detroit dailies, the Chicago Tribune and the Cleveland Plain Dealer sent reporters. Wayne County Prosecutor Harry Toy himself argued the case.

Toy was anxious to perform well in front of the reporters and he needed a big win. It was only natural that he paid a visit to Sol Levine. They talked about prison. Sol didn't want to go to prison. Sol wasn't sure what he'd done that would send him to prison, but Toy explained what an "accessory" was.

To Sol it seemed like a cop's trick to convict him of something someone else did. Sol tried, but couldn't wrap his mind around the concept. All he knew was that it meant prison. Prison meant the Purples would find him, someone, sometime would kill him.

Toy offered to drop all charges if Sol talked. Sol wasn't sure what he would say, a detail which didn't seem to bother the prosecutor. Toy would tell him what he would say. It seemed like a good deal and less than two months after the arrests Sol was sitting on the witness stand delivering his lines perfectly.

The trial held no mystery. He did exactly what Harry had warned he would. Each day his suit was brought to his cell, after dressing Sol was marched to a waiting police car and soon he was on the stand. Sol was at his very best. He spilled his guts; he talked, he sang, his description of a bullet passing "just under my nose" was a masterpiece. Sol did everything but a reenactment.

Prosecutor Toy was very pleased.

Through the entire ordeal one thing kept spinning around Sol's simple mind. He would play the scene in the boat salon over and over. He could hear the bundles of twenties as they fell from the bag on to the table; he could taste the caramels, his fingers held the cigarettes.

Sol knew. He knew where four hundred thousand dollars was hidden. All he needed was an eight hour head start. He could be down to the boatyard, on that boat and gone in no time. He could still take Dolly and to hell with her if she didn't want to come. They could still make it to Toronto.

He just had to get out of this damned jail!

The Purples did their best too. Every bookmaking operation in the city was assessed a two dollar a day "betting service" fee, each bootlegger was similarly assessed. The best lawyers in town were approached. Cops and court clerks were "talked" to.

The money didn't help. The best lawyers couldn't change the facts. No one could get to the jury and the Judge was incorruptible.

Judge Van Zile was all too aware that witnesses might suddenly change their story, that evidence could suddenly disappear and prosecutors have mysterious car accidents.

He pushed the trial hard. It only took a week before the case went to the jury. It didn't stay there long. After an hour-and-a-half of deliberations, the verdict was in. All three were guilty. A week later Judge Van Zile handed down his sentence.

Less than a month after the trial a specially assigned Pullman train arrived at the ornate Michigan Central Station. The three men, waddling in wrist and ankle chains were put aboard.

Waiting to board they noticed the armed guards and armored plates on the engine and few cars. Moments later the train was headed for Michigan's Upper Peninsula. The ride was an express. They only stopped for fuel. Nothing and no one was going to stop the train from moving. In less than a day the Purples began serving life without parole at the maximum security Marquette Branch Prison.

The remaining Purples were livid. They hadn't been able to spring their brothers in crime, but they could get to Sol. And ol' Solly would pay.

The departure of Bernstein, Milberg and Keywell for the long winters of northern Michigan provided little comfort for Sol Levine. He had run the streets long enough to know the score. There were contracts out on him. Small time hoods and professionals alike all were looking for Sol.

He'd been warned by Detroit's finest, there was nothing they could do. This wasn't going to pass, Sol knew the remaining members of the Purple Gang would not rest while he was alive.

Sol had to figure a way to stay alive long enough to get to that boat, preferably, but not necessarily with Dolly at his side.

The danger was too much. In a surprise move Sol simply refused to leave police headquarters. He decided to live on the second floor. The cops weren't happy, but sympathized with poor Sol. Prosecutor Toy knew Sol would be killed too. But Toy wasn't going to turn the building into a boarding house.

It took a bit of effort, but Toy soon finalized a plan to rid Detroit of one more hoodlum. He offered Sol a deal. Leave the country now, under police escort or some charge would appear which would send poor Sol to Marquette.

It was a bitter pill. It meant he'd have to sneak back in a year or so to find the boat. But what choice did he have? Sol took the deal. He was sure Dolly would understand.

In a few weeks Sol was put on a ship destined for France. Toy's plan was a good one; it could have worked. But, the French weren't stupid either. They refused to let Sol get off the boat. On his own, penniless and without prospects Sol tried to go to Ireland.

The Irish and their British overseers weren't any more stupid than the French. After two years Sol ended up headed back to the United States. He died a bum on the streets of New York never having made it back to Detroit.

Chapter 11

Traverse City Michigan is located at the base of the twin forks of Traverse Bay. Begun as a shipping and lumber town it soon became a favorite haunt of a young Earnest Hemingway. The town passed through the lumber industry period, floundered for some years then found its footing when the Northern Michigan Asylum for the Insane was established in 1885. By the time the old Victorian hospital closed in 1989 the city's economy had moved on to tourism. The rest of the State, and the tawny folks of Detroit and Chicago, had discovered the jewel at base of the bay. Now, multimillion dollar homes lined the Peninsula between the forks of the Bay. A single vacant lot with a bit of water and sand and enough room to install a septic tank sold for more money than most people in "TC", as the town is called by the locals, earn in a lifetime.

Just northwest of TC is Leelanau County. Home to vineyards, orchards and the Sleeping Bear dunes. Here life is still a bit slower, though Hollywood types have begun paying outrageous sums for the privilege of losing money in the wine business. Here a few locals hang on. Here too, was the old family cherry farm where Herman James Crenshaw and his sister Sherrie spent the occasional long weekend and traditional mid-August week when their parents packed them up and shipped them off to the grandparents.

By the time Sherrie entered college, both of their grandparents had passed away. Mom and Dad quickly decided that if they were going to be empty nesters then the nest was going to move. Six months later they'd sold their suburban house, bought out the bank's interest on the orchard and traded a hectic life in the city for the lakes and clean air of "up north" Michigan.

Jim had been in the middle of an Air Force career when the bad news arrived; he'd lost both his parents to a drunk driver. The will split the property in two, which meant that neither could live at the orchard. Jim, in exchange for a lifetime supply of cherries, gave his half of the property to his sister and resumed his Air Force career.

It was a bad move financially, but a good one morally, and Jim never regretted it. Sherrie and her husband Gerry immediately quit their successful but stressful careers in Chicago and moved north. Sherrie oversaw the restoration and expansion of the traditional field stone farmhouse and now proudly showed her home to various tourist magazine photographers as the essence of a northern Michigan home.

Gerry hadn't been idle during the home renovation. When not working on the house he renovated the cherry shed, added more processing space, and a small office. He reskinned and reroofed the barn then put new roofs on the smaller outbuildings. When the buildings were complete the two turned their attention to expanding and updating the orchards. Now, several years later they managed a very successful cherry farming business, supplying cherries to packinghouses and individual customers on-line.

It was this expansion of the farm that now had Gerry's attention. He and Sherrie had recently completed the purchase of an additional twenty acres of land, which bordered their orchard's southern edge. The property had been sitting idle for many years and was a bit of a mystery.

The property had been sold by the state, not by a bank or land company. While that did occasionally happen, what really seemed odd was the lack of property records associated with the purchase. Each county in the state maintained a map showing ownership of every square inch of the county, the map, called a 'plot map' was periodically updated. Somehow, the twenty acres in question were missing from the plot map. A title search showed a dead man as the owner as of 1961.

Sherrie couldn't remember having ever seen anyone on the property when she had vacationed at "the farm" as a child. Being landlocked the property hadn't generated a great deal of interest when it went up for auction. It was a fairly simple thing for Sherrie and Gerry to make the purchase. Included on the property was a barn made of brick. The barn was of unknown age.

The lawyer who had represented the state had been unable to supply any information on the building or its contents and had insisted the purchase be made "as-is." Gerry half expected to find a barn full of cow manure.

The purchase complete, Gerry was now assessing the property, intending to lay out a new orchard. He referred to several pages of a soils report he held in one hand. In his other hand he held a soil pH test probe. He took several pH samples and began to walk the length of the orchard. Gerry only went ten feet and stopped. The task was impossible. Before he could begin, Gerry had to satisfy both his own, and Sherrie's, curiosity.

Here Gerry ran into his first problem with the new property. Try as he might Gerry could not find a way into the barn. For the third time he walked around the building. It was long, and somewhat narrow. There were three doors, all firmly locked. A set of, what appeared to be, steel garage doors on the narrower south side and an individual door centered on both the west and east sides. Each door was constructed so that the hinge was on the inside of the building. Gerry found this a bit odd. Around the top of the walls, just below the tin roof and protected from the rain by the overhanging rafters were eyebrow windows. Spaced two feet apart each window appeared to be painted over with black paint. The paint was thin in some areas. Gerry wasn't sure, but he thought he saw heavy gauge wire mesh against the inside of a few of the windows.

Returning to the large garage doors Gerry examined the inset door lock. It was clearly a heavy gauge, solid deadbolt. Gerry thought that a bit odd for a barn. The lock stood out in a round circle of reddish orange. Even if he had the key he doubted the rusted lock mechanism would work.

Disgusted, Gerry returned to his pick-up truck and bounced across the back of the field, opened a gate, passed into the edge of his orchard, found the lane between trees and eventually stopped at his cherry processing shed.

Sherrie walked to the side of the truck and leaned in the open window. After a quick kiss she asked, "Well, did we make a good deal? Or, are we the proud owners of a toxic waste site?"

Gerry grinned. "The land is beautiful. I'm not finished confirming all the soil tests, but the reports are perfect. We're going to have a nice orchard in there honey. But, that damn building. I can't find a way in!"

Sherrie's eyes lit up and she started to laugh. "This is cool! It's like we're on a game show."

"With Bob Barker asking what's behind Door Number One?" Gerry laughed.

He parked the truck and they walked to the house. "I think the only way in is to cut a big hole into those doors."

Sherrie looked puzzled. "Why can't you just break a window and climb in?" she said as the screen door banged behind them.

"Can't. The windows are all at the top of the wall and, you won't believe this, but I think there's heavy wire mesh on the inside." Gerry walked to the kitchen sink and began to wash his hands. Then, without turning around said, "Jim has an acetylene torch doesn't he?"

"I have no idea...and don't even think about using my clean towels to dry your hands. Use a paper towel."

Gerry grinned, "Yes ma'am."

Sherrie picked up her cell phone. "We haven't talked to Jim and Eve in a few weeks. Let's give 'em a call."

Chapter 12

Jim stood at the kitchen counter and listened to the phone message. "Hi guys, it's your loving sister Sherrieeee…" He grinned, this woman was always excited.

"We need a favor pleeease. We just closed the deal on the twenty acres next to us with that big garage on it. If we were to cook steaks and make a nice cherry pie would you bring your acetylene torch up this weekend? We can't seem to get into that stupid garage and Gerry figures the only way is to cut a hole in one of the doors. Let me know, love ya. Bye"

Jim considered himself to be fairly practical, and cutting holes in doors didn't sound quite right. Surely there had to be a way to get in that old building without destroying expensive doors. In any case a trip north was a good deal this time of year. Eve would be excited to visit family, and he and Gerry could get in a little trout fishing. Jim went to the barn to load his torch on the wagon.

Eve's arrival home from work was always an event. Carrying a minimum of two large cloth bags, she would burst into the kitchen, simultaneously calling "I'm hoommme." Then, before Jim answered she would recite the details of her day, beginning with the funniest thing a child had said or done and ending with the stupidest thing said or done by a member of the school's administration or a fellow teacher. The entire process interrupted by their beagle Molly's excited barks and demands for attention.

Jim looked forward to this ritual, he rarely listened in great detail; it was the enthusiasm with which it was told that he loved. Tonight's ceremony was no different, and to Jim it proved once again that all was right with his world.

Eve was surprised and pleased that Sherrie had phoned and immediately returned the call. No one outside the family could tell the two were not immediate sisters, they were "like two peas in a pod" Jim's mother used to say. Twenty minutes of one trying to out talk the other and somehow arrangements were made.

Friday was the beginning of the Easter break. Thursday night Eve left the school as quickly as she could. She hurried home and, upon entering the kitchen announced they would stop at "Cops and Donuts" in Clare for dinner. A quick change of her clothes and she was backing the Jeep up to the trailer almost before Jim had the barn doors open.

Ten minutes later, the Jeep Grand Cherokee, hitched to a small trailer loaded with an industrial sized acetylene torch and attendant tanks, along with two bikes and two kayaks slowly moved down a hundred-yard long driveway.

On the folded down back seat lay a large pillow where Molly sat calmly watching the scenery slide past. She would be curled up and snoring before they came to the end of the long drive. Molly would miss most of the three and a half hour trip north.

Chapter 13

Detroit and the Detroit River business soon returned to normal. The city forgot the Collingwood murders. Harry Keywell, Irving Milberg and Ray Bernstein were gone and quickly faded from memory. Sol Levin soon became the funny story of a scared rabbit who refused to leave the police station. Sol was quickly forgotten by everyone involved with or who had ever heard of the 'Collingwood Manor Massacre.' Everyone, that is, except Dolly Eleanor Grongoski.

Dolly slipped out of the city and moved to Michigan's west coast and the gritty little port town of Muskegon. The town's small waterfront was jammed with ships, large and small, making the run up and down the lake to Chicago. Some of the bigger ones even crossed to Milwaukee or north to Green Bay.

The sailors got hungry and Dolly landed a job at the Dockside Café. It wasn't the kind of café she had seen in the movies. Muskegon was not Paris or New York. The Dockside's walls were nearly as grimy as the coal fired ships whose crews it served.

Behind the building a small pigpen housed three large sows and their piglets. A large boar was kept in a separate pen to the side. The pen provided about half of the ham and bacon for the café and a good deal of ambiance.

Dolly worked four days a week. Five if she could talk Mel, the cheap bastard owner, into giving her the extra day. She made a buck fifty a day plus tips, which she split with the other waitresses and the cook. Sometimes she talked Mel into paying her to slop out the pigpen and that gave her an extra seventy-five cents. She'd been raised on a farm and didn't mind the work, but she hated pigs.

The sows could be mean when they had piglets and the boars could be mean just because. And she thought about what Sol had told her. She thought about having a nice place to live and her hair done by a real woman's hairdresser. And the clothes. She dreamed about the clothes. She thought about warm soft coats, pretty dresses, the fanciest hats and real silk stockings. Mostly, Dolly thought about how close she'd come to being rich.

They had taken the bags into the boathouse and put them on the boat. Sol had said that they were all packed and would leave as soon as he finished fueling the boat.

But she hadn't seen the money, and of course they were packed, she had her two bags and Sol wasn't taking anything.

He'd asked her to get him some razor blades while he worked. She thought about that. He didn't need razor blades. Had he been trying to get her away from the boat?

Maybe he had intended to leave Dolly? But why had he driven all over Detroit to find her? Had he changed his mind? Sol had sent her away for some reason she was sure of it. What was it?

The money. Where was the money? Did he leave while she was gone, get the money and come back? But they were going to leave as soon as she returned from the market.

Dolly mulled the thing over and over. It had only taken her about eight minutes to walk to Jefferson Avenue, turn right and go another block. A store stood on the corner there. Then eight minutes back. If she added five minutes at the store…there was no way Sol could drive someplace and be back with the money. And…he said they were all packed.

She thought about that. She thought about it every day, every time she filled a coffee cup, every time someone only left a nickel for a tip or grabbed her bottom or when her boss told her to take the diner's scrapes out to the pigs in back. They were all packed.

That November, as Sol was being loaded on a boat for Europe, Dolly got her first break in months. She was pouring coffee for a sailor on the railroad ferry.

Suddenly a man burst into the diner and yelled, "Lowel, you lazy sonofabitch, if you don't get your shit loaded now you ain't going to have time when we leave." The sailor didn't move, he just smiled and said, "Hoss, I loaded my gear last night."

Dolly didn't hear the rest of the conversation. The sailor's words hit her like a ton of bricks. It came to her. Just like that. It was so simple; she should have seen it months ago. The money was already in the boat.

Sol had picked her up about one o'clock. He said he'd been looking for her for two hours. They'd gone to Gosse Pointe, then Hamtramck for dinner. They'd stopped at her apartment to pack, drove to his apartment and gone to the boathouse. She'd gone to the market, but Sol hadn't gone anywhere. He didn't have time.

Sol was doing what he said he was doing, putting gas in the boat. He really did just want some razor blades. He must have loaded the money before he picked her up. She'd known it all along, only now she understood it. Sol had loaded it before he came to see her that day.

The boat. She needed to find the boat.

The world was beginning to change. The artisan was being replaced by the big company. The small car companies in and around Detroit were being consolidated. Willie Durant and Charles Stewart Mott were building the biggest company the world had ever seen. Reliant Motor Truck, Pontiac, Oldsmobile, Cadillac all had been taken over, it was just business.

It was just the same in the world of crime. The Purples were just as mean and vicious, but there were fewer of them. No new leaders had been groomed to replace Ray Bernstein or Harry Keywell. Gradually leadership fell to Abe Axler and Eddie Fletcher. Abe and Eddie were loyal soldiers, but they weren't very smart. They began to make mistakes. The loss of leadership, manpower and influence at City Hall was like blood in the water to a Great White shark. The competition began to move in and the Purples were helpless to stop it.

The biggest threat came from the Italians. The Eastside gang was tied into the New York Mafia and Capone's Chicago gang. Slowly they were becoming the dominant gang in Detroit. "Black" Bill Tocco had a special hate for the Purples and pressured them across the city. Muscling in on their gambling operations, prostitution and most of all the alcohol smuggling routes. Imports were down, hijackings were up and 'runners', the boys who delivered the booze to the speakeasies and beer gardens across the city were being killed, disappearing or quitting.

Dolly didn't know of the turmoil in the Detroit underworld that winter. She spent her time thinking about the boat. She'd have to find it. She was convinced Sol had hidden the money on the big Chris-Craft, she just needed time alone with the boat and she'd find it. But that was the issue wasn't it? How to find the boat. Dolly didn't know Detroit. She'd only been to the river once before that night and in their panic and the darkness she certainly hadn't kept track of street names. All Dolly knew was that the boat was in a small boathouse on the Detroit river.

She got another break in mid-December. A truck driver stopped at the diner for breakfast before loading onto one of the ferries crossing the lake. He ate his breakfast, drank his coffee and paid his bill and drove down to the docks. Dolly cleaned up his table and found a packet of maps laying on the seat where the man had been sitting.

She picked the packet up and stuffed it down deep in her apron pocket. Then Dolly poured coffee and waited tables for the rest of the day, the packet totally forgotten.

That evening Dolly took off her shoes and her apron, counted her tips and began to think about making dinner. Suddenly she remembered the packet. Untying the string and unfolding the leather case she found road maps of Michigan, Ohio and Indiana.

There was also a detailed street map of Detroit. Dolly stared at this map for several minutes. This was important, this could help her. Dolly wasn't exactly sure why this was important, but the feeling was more than a suspicion, it was a certainty. She had never seen a map and didn't know how to use one, but she wasn't stupid and she could read. She would figure this out.

She cleared the small table which served as kitchen counter, dining room table, ironing board, and occasionally living room coffee table, and spread the map out flat. Carefully she examined the thing. Slowly she began to understand what she was looking at. After a while it began to make sense. It was just a big picture of the city.

Eventually she found the address of the old boardinghouse she had lived in. She placed her finger on the map. She closed her eyes and imagined walking down the steps, turning left and walking to the corner grocery. She traced her finger along the map. He finger came to a street intersection. If she was doing this right it would be Bagley Street. She searched for the street name. Bagley Street, she'd done it.

Excited, she began finding other places she knew from her year in the city. She found the library, the museum, the streets where she knew the clubs. Then the importance of the map came to her. She could find the boathouse.

Dolly quickly found the Detroit River and began to trace the streets that ran parallel to the river. She remembered a park and the city water works. She'd run past both. Her finger ran along the river. Jefferson. She had run along Jefferson Avenue. Past the water works and, there it was, Memorial Park. That meant the dirt road was somewhere...here. She stabbed the map with her finger.

That night Dolly lay in her bed deep in thought. She could find the boathouse. She was sure the money was in the boat, Sol must have put it on board before he came to get her. She had been in the boat and hadn't seen any bundles just sitting out; he must have hidden it. It wouldn't make any sense to just leave it laying out. Lots of boats were stopped by the Customs police; Solly must have anticipated that. He hid it. The only real question was how well had he hidden it?

It had been months; the Purples must have used the boat since. Surely they'd found the money by now. But, maybe not. Could she really afford to not look? She could spend the rest of her life feeding slop to pigs and waiting tables, the same things when she thought about it. Or, she could take a chance on being rich.

Chapter 14

The first morning of any visit to Sherrie and Gerry's farm was, by tradition and function, an exercise in choreographed confusion. The first person awake made coffee then, inevitably took a seat on the covered porch.

As each member of the foursome made their way to the porch the topic of breakfast gradually took over. It always ended with Jim and Gerry frying eggs, pancakes and bacon, while Sherry retrieved a selection of homemade cherry, apple and berry jams from her pantry. Eve produced a maple syrup from a friend's farm, and then she and Sherrie selected a tablecloth for the antique round eagle claw table, which sat in an equally rounded portion of the covered porch.

When all was ready the four descended on the food. The next hour was spent in a near continuous dull roar as each talked over the other and all laughed at the same stories which had been told countless times before. Jim enjoyed this noise more than anything he could think of. This was his definition of wealth. Finally, he asked Gerry why they had to cut a hole in a barn door. It seemed rather odd.

"Odd? That doesn't begin to describe this place," replied Gerry. "The building is made of brick, not terribly unusual, but still a little different. The windows are all eyebrow windows. They're all at the top of the walls."

"Are you sure this thing is a barn?" Jim interrupted.

"I mean, that sounds like a mechanics shop or something like that."

"You're probably right." Gerry took a sip of his coffee and continued, "There's a pair of steel garage type doors on the south end and both sides have normal entry doors. Which is also a little odd, normally the long doors go on the long side of a building. The thing is that all those doors are made of heavy gauge steel. No door windows and the hinges are all on the inside. I'm assuming the doors open to the inside, but I can't be certain of anything with this place. I'm telling ya Jim, it's a weird deal."

"Are the windows big enough to get through if we can get that high?" Jim asked.

"Sure, but I think they're lined with a steel mesh on the back side. And, they're all twelve feet off the ground. We can't get a torch up that high and cut the mesh."

"We thought about our picking equipment. That could get us high enough, but we don't think they will hold the weight of your torch," Sherry added.

"You've got a front loader on your tractor don't you?" Eve asked.

"Sure, but that's not..." Gerry stopped for a moment.

"We use the bucket to put up Christmas lights," Jim said with a smile.

"That's a great idea! Let's get going," Gerry stood.

"No, lets not," Sherrie cried.

"You guys get the towels, we'll clear the table," Eve confirmed.

In moments the dishwasher was humming, the fry pans were being scrubbed and put away and the counters cleaned.

Gerry's tractor was equipped with a hydraulically operated front loader; an arm on each side of the tractor held a V shaped bucket approximately six feet long and three feet wide. Two levers mounted next to the driver operated the loader. One moved the two arms up and down; the second tilted the V shaped bucket forward and backward.

Sherrie found some moving blankets and packing material in the processing shed while Gerry grabbed two coils of rope. They quickly made a cushioned bed for the tanks of oxygen and acydlene and then secured them in the bucket with chains. Satisfied the tanks would not roll or fall out of the bucket Jim, Eve and Sherrie piled into the pickup truck. Gerry climbed to the tractor seat and soon they were on the way through the orchard to the mysterious block building on the new property. Arriving at the building they surveyed the exterior for several minutes.

"This thing is a regular Fort Knox!" Eve exclaimed. All nodded in general agreement.

"I've always wondered about this place," Jim said. "Did the title search tell you anything?"

"Its been owned by the state for the past thirty years. Apparently, the state got it because the property tax wasn't being paid. When the title was transferred it seems that whatever office is responsible for government property was never notified. The lawyer told us the State of Michigan didn't know it owned this land. No one knew about the property until an alert auditor found it during an inspection of the Secretary of State's records. This popped up," Gerry explained.

"How did the county not collect property taxes?" asked Eve.

"That's a mystery to me too," Gerry answered. "When someone figures out how to pull that trick off let me know."

"From what we could tell this building isn't on any tax role. And, the property owner in the sixties was a guy named William Tocco. Apparently he died and this piece wasn't processed with the estate," Sherrie offered.

"Well, it's a nice piece of property," Jim said glancing around.

They all admired the view for a moment, then Jim said, "You ready to do this? Pick the window you want to replace."

They settled on a spot where the ground looked firm, Gerry squared the tractor to the building and tilted the loader so that the point of the V sat on the ground. Jim climbed in and knelt on one knee. When he was ready he signaled Gerry to lift the bucket. Slowly the bucket reached its highest point, Jim was just below the window. Gerry then tilted the bucket forward a few inches leaning the bucket against the barn's wall.

Taking a pipe wrench in his right hand, and covering his face with his left, Jim reached out and smashed the wrench into the window. Glass cascaded into the bucket. Behind the painted glass was a heavy wire mesh. Jim set to work on the remaining glass, removing it from the steel frame. After several minutes the frame was clean. He then lit the torch and began to cut the heavy-duty wire mesh, a few minutes later it fell away to the floor of the building.

Gerry lowered the bucket and Eve and Sherrie took a ladder from the back of the pickup and placed it in the bucket. Eve then climbed in next to Jim and the bucket was raised once more. Jim secured a rope to the top of the ladder while Eve tied the other end to the bucket. Satisfied with their knots, Jim and Eve pushed the ladder through the window then gradually lowered it to the ground.

"Ready?" Eve asked.

"Almost," Jim replied.

He finished tying a bowline knot, slipped the end of

the rope around his chest and passed it through the knot.

"Loop it there," he pointed.

Eve quickly looped the line around the hydraulic arm, then snubbed the line as Jim squeezed through the window, hung from the windowsill, and found the top of the ladder with his toes. "Okay, give me some slack," he called.

Chapter 15

Dolly was determined to find the boat. Unfortunately, she was two hundred miles from where ever that boat was hidden. She needed to eat and the only way she could do that was to work at the diner. But, she needed time off too. Her boss was the problem. Mel rarely scheduled any of the diner's crew for more than five days in a week, but he never gave them two days off in a row.

That would not work for Dolly; she set about convincing him she needed her days off together to visit a sick aunt. Mel didn't believe it. He was convinced she had a boyfriend somewhere. He was certain she would be married or pregnant soon. At first, he didn't want her to leave and considered never scheduling her days together.

But Mel had a surprising soft spot for young girls in love. He pretended to buy the story about a sick aunt and soon Dolly had two days off a week, back to back.

It was perfect. As soon as her shift finished Dolly would hurry back to her room and pack a small handbag. It was a long ride from Muskegon and there was always the fear that someone from the Purples would recognize her, but Dolly was determined.

She stayed away from anyone or anyplace she had ever known or visited. She dyed her hair and tried to blend in with the other people walking the streets. She did her best to keep out of sight. She was certain that no one recognized her.

It took two trips and a lot of walking to find the boathouse. Finally, on a Tuesday morning, just before lunch, she found the corner store. From there it was easy.

She retraced her steps from all those months ago to the tool shed. And there it was, the boathouse where they captured her Solly.

That first morning she had nearly been caught. She hadn't expected the Purples to post a guard on the boathouse. She had nearly blundered into him. Only the sound of a passing barge had distracted the lookout. But, she hadn't been caught and now she would bide her time and find that money.

And so it went. Dolly would travel to the boathouse almost every week. Carefully she would slip into the same shed and sit on the same stool from which she had watched Sol arrested. She would spend every minute she could in that damned shed. On the second day, about five o'clock she would slip out of the tool shed, creep low behind the wooden crates and race away through the alley between the warehouses. An all night train ride later and she was back home in Muskegon.

As summer began to turn to fall, Dolly began to plan for the coming winter. In late August she began knitting a heavy sweater, a new hat and heavy mittens. She visited the church and found a good winter coat in the charity box. She knit two pairs of wool socks and then, when no one was looking, stole a pair of men's winter boots. She was ready.

That winter she visited the Detroit riverfront whenever she could get away from the diner. She felt like she was hunting deer with her father. She would sneak into the tool shed and sit and watch the boathouse for hours. It was guarded night and day. She couldn't be sure the big cruiser was still inside.

She didn't see the boat at all that winter. But her father had taught her how to hunt. She'd sat on a deer stand many, many cold mornings waiting for a big buck. She knew you could go an entire season without seeing a deer, but they were there. She was certain the boat was there too.

Dolly didn't have a plan, but she had plenty of time to think. She thought about how to search the boat once she made it inside the boathouse. Where she would look, how she would search. She thought about tools and saws and drills. But the more she thought about it the more she realized how long it would take to really search the boat.

Finally, her mind was made up. Searching the boat made no sense. Why not do what she and Sol had intended? She decided to steal the boat and go to Canada; just like Sol had planned.

She began to study boats. She visited the library and read everything she could about boats. She especially liked the magazines, they showed lots of pictures of Chris-Craft boats. She found one picture that included the controls and she familiarized herself with them all. It didn't look hard, she had driven the neighbor's tractor; she could do this. She talked to the sailors about boats. She asked questions about motors and steering. She showed them pictures of powerboats and asked about the controls.

Dolly figured it out.

One evening Dolly was in the town library reading about ships and sailing when the question of navigation began to nag. She'd not thought about navigation, Sol was going to do that. Dolly went to the card file and quickly found several books about maritime navigation. It was complicated, it took a lot of figuring and she felt as if she'd hit a stone wall. She wasn't good at math and didn't know the names of any of the stars except the North Star. Dolly began to doubt she would ever understand latitudes and longitudes and sextants and all the other things associated with navigating a ship at sea.

A week later Dolly was pouring coffee for one of the sailors and decided to ask for help.

"Honey, I don't use none of those tricks. Hell, if I want to go to Chicago I go south until I run into it. If I want to go to Milwaukee I go west until I git there. Ain't that hard."

Dolly thought about his answer the rest of the day. It made sense. She would be in a river or a lake, not an ocean. There's only two ways to go on a river, up stream or down. And on a lake, well, even a big lake like Erie, she would eventually come to the other side. Dolly had renewed hope.

One morning Dolly was sitting in the tool shed watching the comings and goings of the riverfront. The gang's boathouse guard sat on a stool, leaning back against the building's wall, and smoked a cigarette. Dolly watched the boats on the river. They always stayed between the colored buoys. That was it! There was a road out there defined by the colored buoys.

Back at the diner she tested this theory with the sailors. One, a sailor named Brian took the time to explain to her about the colored buoys. "Red, right, returning" is the saying he told her, "keep the red buoy on your right when in the river or the channel, it's where the deep water is." Seemed simple enough. She kept repeating it to herself. "Red, right, returning."

She found an atlas of the United States at the library and poured over its maps. After a while she decided that if she kept in the middle of the river, between the buoys and headed south, turned left when she got to Lake Erie and went east until she was low on gas that should get her out of danger. She'd get gas wherever she ended up and continue until she got to Buffalo or Toronto whichever came first. She decided to buy a road map of Canada, at least she'd know where Toronto was.

There was only one problem. If she was going to steal the damn thing she had to know where it was. She hadn't seen it since the morning they arrested Sol and the others. She spent every minute she could in the tool shed. Sometimes, she spent the entire night in the boathouse, shivering and watching. Maybe it wasn't there; maybe she was a fool. She didn't know, but she was determined to get a look inside the building.

Finally, in late April she got her break. Mel had given Dolly three days off in a row in the middle of the week. She wasn't happy about it, the extra day off was a day without pay, she needed the money. However, it did give her an extra day to watch the boathouse.

That Thursday afternoon four cars - two Chryslers, a Ford and a Packard, arrived within minutes of each other. Several men got out and stood around the empty lot talking and smoking. One man from each of the vehicles went inside the boathouse.

Ten minutes later she heard the low rumble of a big engine. Not sure what the sound was she tried find a hole in the shed wall that would let her see further south. It was no good. Then, like an evil monster crawling out of the swamp, the cruiser crept north up the river, swung its bow toward the shore and slid into the darkness of the boathouse.

A man came to the door and waved his arm.

Immediately all the "extras" standing around their cars dashed inside. In less than a minute they were back, arms full of cases of whiskey, gin, and vodka. Dolly watched it all.

As the last Chrysler drove away she scanned the area around the boathouse intently. No one. They hadn't left a guard. She waited; maybe he was inside. Five minutes passed. She eased herself through the tool shed's door, moved right to the edge of the water and knelt behind a stack of wooden crates. She carefully studied the boathouse and the shadows beyond. The building looked deserted. Moving around the crates she put two large barrels between her objective and herself, then crawled to the barrels. Peering between them she again studied the boathouse. No one was there. Now what? Inhaling deeply Dolly stood. Slowly she walked toward the boathouse, then veered to the water's edge. She knelt and picked up a stone, just an innocent girl at the river edge. She threw the stone into the river. Casually she glanced around; she was alone.

Chapter 16

Eddie Fletcher sat in the back seat of his Packard Light Eight. "That was a good run Fred," Eddie said. "We'll get the rest tonight."

"The boys said they didn't see anyone else on the water. Joey thought someone was tailin' em in Windsor. They got eyes over there Eddie, it ain't gettin' easier,"

Fred's eye's flicked between the rear view mirror, his boss' face and the street ahead.

The Tocco gang had hit two of the last five runs. Hijackings were up, the Purple's had competition and Eddie didn't like it. He reached for his cigarette case; it wasn't in his jacket pocket. He looked on the seat, then the floor. He felt his pants for his Zippo. Not there.

"Fred, turn around." Eddie said to the driver. "I left my damn cigarette case and lighter on the boat."

Fred did as he was told and the new Packard did a U turn in the middle of Woodward Avenue. Ten minutes later Fred parked the car on the hardpack dirt outside the boathouse and Eddie got out. He took several steps and then stopped. A loud rumble erupted from inside. Shock then anger washed over Eddie. He screamed, "What the hell...!" and watched the big Chris-Craft slowly back out of the boathouse.

Eddie ran to the waters edge. The cruiser was already sixty feet into the middle of the river. Slowly the bow came round into the current as the driver increased the power.

"You son of a bitch!" Eddie yelled as he pulled his pistol from a jacket pocket. A short man in a heavy coat stood at the boat's controls. The boat began to pick up speed and Eddie fired four quick shots with no apparent effect. The rumble turned to a roar, the stern of the boat erupted in white foam and the bow lifted. It seemed to pause, like the moment just before a sprinter explodes from the blocks. Then the Chris-Craft shot forward and sped south down the Detroit River.

Dolly let out a scream of joy, she had done it. She pulled her hat off and let her hair blow in the wind as the boat's motor settled into a content throb. She'd seen a man on the shore, he'd pointed a gun at the boat. She was certain he'd fired, she'd seen the gun flash. But she hadn't heard any gun shots and she certainly hadn't been hit by any bullets.

She headed toward Fighting Island. In a few minutes the island flew past and the passage at Stony Island appeared. The wind made her eyes water and the bouncing of the boat scared her, but she had never, not once in her life, felt this alive. She screamed at the wind, she punched the air.

Slowly Dolly began to relax. The adrenaline rush she'd experienced at the boathouse began to subside. She pulled an atlas from under her coat. Holding the atlas with her left hand and the steering wheel with her right she found Bois Blanc Island. Squinting through the sun and the spray she studied the river. Moments later she spotted the island. Lake Erie wasn't much further, after that Canada.

After his last shot Eddie knew he'd been had. He sprinted to the car, yelling at Fred. "Tocco! The SOB took the boat!" By the time Eddie reached the car Fred had the trunk open. Eddie grabbed a Thompson submachine gun and ran back to the river's edge. Too late, the big boat was too far away. Eddie was furious. Swearing, he ran back to the car yelling, "The Wyandotte boathouse! I'm gonna kill him! I swear I'm gonna kill him."

When Fred's confusion showed Eddie shoved the machine gun in his gut and yelled, "MOVE! Now, you fool!" Fred suddenly understood the urgency of his boss' demand and ran to the driver's door. Spraying gravel and dirt, the Packard shot up the hill, bounced over the curb and rocketed out of the side street onto Jefferson.

Fred dodged traffic and ignored traffic signals. Cops walking the beat blew whistles but no one gave chase. In twenty minutes they swung into a small riverside lot next to a large warehouse. Both Fred and Eddie ran from the car to a ramshackle boathouse standing some twenty yards to the south of the warehouse. Five minutes later a Gar Wood Runabout Model 30 launched from the boathouse.

Eddie turned south. He pushed the throttle as far forward as it would go. The little boat instantly began to skim across the water, the occasional wave nearly bouncing the two men overboard. He shot between Grosse Ile and Stoney Island and searched for his target. He tried to decide if the boat was south or north of him; he wasn't sure so he kept racing south. After ten minutes he thought he saw the big cruiser in the distance. He pointed, told Fred to get his Thompson ready and adjusted his course a bit to the east.

Dolly spotted the small speedster just as she turned east into the lake. It was coming fast and she knew; she knew deep in her heart that it was the Purples. They weren't going to let her get away. People like her never got away. Her father had died when their one horse had kicked him in the head. Try as he might he'd never been able to get off that damned, broken down, good for nothing farm. He was even buried there.

There really was no fighting it. She wasn't going to get

away from her hopeless life either. She screamed, she cried, she pushed the throttle forward so hard the metal bent and her hand and arm ached. Still the little runabout was catching her. She edged closer to the Canadian shore. The road map showed a small inlet to an area called Big Creek. If she could get in there she might have a chance, it would be dark soon. Maybe she could hide the boat in the cattails and bulrush.

The runabout was closer, the daylight was fading, she thought she saw the inlet and turned toward it. The Chris-Craft sped toward the narrow gap. Suddenly a loud bang, the boat slammed to a stop and Dolly was thrown forward onto the dash. It took a moment to clear her head and then to her horror she realized she'd missed the inlet, she'd hit a rock. She could hear water flooding into the front of the boat. The little runabout was fast approaching. The shore was just a hundred yards away, maybe she could swim for it.

Dolly ran forward and jumped into the cold water. A second later she shook off the cold and started swimming. It was a valiant attempt, but it wasn't going to succeed. The men in the boat saw her. They followed her, staying just ten yards away, not saying anything. It didn't take long. Exhausted she began to tread water, then she floated and tried to rest. The runabout idled closer. Eddie was a little surprised the thief was a woman, but business was business. Fred stood, took careful aim and fired the Thompson. Dolly's body slowly sank to the bottom.

Chapter 17

Jim balanced on the top step of the ladder. "Hold tight," he called to Eve. Then, arms outstretched hard against the wall he balanced on one foot and lowered the other to the next step of the ladder. Beads of sweat formed on his forehead. The still heat of the building was oppressive. Some light leaked through the blacked-out windows, but it wasn't enough to see anything more than vague shadows. He lowered himself one more step and stopped.

"You alright?" Eve called.

"Yeah."

Jim considered. Then, after a moment he climbed back to the top step, "Eve?"

She leaned in the window. "You forgot something didn't you?"

"Hon, ya got a flashlight?"

Eve thought a moment then said, "You climbed all the way up here and forgot a flashlight?"

"Yeah, well, I thought more light would come through the broken window."

Eve grinned. "Good thing I know you." She said and, reaching behind her back she removed a flashlight she had stuffed into her belt in anticipation of this very request.

"Thanks hon! Oh, I'll need some tools too."

"How did you expect to open the rusted shut doors without tools?"

"Eve, I was just going to look around, then I'd get the tool I needed. It's a process, very well thought out and methodical. Don't you see?" Jim did his best to look innocent.

"Oh brother, it's getting deep and I'm ten feet above the ground!" Eve grinned back, turned and shouted:

"Sherrie…in the truck. Jim needs the tool box."

Sherrie was back in a moment. Gerry lowered the bucket and Sherrie handed the box to Eve then climbed into the loader. "I want to see what's going on," she said as she surveyed the inside of her metal steed.

Both women knelt on one knee, grabbed the sides of the steel box and gave Gerry a thumbs-up. He gently touched the control lever, raised the tractor arms, and set the box against the wall. Then Gerry watched as the toolbox was pushed through the open window and lowered to Jim.

A moment later Gerry was staring at the backsides of two women who had their heads thrust inside a broken window. He grinned, took his cell phone from his pocket and snapped a picture. "This will be a great Christmas card," he said to no one in particular.

Jim stuffed the flashlight in a pocket and gripped the toolbox with one hand. Using the other hand he slowly climbed down the ladder, put the tools on the floor and scanned the building with the light. Immediately Eve and Sherrie let out a gasp. The flashlight illuminated a large wooden cabin cruiser.

"Are you guys seeing this?" Jim shouted as he moved closer to the boat. He flicked the beam of light across the craft as he walked. Finding a dusty metal name plate Jim used his free hand to wipe off a layer of dirt. Slowly the words 'Chris-Craft Express Commuter' emerged. He stepped back and tried to get some perspective on the large boat. The darkness was too much. He couldn't take it all in.

Jim slowly walked around the boat. Rounding the

bow of the craft his flashlight found a small stack of crates against the block wall. The crates were covered with dirt and he couldn't tell their contents. Jim suppressed his curiosity and began looking for the building's doors. Spotting the main doors he was about to pick up the toolbox when his light swept the bow of the cruiser. A hole had been smashed into the left forward area. The damage was about four feet long and two feet wide. It appeared to be fairly deep and Jim wondered at the story he would never hear.

Focusing on the immediate task Jim recovered the toolbox and went to the large garage doors on the end of the building. After a short examination he found two spring loaded latches, one secured the top of the door to the frame and the other at the bottom secured the door to the building's concrete floor pad. A chain extended from the top and Jim used it to release the latch. A bar extended up from the floor latch and he pulled it up and swung it out of the way, releasing that latch. Jim then pushed on the doors, but only succeeded in flexing them outward a few inches. He pulled on the doors and didn't do much better.

Examining the door handle he found a steel cylindrical lock. It looked completely rusted and Jim was certain it was unusable. Taking a flat head screwdriver and a hammer from the box he was able to knock the cover off the rusted lock. This revealed an inner steel cover plate and a portion of the lock's bolt as it extended into the lock plate on the opposite door. The bolt was covered with rust. This gave Jim an idea.

Removing the tray from the top of the toolbox he began searching through the larger items beneath. Eventually Jim selected a large ball peen hammer and a cold chisel. The chisel, designed for metal, not wood, would cut the rusty deadbolt. Placing the blade of the chisel against the bolt he set to work. Two sharp blows with the hammer and the bolt snapped. With a smile Jim pulled the doors open and the first daylight to enter the strange block building in years flooded past.

Chapter 18

Abe Axler and Eddie Fletcher stood in the wheelhouse of a large towboat. It was just after midnight and the current leaders of the Purples were staring hard into the night. Phil Bronski, the boat's owner, hadn't found a lot of work for his boat in the past two years. The heavily built craft had been designed for pushing barges and other workboats of various types around the construction sites of the new Detroit-Windsor tunnel.

That work was gone now. The tunnel, nearly a mile long, had taken just two years to build and had finished in November 1930, a year ahead of schedule. A fact that both the Purples and Phil bemoaned.

As the work had dried up Phil had been forced to work harder and harder to find fewer and fewer customers for his boat. Gradually he began to find the bottom of a bottle. Now, his tab with the Purples dangerously high, he was thankful for any chance to work some of the crushing debt off. Even if that chance involved a small invasion of Canada.

"It should be in here someplace." Eddie said.

"Ready your light," Phil called to his deck hand.

The boat coasted gently into the night. "How far are we from shore?" Abe asked.

"I'd guess about a hundred forty, maybe a hundred fifty yards. See the edge of the beach there?" Phil pointed.

Only a few brave stars shown in the black sky, but to Phil the night was bright. To Abe and Eddie it was dark as a coal mine.

"There!" Phil called and pointed. "Light to port, just off the bow. You got it?"

In answer a deckhand had shined the spotlight in a zigzag across the water, finally resting on the Chris-Craft. The boat sat with its bow above its stern and pitched on its left side twenty degrees. The surface of the lake strained to reach the stern rail but fell short by a foot. They quickly dropped anchor and tied to the wreck.

Few words were spoken. One member of Phil's crew jumped to the stranded cruiser while another passed tools, a large tarp, and a long, wide-mouthed hose. Then they attached a line to the stern cleats and prepared to pull the boat off the rock that had doomed Dolly Grongoski.

When all was in readiness for the pull the tarp was lowered into the water and pulled under the boat with lines affixed to each side. These lines were then tied off on the boat rails so the tarp hung under the boat like a sling.

A voice from inside the Chris-Craft called, "Start the pump!" Another man, stationed at the bow of the towboat gave a sharp tug on a pull cord starting a small gasoline engine. The engine caught and soon a rhythmic clatter filled the air. An instant later the discharge hose of the pump filled, gushed water and settled into a steady stream.

Once Phil was satisfied the pump was working he backed the towboat's engines. The Chris-Craft slowly slid off the rock. The stern nearly swamped, the bow bobbed up and down but the cruiser eventually settled bow down in the cold water. Immediately water tried to rush into the hole caused by the rock. They were ready for this. Two men ran from line to line and pulled the tarp tight against the hull. The pump caused a slight decrease in water pressure inside the hull, the natural displacement of the craft caused pressure outside the boat and pushed the tarp into the hole. Immediately the gash was sealed.

The pump did its job and slowly emptied the flooded craft. Gradually the bow raised itself out of the water and the boat leveled. Both Abe and Eddie smiled and shook Phil's hand. "Impressive Phil," Eddie said with a grin.

"We ain't done until she's back in her happy little boathouse," Phil replied. He knew that his job wasn't done and they had a long way to go across a sometimes angry lake. More importantly, Phil knew that seeing the morning sun wasn't a sure bet until the Chris-Craft was back in the boathouse.

"Yeah, well…this is a good start ol' buddy," Abe replied.

They began the long tow back to the boathouse. Forty minutes later Abe leaned over to Phil and said, "Put in at Grosse Ile." Phil started to question the change, thought better of it and kept his thoughts to himself. Slowly reducing the throttle Phil gradually approached the haul-out bank.

Several men directed the Chris-Craft into position using a combination of ropes made fast to the bow and stern. Finally, the big cruiser was in place and a pair of lines were directed forward to a matching set of winches, began to tighten. Gently the boat was pulled forward until it came to rest on a wooden boat cradle. The cradle sat on a steel wheeled dolly, which rode on a pair of rails. A large engine turned a drum and a cable attached to the dolly pulled tight. Gradually the dolly was pulled up a shallow incline until the Chris-Craft sat in a cradle on dry land.

Phil was impressed with how efficient the operation had gone, but this was not terribly new or unusual to a man who had spent his life around boats and boatyards. Then the unusual did occur. A large diesel powered crane roared to life and came rumbling toward the Chris-Craft. As it approached, a truck with an oversized flatbed trailer drove into position next to the crane. Men swarmed around the Chris-Craft. Six-inch wide straps were strung from side to side and over the top, culminating at a single universal hook, which was then attached to the crane's lift cable.

Moments later the cruiser lifted from its cradle, swung through the air and was gently lowered to a similar cradle on the back of the truck.

Abe Axler and Eddie Fletcher had left the towboat and were supervising the loading of the Chris-Craft from next to the cab of the truck. As the last cable was being secured to the side of the truck trailer Eddie grabbed the driver's arm.

"Forget what you've been told. I want you to take it to the orchard. One of the boys will have the equipment. Change the paint, I want the top blue. Change the name; call it…" He stopped, searched the yard for Axler then called, "Hey Abe! What the hell was that horse's name? You know, the Derby winner?"

Axler flicked his cigarette. "Eddie, how the hell could you forget a name like Burgoo King?"

"Have 'em paint Burgoo King on the back. Then put it in the shed and lock it up. We'll get back to it next spring." The driver nodded.

"I don't want anyone seeing it go in the shed, understand? That means you do all this at night. In fact, you drive only at night. Take the back roads, no state roads. You got all that?" Eddie jabbed a finger into the driver's chest. The man's eyes widened slightly.

"Yeah. Night, no state roads, backroads only. I got it Eddie."

"Good, don't screw this up." Eddie pointed and lifted his thumb, the universal sign of a gun. "Or..." His thumb flexed forward.

"Really, I got it Eddie, no worries."

Eddie grinned and slapped the man on the back. "Good" he said.

Several minutes later Abe and Eddie watched the truck leave the boatyard. "We all good here?" Abe asked.

"Yeah."

"What about Phil?" Abe glanced in the direction of the towboat.

Fletcher thought for a moment, then decided, "He's okay. Who knows, maybe we'll need him again."

"I'll tell him." Abe said, then turned and walked back to the towboat. "Phil" Abe yelled the name as he jumped from the dock to the boat.

"Yea...Yeah?" Phil could feel his chest and throat tightening.

"Phil, you know you owe us a good amount of money? We've extended a lot of credit."

"Ah geeze Abe. Times is hard. I'll pay you back as soon as I can, I promise I will." Phil could feel his bladder convulse and wondered if he was going to wet his pants before they killed him.

"I don't like debt Phil." Abe stopped. The silence nearly crushed Phil as he shifted his weight from foot to foot. Abe was enjoying Phil's discomfort. "Phil, I don't like debt, yours or mine. And if I didn't pay you for tonight's work, I'd be in debt to you right?"

"No, no Abe. Really, consider it a favor, really."

Phil could feel the warmth on the inside of his leg.

"Phil, I don't do favors and I don't want favors. You

understand Phil?"

"Yeah, yeah, sure Abe. But I was just considering this to be among friends."

"I don't have friends Phil." Abe studied the man. Several seconds passed, Phil began to shake. Urine began to run down his leg. Finally Abe said, "Well Phil, tell you what. You did us a favor tonight. We'll call it even."

Phil couldn't believe his ears. He could feel his heart pounding. He thought about his wet leg, then he smiled, and then he slumped back against the rail. "Thanks Abe. Thanks. Any time I can do something for you boys you just let ol' Phil know." His relief was palatable. Phil knew he could just as easily have ended the night as carp food.

Axler and Eddie Fletcher didn't get back to the Chris-Craft the next spring. The raging war among the Italian Mafia spilled into Detroit. The East Side Gang became the Detroit Partnership. As time slipped by Charles "Lucky" Luciano took over the New York organization and the Mafia war ended. Luciano formed 'La Cosa Nostra' from the nation's twenty-four most powerful Mafia crime families. The Partnership was one of them. The organization was too big, too powerful for the Purples or anyone else. In November, Abe and Eddie were taken for a ride. Their bodies were found in a car on an isolated country road. It was just business.

Chapter 19

Cole David Prestcott was, by any definition of the word, an exception. A man that, by breeding, intellect and disposition should have been a penniless leech on society was, from all appearances, doing exceptionally well, thank you very much.

Cole had barely graduated from Petoskey High School, located in the town of the same name on northern Michigan's west coast. No one was sure which was worse, his academics or behavior. Fortunately, Cole did have one talent. He was a hockey phenom. His grace, power and skill on the ice led to several scholarship offers by the top hockey schools in the upper mid-west. Eventually he chose Ferris State College, a school which always threaten a deep run in the national championship tournament.

School would have been a disaster had it not been for hockey. Coach Guy Boucher had strict rules about study hours and curfews. Woe be it to any player that ignored those rules. Suspension from the team was never considered. Extra hours on the ice, skating endlessly from one end to the other, stick in hand, puck constantly moving was.

The formula worked. Cole completed his Bachelor's degree at Ferris State College. Sadly, his size and a shoulder injury his senior year, kept him from the pro hockey game. Lost and adrift he attempted a Masters Degree at Michigan State University, but too much drinking, too many girls and not enough studying quickly put an end to that idea. After a year with a small parts manufacturing firm in the auto town of Dearborn he decided to move back to Petoskey. Cole

struggled. Jobs in northern Michigan are few and far
between. Life was hard and dollars scarce. Cole was reduced
to pan-handling when he couldn't pick up some sort of day
job.

An old proverb holds that "sometimes even a blind
squirrel finds a nut" and Cole David Prestcott proved the
validity of that observation. A man from down state hired
Cole to paint his lake cabin. In payment, Cole was given a jet
ski. This was perfect, it filled his unemployed summer days
and all the girls wanted a ride. Soon family, friends and then
complete strangers were asking if they could rent the
machine.

Cole purchased three more and began renting the
speedy watercraft to the tourists who swarmed northern
Michigan's lakeside villages from Memorial Day to Labor
Day. It didn't take long before the business was expanding,
then doubling, and doubling again.

He had found a niche. He rented ski boats, then large
party boats. Cole bought out the competing Mom and Pop
boat rental businesses. Those that would not sell found one
of Cole's ultra modern, rental "salons" being built next door.
Soon the family boat rental shops faced cut-throat prices and
newer inventory. Within ten years Cole dominated the boat
rental business from Houton Lake north to Mackinaw Bridge.

Life was good. Cole married the stunningly beautiful
Elaine Mary Johannsen from Grand Rapids. He had it all and
Cole was not afraid to show it off. The irony of the thing was
not lost on him. Born to a typical middle class family Cole
had been a disappointment to his domineering father and
never-to-be pleased mother. His older brother's law degree
had only added to the pressure. Now, they could all go to
hell. Cole was the one with the multimillion dollar house and

business.

Elaine and Cole were cut from the same cloth. They met on a Wednesday night at one of the many East Lansing pubs catering to college students. She was a premed student who had been bested by the first test in her second semester of organic chemistry. She had been sitting alone at a table full of girls, contemplating a grade point average fading into the "we're sorry, but you do not meet our academic standards" range. He was back in his favorite bar after a day looking at used boats. Elaine was drowning her sorrows in mixed drinks with words like "Fuzzy, Sunset, Pink, and Lady" in their name. She had spent the better part of that afternoon in a tear filled discussion with her less than honest roommate. By nine that evening Elaine had decided that a "Mrs." degree was much easier to obtain than an M.D. degree. Her roommate readily agreed since she was also a pre-med student and there were only a limited number of students carried forward each year.

Cole's timing couldn't have been better. It had not been Elaine's pre-med brain that attracted Cole. Which was fair since it wasn't Cole's brain that attracted Elaine. What attracted Cole was the fact that Elaine was a twenty-one year old gymnast and football cheerleader with a figure that had caused more than one out-of-bounds player to momentarily forget the game.

What attracted Elaine was Cole's larger than average wallet. Time passed. Cole got his trophy wife and Elaine got her "Mrs." degree.

Cole joined the local Chamber of Commerce, the country club, the Rod and Gun Club and was often seen skiing, boating and playing on the lake with various friends and associates from the local business community. To them,

Cole was a great guy.

To his wife he was a no-good, two timing SOB, who had imprisoned her in the uncultured hinterlands of northern Michigan. But she liked the money, had no skills outside of the bedroom and at the age of thirty-four had never earned a paycheck from anyone other than her husband. Elaine was not a fan of working for a living, though she had worked full time in the business until recently. She still did some occasional work for the company, but only when it suited her. And, it suited her only when opportunity presented itself. Elaine couldn't conceive of working for a living, so she stayed with him, or so Cole thought. But then, Cole didn't think too hard about people.

Cole's ego matched the size of the Great Lakes. In a few years he sold his home in Petosky and moved several miles south to the shores of Lake Charlevoix. Here Cole let his imagination and wallet run wild. Cole intended that everyone cruising those bright blue waters knew that Cole Prestcott had hit the big time.

He purchased seven acres of land jutting into the western end of the lake near the little puddle known as Round Lake and the canal which led to Lake Michigan. He tore down the nine hundred square foot cabin that had occupied the lot for seventy years and replaced it with a modest home. Modest only in the sense that it wasn't as big as Oprah Winfrey's Chicago home.

Built to impress, using the most eco-friendly technology available, it was a six thousand square foot Northern Michigan white cedar log cabin with gray slate roofing. It held six bedrooms, three massive stone fireplaces, one each in the living room, master bedroom and in front of the full length bar in the "man cave" basement plus a game room, family room and formal living room. The home was, of course, professionally decorated in a dual logging and maritime motif that captured the heritage of the area perfectly. The fact that Elaine could stay at home, yet go days without having to see Cole had a certain appeal to her.

The "cabin" was truly beautiful. Elaine hosted several dinner parties each year; parties meant more to cement their role in society's elite than to fraternize with friends or each other. And, while Cole loved the status conferred by the most elegant house on the lake, he was less impressed with "his cabin" than he was with his boathouse.

The boathouse was massive. Constructed of white cedar logs to match the "cabin" it was two stories high, its east and west sides lined with tinted glass allowing the morning and afternoon sun to filter in and illuminate the space for the entire day. The building, actually two buildings, one on each side of a waterway covered by a roof, had been built on concrete pillars sunk into the lakebed. The walls were festooned with oars, paddles and fishing poles of various types. On the south, or land side, of the structure the left and right corners contained an office and machine shop respectively. Protruding some forty feet into the lake, the northern end contained storage and machinery rooms. A deck, with four docks forming berths stretched around the building in the shape of the letter U. Boats entered through the chain driven overhead doors at the open end of the U and rested comfortably in the eight cozy berths. Cole had dredged the lake bottom and designed the structure to allow his deep draft sailboat to be housed between the berths, lengthwise in the U. The mast extended neatly through an opening in the ceiling like a straw in an ice cream float. The docks were where Cole kept his current favorite watercraft ready to exit through the "port" as Cole called the north opening; "door" as his wife called it.

While the floor plan and dock system were impressive, what Cole really counted on to impress his visitors was the hoist system. Cole's people could lift a boat out of the water at four berths and suspend it over the water underneath. This allowed another boat to slip into the now vacant dock space. Cole employed two "deck hands" in the boathouse to complete the maintenance on the various boats, most of which were wood and required a considerable amount of care. The deckhands also maintained the boathouse and moved the boats here and there on the hoist. At present, Cole's boathouse held six different boats, not counting of course the numerous kayaks, canoes and wave runners which were suspended from the ceiling or placed on racks along the shore side wall. Cole had everything from a thirty-foot sailboat to an eight-foot canoe under one roof.

His pride and joy however was a perfectly restored 1922 Standard twenty-six foot Chris-Craft speedboat which he used to visit friends, lovers and the grandiosely named small town of Boyne City at the opposite end of the lake. Cole loved everything about the boat and was a fanatic Chris-Craft boat owner.

That Cole was an expert on the Chris-Craft line of boats came as no surprise to the few childhood friends he had, emphasis on the past tense. Cole had always viewed a Chris-Craft boat as the definition of luxury. Movie stars, captains of industry and the rich and famous of all brands had once made Chris-Craft the definitive mark of success.

As a young man Cole had decided he would someday own one and it would be perfect. As Cole's fortunes had improved he'd never forgotten that dream. He had often taken the Standard to owner's conventions and shows around the country. Cole even had an enclosed trailer specially made to transport the boat from his home to boat shows across the country. Should someone question a part, finish or color on the Standard, Cole immediately accessed his large library of original drawings, parts lists, brochures and manuals. Cole's boat was perfect and he made certain that everyone knew it.

Chapter 20

Cole had certainly found the proverbial nut. Unfortunately, he had never heard of another proverb which held that "pride goes before a fall." The Horton Bay Boat Company was a small, family owned firm located on the opposite side of the lake. The Schultz family began building wooden canoes during the post war boom years of the 1950's. The company was perfectly positioned as the auto industry created a huge middle class anxious to play on the hundreds of lakes scattered across the state. Soon easily operated, family friendly ski boats from the Schultz factory could be found on every lake in the State.

Otto Schultz had run the company since his father died in 1977. Otto had two children, both boys. Sadly, the oldest was one of the few Americans killed during the first Gulf war. Otto's younger son eventually married and had two children of his own. A plane crash took the family several years ago. Now, Otto and his wife planned to move to the Florida Keys and never shovel snow again.

In time he approached Cole about purchasing the business. The price was steep, but the business was sound and the idea of building boats began to consume Cole. Unfortunately, Cole was already saddled with a large debt from the construction of his home and boathouse. He had mortgaged his business and carried a heavy debt on the property. It all added up to a bad risk. Cole was turned down by several banks; he could not swing the deal.

There are no secrets. It's a law of nature. People who truly knew Cole for what he was knew the state of Cole's finances. But bankers are as greedy as any scavenger and Cole soon found the perfect partner.

Alan Wisecup's career had stalled. He had begun working for the bank as a teller while he completed a two-year degree in accounting at the local community college. Upon graduation he had been promoted, the first of several. But now Alan had reached the top of the ladder, the top for a community college graduate in any case. As deputy chief loan officer of the Traverse Savings and Investment Bank Alan's only hope of moving up was to earn tremendous returns on his portfolio...or for the old bastard he worked for to drop over dead. Alan was a lot of things but he wasn't a killer. The boat building business was the perfect deal. The company looked sound and Cole Precott seemed to know his stuff. Returns from this deal were a sure thing.

Alan began making 'adjustments' to the Horton Bay Boat Company books. The debt load wasn't so much, the property suddenly became 'prime waterfront' and the tooling was new and could be depreciated...again. The asking price was a steal.

Cole's assets also underwent a transformation. Miraculously his debt load was gone and stores were expected to continue growing at a double digit rate. Cole's house doubled in value and his boathouse became a company asset. Only a fool would turn down this loan.

Cole sold his boat rental business, bought the Horton Bay Boat Company and began building boats. Cole's luck held. While he carried an unusually large interest rate on his loan and his payments were extraordinary, his boat sales were able to generate the income to service the debt and keep Cole and Elaine living the lifestyle they had only dreamed of. Cole's mistresses were happy, Cole was happy and his wife, he thought, was kept out of the loop.

For the next three years the business thrived. The day to day operations and main source of income for the company was a line of sport fishing and ski boats sold to auto workers and lower level executives from the southern part of the state, Ohio, Indiana and Illinois. The fishing boats were strong, powerful affairs intended for lake trout miles off shore in the Big Lakes. Sales were steady and profits good. The occasional luxury yacht order spiced things up a bit and the boat yard and repairs filled any gap in orders for boats. It was a good business.

Best of all Cole was able to dabble in Chris-Craft restorations. The work was slow, tedious and didn't make the company a lot of money, but Cole loved it. His restorations were gaining a national reputation as being as close to perfect as could be achieved.

Unfortunately, when a group of junior geniuses at the world's largest banks decided to sell each other bundles of worthless mortgages, the global economy shuttered and nearly collapsed. Michigan's auto industry did collapse, taking with it hundreds of small business owners and executives from the Big Three. Brokerage firms issued margin calls in numbers not seen since 1929. Millionaires across the country found they weren't millionaires anymore.

The first thing to go were the orders for sport fishing and ski boats as the middle class saw their homes collapse in value and their jobs disappear. The highly paid skilled tradesmen of the auto industry were laid off. Tool and die makers, electricians, machine operators of all types lost their middle class life style in a matter of weeks. Not far behind were the once powerful executives. The yacht construction and Chris-Craft restoration business collapsed.

The boat repair and storage business disappeared as people abandoned the boats and invited banks to foreclose on the loans. Within six months Cole's business was on the ropes.

He was forced to lay off nearly all of his employees, except of course his secretary. She of the 36C cups, meager ability to use a word processor and skills in the bedroom that were truly amazing. Soon Cole found himself with no staff, nothing to sell and debt threatening to swamp his otherwise perfect life.

He considered selling several of his prize boats. Then realized the money received from the boats would not approach their worth. Besides, if he could sell those boats he should be able to sell new boats. He couldn't; so that was that. The cabin and boathouse approached his debt, but he loathed the idea of losing his most prized possessions. And, with the economy as it was, there was little hope of getting full value from the property anyway.

Cole David Prestcott was, in his own words, screwed.

Chapter 21

Gerry had already lowered Sherrie and Eve to the ground and the three now stood at the garage doors. Sherrie and Eve quickly blocked the doors open using two large fieldstones and the four began their exploration of the building.

The boat appeared to be over thirty feet long. It was sitting on a wooden cradle with its bow toward the large double doors. To the right, between the boat and the wall stood a small stack of crates. To the left of the boat was a bit more space; against the exterior wall and running the length of the building was a wooden workbench. Tools, cans of nuts and bolts and assorted implements lay scattered on the bench. Three stools were positioned at random along the bench front.

Jim climbed the ladder, untied the rope and then moved the awkward beast to the side of the boat. Soon the four had scrambled up the side and were standing in the command console area of the boat. Dark green cushioned benches lined the exterior walls and a galley way door hid in the center under the mahogany framed windows. The cushions were clearly the home of numerous mice.

"This is nice, well…it was nice!" Sherrie gasped.

"We could have a heck of a party on this couldn't we?" Gerry said as he examined the settee.

Jim ran his hands along the smooth mahogany wood, admiring the workmanship then moved to the bridge deck. Eve quickly followed and spotted the ship's wheel.

"Check this out! Look how this thing is flat," she said

to Jim. The ships wheel was mounted parallel with the floor on a chrome column extending to waist level. A matching chrome drum stood on the console in front of and to one side of the wheel. It held the throttle mechanism. Jim tried to move the wheel, it barely budged. "It's stuck," he said to the group.

"Might be how this thing ended up with a hole in the front," observed Sherrie.

Eve then opened the door to the interior cabin. Dark green cushions, again the home of mice and what appeared to be sleeping berths.

"Nice boat once, what a waste it's just sitting here," Jim sighed.

"I wonder how it got here. I don't ever recall any mention of this thing when we were kids," Sherrie looked at Jim.

"I don't either. But, come to think about it, I really didn't know anything about this place. Dad just didn't want us crossing the fence and for some reason that was one of his rules that I never broke. This place always had bad karma, ya know what I mean?" Jim explained.

"I DO! I always felt the same way. Denise and I used to pick blackberries all up and down that fence, but I never would go on the other side."

No one could come up with an adequate explanation of how this boat ended up ten miles from Lake Michigan and soon they resumed their exploration. It was a cabin cruiser, obviously a high-end antique boat. Except for the damaged bow section, years of dirt, lots of mice and what appeared to be a mummified raccoon it appeared to be in remarkably good shape.

"This thing has to be worth a lot of money," Jim

remarked.

"I'll bet you're right," Gerry said. "We'll have to get it appraised.

Jim and Gerry climbed down the ladder and inspected the damaged left front of the cruiser. Gerry ran his hand along the gash, examining the damage in detail. "Jim, this looks like someone ran the boat onto the rocks. Look, the front part of this impact point splintered the wood, caved in several boards and then dragged back along the bottom of the hull."

Jim studied the marks where Gerry pointed. "I think you're right. And look here, this board is pulled the opposite direction. This boat was pulled off the rocks."

"Wonder why it didn't sink?" Gerry mused.

Jim grabbed a stool from in front of the workbench and sat looking at the damaged bow. Finally, he said, "Maybe it was being supported or floated somehow. I've heard of sailors wrapping a sail over a hole as a plug. But, to be honest, I have no idea."

"Well, somehow somebody did it," Gerry murmured as he tried without success to reach inside the damaged bow. "I'm wondering if we can fix this."

"If the keel is sound...if it's just this hole and refinishing the old wood, maybe some motor work, yeah, we could do it. Shouldn't be too hard." Jim said with an ironic grin. "Going to be expensive; that's mahogany. And "it ain't cheap" as they say."

They finished exploring the boat then climbed down to the barn floor. Jim edged over to the tool bench and began exploring the antique tools and other objects.

Sherrie and Eve found a broom and began clearing dirt from the boat. Gerry began surveying the building. Eve appeared at the toolbox, removed a claw hammer and disappeared again. A few moments later a sad moan came from behind the boat. "Awwww…Darn, I thought we had something!"

Walking around the boat Jim and Gerry found the women sitting on two crates, another two crates were open and they were attempting to open a third.

"These are all Canadian Whiskey crates, but they're all empty!" Sherrie explained.

"You were looking for cheap booze weren't you?" Gerry pointed an accusatory finger at his wife and laughed.

The group examined the whiskey crates. "Lots of empty booze boxes," Gerry said. "I kind of like the old wooden crates, they're sort of interesting. Think we could use some around the house as decorations?"

"I don't know, but I'll bet we can get rid of these in a garage sale in about a minute," Sherrie observed.

Jim had become fixated on repairing the boat. "I'll bet I can fix this," he said to himself as he studied the damaged bow. A moment later he was climbing the ladder and reentering the cabin. After several minutes Jim yelled, "Hey Gerry, do me a favor and bring me the tool box and flashlight."

Gerry grabbed the box and soon found Jim on his hands and knees in the forward cabin of the craft, his head and shoulders wedged under a small settee.

"I should be able to access the bilge from somewhere around here. If I can, we should be able to see the frame and the backside of that impact point. We should be able to tell how big a deal it will be after seeing that."

Gerry agreed with the plan and the two began looking for the bilge access panels. Soon Jim found the latch and pulled a three-foot long by two-foot wide piece of cabin sole from its frame. The two examined the inside of the bilge. Gerry looked at Jim but didn't say anything.

"That's odd," Jim said.

"What is that?" Gerry asked.

There was no bilge. Instead, another panel lay just under the cabin sole they had removed. Gerry shinned the flashlight along the new panel. Finally, he spotted four large screw heads, one at each corner. Jim grabbed a screwdriver and they removed the cover. Inside they found six crates of Canadian Whiskey, only these were full.

It took a moment for Eve and Sherrie to climb the ladder and join Jim and Gerry in the boat. Soon the four had removed the six cases to the floor of the barn.

"I think this is a smuggler's boat. That extra little storage area must have been added to the boat after it was built," Jim said while climbing back up the ladder.

"You really think so? That's too cool!" Sherrie said.

"Bet there's more," Eve added.

"What makes you say that?" Gerry asked.

"Well, if I'm going to all the trouble to outfit this big boat to smuggle booze I'm going to take a lot, not a little. And let's face it, six cases is really not that much." Eve seemed confident in her guess.

Jim studied Eve for a moment, "You're right, that makes sense, let's keep looking." It took nearly thirty minutes, but they found five more compartments. All were empty save one, and it held an additional four cases of hard liquor. By now there was no doubt, this was indeed a bootlegger's boat. They loaded the ten cases of liquor in the bed of Gerry's truck and returned to the barn.

Jim and Gerry climbed back into the boat and began

to examine the false bilge. "This might give us a better chance to see the inside framing," Jim said to Gerry. He stretched out on the floor. Then, on his back, Jim slowly inched his head and shoulders inside the large compartment hidden in the bilge. The walls were made of pine boards with several coats of shellac to seal them from bilge water. Using the flashlight Jim examined the compartment interior. Solid walls. He would have to drill a hole.

Gerry sat on the settee next to where Jim lay. "See anything?" he asked.

"Nothing, we're going to need a hole saw to get past these walls."

Chapter 22

As the nation's economy sputtered Cole's days had become increasingly empty. There simply wasn't anything to do in the shop. He did his best to hide it. Each morning began exactly the same. Elaine, the master of the cutting remark, made some comment about how she wanted to move to Grand Rapids, Chicago or Ann Arbor and he pretended there was something important to do at the office. There wasn't. There hadn't been anything to do there in months, but Cole felt like he had to keep up the appearance. Normally he slipped out of the office about noon. He'd head to the golf course or take a turn of the lake on one of his boats. Although lately he'd spent more time on a sailboat than a powerboat. The days of burning a hundred dollars of gas in an afternoon were coming to an end.

This morning however he did have an important meeting. His banker, Alan Wisecup, seemed to be very concerned about Cole's loan payments. To Cole, Wisecup was the perfect banker. He wasn't young. He was youngish. Which meant that he should have been promoted long ago. He hadn't been which meant he wasn't very good and he was still young enough to be stupid. He seemed to be a bit of, well, he seemed like a pencil pushing geek. Cole always had to work at not laughing outright at the man. Young, pencil pushing geeks were good, they could be pushed around.

Cole knew Wisecup was coming with bad news. The loans were coming due in less than ninety days. But, he was certain he could either talk the tight wad sonofabitch into an extension on the loan or simply refinance the entire thing.

This was important. The small amount of cash the business generated from boat repair, storage and commission sales wasn't covering the note. Hell, it barely covered his house payment and the payroll for the four remaining employees.

At ten o'clock sharp Alan Wisecup, deputy chief loan officer of the Traverse Savings and Investment Bank walked through the door of Prestcott Boats. The secretary, Donna LeGrange, directed him to a seat in the waiting area in front of her desk. A move which annoyed Mr. Wisecup; he'd expected to be shown right to Cole's office. Donna offered him water, not coffee, which also annoyed Wisecup. Then she disappeared into Cole's office.

Alan hated Cole Prestcott, hated him more than anyone or anything in this world. A year ago his promotion looked certain, now this loan made him look like a fool. Worse yet the auditors might find how he had altered the books and made this incompetent show horse look like the second coming of Warren Buffett.

He had tried to force Prestcott to pay his bills, but it hadn't happened. Now all he could hope for was to break even. He opened his briefcase, a shabby, tattered brown affair and removed a multicolored spreadsheet. The payment history was bad, Prestcott hadn't made a full payment in the past five months. The cash flow looked worse, maybe if he took the house there would be enough there. Wisecup grimaced. He had to get this loan off the books before some auditor came snooping around. The house, the boathouse, the boats, the company. Maybe he could save his job and stay out of prison.

"Cole baby, the banker is here" Donna was a constant source of amazement to Cole. She knew the situation; she couldn't help but know the situation. She had to know the business was in trouble. She had watched the parking lot empty itself over the past six months. Hell, she'd typed the lay-off notices. Now there were only five cars if you counted Cole's, four if Jim Abbot rode with his brother. But she never mentioned it, never asked Cole about it and never treated a banker any better than dirt.

Cole could only shake his head in amazement; either the woman was as stupid as a post or she simply didn't care. In either case, Cole liked it.

Today he was feeling cocky, he'd played the scene over and over in his mind, and he was certain he knew how the conversation would go. He pulled Donna to his lap and kissed her. "It's alright honey, send him in," Cole whispered as he slipped his hand under her white polyester blouse and squeezed her right breast. She smiled and whispered, "Later sugar."

Cole then lifted a knee and tipped her onto her feet. "Okay, send him in; I've got a few minutes this morning."

Donna smiled, kissed Cole once more and returned to her desk. "Mr. Prestcott will see you in a moment," she said. It was always best to let them wait a little bit. She settled herself behind the desk, studied the banker for several moments, took a measured sip from her coffee cup, then picked up the phone. She listened intently to the silent line for a long moment then said, "He's ready now." Donna then escorted Wisecup into the office of her boss.

Returning to her seat she opened the bottom drawer and pulled out a Barbara Cartland novel. Her day had begun.

Chapter 23

Elaine Prestcott stepped out of the shower, pulled the towel from the heated towel rack and began to dry herself. Glancing at her reflection in the mirror she smiled. She liked what she saw. Her stomach was flat and firm. Her breasts large, but not overly large and, she was happy to see, they didn't sag. She half turned and looked over her shoulder. No sign of cellulite.

Elaine had a secret. Not the kind of secret that brought down empires or ruined the lives of politicians that couldn't keep their pants zipped, but a good one nevertheless. She knew exactly what the bank, or more accurately Alan Wisecup, was going to tell Cole. It really didn't take a rocket scientist to figure it out. There wasn't a snowball's chance in hell that any legitimate bank would refinance Cole. Even the corruptible bankers whom Cole did business with had their limits, and they'd reached them.

An afternoon in a Petoskey bed and breakfast had not only relieved her 'tensions' but also given her all the information she needed. Elaine had seen all the documents, all the finances of her husband's business, and decided that now was the time to move on with the rest of her life.

The years since her marriage to the cheating SOB had been good to Elaine. She had her figure, her hair fairly glowed in the sun and the lines around the corners of her eyes were only just starting to appear. In the beginning Elaine had held out hope that this self-arranged marriage could become, if not a loving one, at least a tolerable one. She had envisioned children whom she could love, and possibly she would come to accept Cole as a lover. The years had proven her wrong. Happy, or at least acceptable, endings only happened in second hand bookstore novels. She would have to endure or get out.

Thinking about it now she could pinpoint the exact day she decided to screw the bastard. It was a Wednesday, just six weeks after they had returned from a honeymoon in Key West. A normal morning, a normal day. But by lunch she had stumbled into Cole's hidden world. He had an early meeting and had rushed out of the house. Elaine had been dressing for a Pilates class when Cole left. Passing the kitchen table on her way to the garage Elaine spotted Cole's cell phone. Deciding to take it to him she scooped the phone, along with her keys and makeup, into her purse and left the house.

When the class was over she gathered her things from her locker and walked to her Firebird. The cell phone buzzed just as she opened her purse to find her keys. It was the phone's voice mail notification. Elaine swiped her finger across the phone then pressed the keypad. The cell phone immediately launched into a recitation of the date, time and phone number from whence the voice mail sprang. Then a woman's voice, dripping with honey, asked Cole when he was coming by again, mentioned the 'shivers' his touch gave her and dinner. Elaine listened and knew exactly what had happened.

The previous night Cole had attended a Chamber of Commerce meeting, or so he had said. He had come home very late and taken a shower before coming to bed. It wasn't the first bed Cole had been in that night.

Elaine opened the car door and got in. She sat there for several minutes letting rage and hatred build. Then, she began to relax. If she really thought about it she didn't love Cole anymore than he loved her. This was a marriage of convenience.

Elaine then began a cold, dispassionate assessment of her life. She had failed at her dream of entering medical school. She had left college to marry. In truth she had married for money so it only seemed logical that she start getting it.

She knew from the first time he'd brought her to Petoskey that his business would be a cash cow. Even while they had dated she could see the business growing. It seemed to double every week in those days. Now, her husband of less than two months was sleeping around. Elaine had thought about that, he was a cheater. In truth she'd known from the start that he would, and she knew he would never stop. She had no prospects and she could see the business making them very wealthy, very soon.

Twenty minutes later Elaine had her plan. She drove home, opened Cole's side of the garage and drove in. She then placed the cell phone behind the car's front tire, got back in the Firebird and backed out of the garage.

When Cole came home that evening he would find the crushed cell phone and think he'd dropped the little unit that morning. All evidence that Elaine had listened to his voicemail would be gone.

The next day Elaine waited until Cole left for work. Then she drove to the home of a woman she had met at one of the numerous socials she attended. The woman, fifty-six years old, had divorced her husband, a modestly successful housing developer, six years ago. She lived in a large, seventy-five year old field stone mansion overlooking Lake Michigan, was a board member of two country clubs, a prominent member of the local Democratic Party and known for her philanthropic giving.

This intrigued Elaine. The woman had never worked a day in her life and the husband's business hadn't been that successful. Two hours later Elaine knew why the business hadn't shown great profits. She left the big house and drove the sixty miles south to Traverse City. There she opened a bank account and visited her new friend's financial advisor.

A month later Elaine put the second part of her her plan into motion. Over coffee and a bowl of Cheerios she mentioned to Cole that staying home while he was at work was boring. She thought it would be much better if she worked with Cole everyday. He resisted the idea at first of course, she knew he would. But she patiently explained what a bookkeeper would cost the company. Besides, she had the skills and they might as well keep the money in the family. Put that way, Cole couldn't resist.

Elaine quickly took over all the company accounting and purchasing. On every purchase Elaine padded the price, adding a few dollars to small purchases, a few hundred to larger ones. She then skimmed the excess from the company books and sent the money to Mr. David McFain of Growth Financial Management on Front Street in downtown Traverse City.

Mr. McFain, of course, used only the back door of the building, he being the same disbarred attorney who once held the position of budget director for the Detroit mayor's office. McFain had been convicted of violating Rule 10 of the Commodities and Exchange Act, trading based on insider information. Eighteen months of cutting the grass and raking leaves with Wall Street's best at Maxwell Air Force Base's minimum security prison earned David a Master's degree in stock manipulation. McFain was now very good at avoiding detection, and still had his Rolodex. Elaine was very pleased with the results he was able to provide.

Chapter 24

Dinner at the orchard consisted of leftovers, beer, and chips. The barn, the boat, and the whiskey were the sole topics of conversation. Gerry and Sherrie couldn't decide if they were suddenly the proud owners of an antique treasure or in need of a dump truck and several cans of termite spray. Jim and Eve were excited for them and curious about the boat.

"We've got a mystery here," Jim said, sipping a bottle of beer from one of the local microbreweries.

Gerry nodded his head. "That's for sure. I'd sure like to know more about that building. I don't know anything about the property other than what the attorney said about it not being on the tax records.

And the boat! That is one cool boat. We should probably find out where the boat came from…and do Sherrie and I own the boat since it came with the building? I think we do but don't really know the law."

Sherrie handed him a cantaloupe and a large knife.

"I can't imagine you don't," Eve offered. "But I think you have two big issues. First, ownership of the boat. It seems logical that you own the boat, you own the land, and it was part of the deal, wasn't it? It should be yours.

Second, and I think your bigger issue, is the whiskey. It must be illegal to have all that booze? There aren't any stamps on the bottles. I'm betting it's moonshine."

"I think you're right hon, the boat is probably theirs. You guys better check with a lawyer though, which of course will cost you an arm and a leg. But still better safe than sorry.

You'd hate to spend money fixing the thing up, getting it to the water and then have someone come along and claim it's theirs. And, you'd really be in it if you sold the damn thing, then someone could come after you," Jim said.

"Ahhh…I hate lawyers, they charge so much for everything and act like they're doing you a favor! The regular guy can't afford a lawyer anymore," Gerry moaned.

"Suck it up buddy. It's the way of the world," Jim grinned. Turning to Eve he said, "Bet that isn't moonshine. Those labels all look professionally printed. All the bottles are the same, all have the same logos in raised glass. I'm going to guess that those are legit Canadian Whiskey bottles, but they were smuggled in from Canada. No U.S. taxes were paid on those bottles."

"Prohibition era booze?" Sherrie asked. "Woo…we've got Al Capone stuff here!"

"Sure, why not?" Jim replied. "Hidden booze, no tax stamps, the boat is from the right era, you've got to admit it all fits. It could be the real deal."

Sherrie glanced at Eve, "You think he's serious?"

"He thinks he's Sam Spade but I must admit, he's more often right than wrong," Eve laughed.

Jim thought a moment then said. "Sherrie I never saw anyone over there when Dad and I hunted that side of the farm. Did you ever see anyone there?"

Sherrie traced her fingertip around the lip of her wine glass. "No I didn't. And I spent a lot of summer afternoons on that side of the orchard. We picked berries there and I played over there with my friends."

"I'll bet that boat has been there all these years," Jim said.

"I wonder who we contact about illegal booze?"

Gerry said.

"Gotta be the FBI," Eve replied. "Prohibition was a national thing, it was in the Constitution, and the tax thing has to be the federal government. Is there an FBI office in Traverse City?"

Gerry shrugged. "I don't know, probably not. Might be one in Lansing or Detroit, but I can't imagine one in TC. I'll go into town tomorrow and find out. I'll stop by the police station and talk it over with them. Should be interesting, I'll bet they've never handled bootlegger booze before!"

Conversation lagged as everyone tried to imagine the story behind the Chris-Craft in the barn. Finally Jim said, "It's probably putting the cart before the horse, but I'd like to get a professional to look at the boat. It would be nice if it could be repaired. Maybe the engine can be started. But we may have to overhaul it. That cruiser would make a nice summer toy on the bay. The sooner we get a handle on the damages and the worth the sooner I can fix it up for you."

"For us buddy, we're going to run that boat together," Gerry laughed. "I'll check with the lawyer I had working on the land title about boat ownership on Monday. And, I'll see if the state guy has any more information on the property, the barn and the boat."

"Sounds good to me," Jim said. "Know anyone that really knows boats?"

Gerry thought a minute, "Well, yeah, I do. I met a guy at a Chamber meeting awhile ago. He repaired boats or sold boats, something like that. From what we talked about the guy is really into antique boats. I've got his card someplace. I'll find it, then let's give him a call."

Chapter 25

Cole sat alone in his study. On the walls were pictures of Michigan lighthouses, a picture of the Edmond Fitzgerald plowing through rough waters, its destiny not yet decided, and a marine chart of Lake Michigan. All were illuminated by subtle wrought iron picture lights. It was a beautiful room. Cole didn't see any of it. He focused on the two bottles of scotch sitting in the middle of his desk.

It hadn't gone like he'd expected; not even close. Wisecup had taken his seat, skipped any pretense of friendliness, opened a briefcase and began unloading a stack of papers. When the stack reached four inches he began reading parts of each document to Cole.

He spent several minuets on each and every one. He pointed to every place Cole had signed his own name, he pointed to dates, he highlighted past due payments, amortization schedules, current cash flow sheets, business expenditures and current billings. Then he went back to the sheet with payment dates, but no payment. After each and every paper the bastard would look Cole square in the eye and ask him if he understood what he'd just been told. Of course he understood, he wasn't stupid, but where was the money going to come from? No one was buying boats; the whole damn state was laid off or about to be laid off or had been laid off. They'd been out of work for so long they'd forgotten what a boat even was.

Wisecup then opened a laptop and showed Cole pictures of similar buildings and what they were selling for. He could sell this building for X. He could sell that building for Y and the boats for Z. But X plus Y plus Z wasn't enough.

Cole pushed for an extension on the loan, but Wisecup wouldn't talk about that. Cole tried to refinance the entire load for a higher interest rate. Wisecup refused that. He kept putting that damned spreadsheet under Cole's nose. He kept telling Cole that the small amount of cash the business generated from boat repair, storage and commission sales wouldn't cover the current note. It barely covered the payroll and his house payment. There was no way it could cover a new note.

Cole argued. It did no good. He cursed. It did no good. He tried to reason. It seemed as if Wisecup enjoyed his pain. Finally, when there were no new forms, no spreadsheets showing the same debt in some different way, when all the contracts and papers had been examined, each and every one presented with just the right twist to pull the maximum humiliation from Cole's gut, only then did Wisecup stop. He told Cole that unless a substantial payment was made and soon it would all come crashing down, he'd lose the company, the house, the boats, everything.

Slowly, ever so slowly, Cole reached out for the scotch. Gradually the two bottles in front of him merged into one. He fastened both hands around the bottle, found his glass and recharged. Raising his glass Cole muttered, "To renting God-damned runabouts again." He slammed the scotch back in one quick, sloppy, shirt soaking gulp.

Chapter 26

In any war sacrifices are made for the greater good. At least that's what Elaine told herself as she inserted the key into a heavily tarnished brass lock face. Information, especially important, sensitive information, didn't come cheap. Margaretha Zelle, better known as Mata Hari, learned that. Still, Margaretha had been on to something, there were ways to learn things that didn't cost money.

The lock secured the entrance door to room number six of the Torch Lake Waterfront Motel. The motel, built sometime in the early 1960s, had been family owned for three generations.

Elaine entered the room, pulled open the window and, had her purpose here not been so utterly boring, would have enjoyed the beachfront view. Turning back to the room she dismissed the starving artist painting over the bed. Elaine studied the room with a practiced eye. It was apparent this generation of hotel ownership didn't believe in fresh paint or, for that matter, carpet. The floor was dark linoleum. Probably installed by the original builder so that housekeeping could easily sweep up the beach sand tracked in by waves of vacationers.

She walked to the bathroom, ran the shower, the water was hot; flushed the toilet, it didn't back up, then returned to the main room. The TV worked; sixty-five channels including the Adult Network. Turning to the bed, Elaine lifted the bedspread and stripped the sheets back to reveal the mattress. Then she inspected the mattress, sheets and pillows for bedbugs. Satisfied she remade the bed, picked up the ice bucket and went to the ice machine. Five minutes later she sat in the room's one chair watching "Ellen," a bottle of Southern Comfort soaking in the ice and a six pack of Coke waiting.

Thirty minutes later, and fifteen minutes early, a gentle rap sounded from the door. Elaine took a large gulp of her second drink, steeled herself and opened the door. Alan Wisecup immediately pushed into the room, and, without closing the door wrapped his arms around her. He kissed her fully, his tongue exploring her mouth, his hand pulling her skirt up at the same time.

"Close the damned door first you idiot," Elaine hissed, pushing him away. The door slammed shut. Wisecup's shoulders slumped. "I'm just glad to see you," he whispered.

Elaine let disgust and triumph and pity wash over her for a moment then forced a smile. "I know, baby," she cooed. "We just can't let people see us and the door was open. Where did you park?"

"At the Quick Mart like you told me," Alan said.

Elaine turned and walked to the ice bucket. The idiot walked a mile to get here she thought and smiled. It was her own little game. "Would you like a drink?" she asked. She poured two fingers into a glass, mixed in the Coke, deliberately skipped the ice and handed the tumbler to Alan. Then she refilled her own. She didn't make any move in his direction. "Why don't you take a shower baby, you're all sweaty."

Alan smiled and kicked off his shoes. He pulled his tie off then stripped his shirt and tee shirt off. Elaine sat and watched this strip tease and smiled. Alan began to dance; slow, jerky, uncoordinated and smiled back.

"You're an idiot," she said and grinned. Alan took it

as an expression of endearment. Elaine meant it for what it was.

He stripped off his pants and jockey shorts then headed to the shower, still wearing his black socks. Elaine watched him walk away. Alan was pale, almost white. His shoulders weren't girlish, but no one would call him broad chested or big shouldered. He was thin, Alan liked to run 10K races in the summer. He was in reasonably good shape, though not muscular. But most of all Alan was a nerd.

Ten minutes later Elaine sat on the edge of the bed and watched Alan towel himself off. "How are things at the bank?" she asked.

"Oh, you know, nothing much. Mark is still a jerk. The guy thinks he's God's gift ya know. Yesterday Debbie brought in donuts. I was out front for ten minutes. When I came back he'd eaten three. I didn't even get one."

She didn't care. "You met with Cole?"

"Yeah. Same old stuff." He said as he hung his towel on the rack.

Elaine unbuttoned her blouse, hung it up then slipped her skirt off.

"How does it look?" she asked.

"I really shouldn't talk about it. But I'll tell you this, you might want to get separate bank accounts."

"Could he really be this stupid?" she thought. "So it's that bad huh?" she said.

"Oh yeah, it's bad." Alan returned to the bed and began to stroke her hair.

Still in her thong and bra she kissed Alan. "I'll pour us another drink." Elaine picked up his glass and crossed the room. She poured more Southern Comfort into Alan's glass, then slipped a little blue pill from between her breasts and dropped it into the drink. "Might as well enjoy the evening," she thought. She picked up the TV remote, turned on the Adult Network and handed the drink to Alan.

She took off her bra and pushed the glass to his lips. "Drink up baby."

Alan did as he was told, his eyes darting between the TV screen and Elaine as she slowly pulled off her thong. He drained his glass in one big gulp and laid back on the bed. "C'mer honey," he coughed.

Elaine straddled his ankles, took him in her hand and bent forward. Then, her hair brushing Alan's thigh she said "Tell me more about your meeting with Cole."

Chapter 27

On Saturday, Sherrie and Eve headed to the farmers market. Jim took the ATV out to the new barn to examine the boat. Gerry went to his office in the cherry shed and began searching his collection of business cards. If his memory was correct, he had met the owner of a marina or boat restoration something company at a Chamber of Commerce meeting some months ago.

The two had, as is custom, exchanged business cards. Unlike ninety-nine percent of all business cards this one was not thrown into the trash. Instead, Gerry had filed it away just in case Sherrie ever agreed to buy a boat. He figured it didn't hurt to dream. Finding the card he dialed the cell phone number and Cole Prestcott answered.

The ringing of the cell phone blasted through Cole's dehydrated, alcohol soaked brain. He lay on the floor next to his desk, his head on top of an Air Jordan shoe with his shirt laying over it. The phone rang a second, then a third time and Cole, having become addicted to cell phones couldn't resist answering the nagging little machine.

"Hello? Have I reached Prestcott Boats?" A voice seemed to shout from the phone.

"Hello…?" Cole's years of renting boats to straight laced vacationing parents paid off. It only took him a moment. Cole cleared his throat, then using all his will power commanded his voice to sound steady, serious, the epitome of a respectable business owner. "This is Prestcott Boats, Cole Prestcott speaking."

"Cole, we met at the Chamber of Commerce meeting

a few months ago," the voice continued. Cole pulled the cell phone from his ear and glanced at the small screen. "Gerry, of course, I remember you. How's the cherry business?"

Gerry was impressed; the man had remembered his name and business. The fact that Gerry's name and the words "Cherry Nation Orchard LLC" appeared on the caller I.D. completely slipped his mind.

The two exchanged small talk for a few moments then Gerry came to the point. "Look Cole, the reason I'm calling is a bit odd. Do you think you could come over here and give an assessment of an antique boat? I'm going to need a good idea of the value next week and so, well, if you could come today or tomorrow I'd appreciate it. Sorry for the inconvenience."

Cole's first instinct was to tell the jerk on the other end of the line to stuff it. "Well, look Gerry, we're pretty busy and…I'll have to look at the schedule and get…"

Gerry cut him off. "Cole, I know it's an imposition. Look, we just we found this old Chris-Craft, it's a big boat, it's in pretty decent shape, and I thought you mentioned something about knowing Chris-Crafts."

The idea that someone was calling him about a "big" Chris-Craft fired Cole's alcohol soaked brain. "How big do you think this boat is Gerry?" he asked.

"Geeze, I don't know for sure, maybe thirty-five feet." Gerry really was guessing.

A cruiser! It had to be. Cole loved the cruisers. They were the classics of the classics. Today they were few and far between, but oh they were sweet. Besides, going to look at the boat was a good excuse to get out of the house. At least he wouldn't have to put up with the dragon queen's nagging about his drinking.

"Sure Gerry, I'll check with my staff and see if anyone is available. Give me a minute." Cole put the call on hold, went to the bathroom then the kitchen. Gerry sat at his desk and counted the minutes. Time dripped past. Gerry put the phone down, turned on his computer and fished a box of receipts out of his desk drawer. Phone wedged between his shoulder and ear he tapped at his keyboard and wished he'd called on his cell phone so he could put the call on speaker.

After an overly long number of minutes Cole returned to his desk with a fresh cup of coffee. He sat down, took a sip of the brew, then reached out to the phone and pushed a button, "Gerry, we're pretty busy so I'll have to come myself. I can get over there this afternoon. Ahhh, Gerry, I'll have to charge you a weekend rate, sorry about that." Cole was pleased with himself; he thought his line about being busy was brilliant.

Gerry glanced at the screen on his computer. The accounting program showed the current checking account balance. He cringed at the weekend rate idea but said, "That's great. A weekend rate isn't a problem. Thanks so much. What time should I look for you, it's about what, forty-five minutes, maybe an hour and fifteen from Charlevoix? If you go to our web site the orchard's address and a map are posted there."

A few moments later, small talk ended Cole had agreed to be at the orchard later that afternoon. Gerry thanked Cole again, put the phone back in its cradle, picked up his keys and started into Traverse City to speak with the police.

Chapter 28

Cole put down the cell phone and took a drink of his coffee. This was good, he could squeeze a few hundred out of this little deal. He wondered how long Elaine would stay once she knew he was broke. Who was he kidding? She'd be gone the same day and they both knew it. He pushed back his chair and walked to the porch. Elaine was reading something on her iPad and sipping her Kahlúa flavored coffee. "I've got to go to TC. Work." he said to his wife.

"Sure baby, you going to be home by dinner?" she asked.

Cole was stunned. She sounded like she cared, which he was sure she didn't. Nothing about his drinking, nothing about him sleeping on the floor and looking like a wreck. Maybe she'd not noticed? Impossible, she had to know.

"Naw, I'll eat on the way home, don't worry about it." Cole eyed her. She had returned to her iPad. Nothing unusual. Something was up. Elaine swiped her finger, the iPad showed a different page. Damned if he could figure it out.

Elaine suppressed a smile. For the past fifteen years she'd endured a two-timing, ignorant husband who couldn't carry on an intelligent conversation about anything other than himself and boats. Fortunately, she'd figured it out early. She looked back at Cole. "Okay, if you're sure. I can leave a plate in the 'fridge if you want?"

Cole paused. "Maybe she was taking her happy pills again," he thought.

He pulled his keys from the kitchen drawer. This was

odd; what the hell was she up to? "No, no, I'm good, thanks. See you tonight," he said and headed for the garage.

Elaine nearly laughed out loud. He was a fool. Then she thought about what could have happened and thanked her lucky stars it hadn't. She'd done three things that guaranteed her a life. First, she'd made sure she didn't have this idiot's kid. Elaine figured the Spartans had it right, only her standards were higher. In fact, she had never met a baby that shouldn't be put outside the walls.

Second, she made sure Cole's banker was her banker. Not that Wisecup would ever touch her money; she didn't trust him anymore than she trusted her husband. Wisecup was her source of information. She paid for that information. Well, 'paid' might be too strong a word. She slept with him. Fortunately, he was surprisingly satisfying, which kept her happy and him under control. As a result, though her name was missing on every account Cole and the business had she had access as if it were.

Elaine fingered her smart phone. A little bit of electronic magic that held the key to the third and best decision she'd ever made. It held the passwords to the investment accounts established by Mister David McFain. Now, those accounts were well into seven figures and it was time to drive the stake in the heart of the idiot she'd married.

Elaine rinsed her coffee cup in the kitchen sink and watched Cole's car back out of the driveway. He turned left and headed to the marina. She headed to bathroom. There she brushed her teeth, applied whitener to fight coffee stains and dressed. Then she placed two phone calls, one to her investment advisor and another to a moving company.

Chapter 29

Cole Prestcott arrived at the orchard gate at one o'clock as promised. He had driven one of the shop vans used for work at various marinas in the area. The van looked like the mobile boat shop it was. The vehicle was packed with parts and power tools of all sorts. On one side of the van a cage had been installed which resembled a bookshelf. It held two rows of reference books and parts catalogs. Each book was devoted to a popular marine engine, brand of boat, or specialized marine parts supplier. The worker could find schematics and order parts without returning to the shop.

He met Gerry and Jim at the orchard office. After handshakes and a bit of small talk Jim said his 'Good-byes' and drove into TC. Gerry escorted Cole into the orchard office, poured two cups of coffee and began to recount the discovery of the boat. The group had previously agreed not to mention the bottles of rumrunner booze, but Gerry did describe the additional hidden storage holds they'd found.

"That's an amazing story Gerry," Cole announced.

"I'm certain that you've got a fairly rare example of a Chris-Craft cruiser. Well, now they're all rare, but you know what I mean. So, let's go take a look?"

"Sounds good Cole, we can take my truck and..."

"No, Gerry. Thanks, but I'm going to have to take my van, it has everything I need. I'll follow you."

Cole followed Gerry's truck across the back of the property, down a two-track path between rows of cherry trees and stopped at a fence gate. Gerry opened the gate, let Cole through, then drove through himself, stopping to close the gate behind. A few moments later they were parked next to the old brick barn. Gerry walked to the large set of doors while Cole took a tape measure and various other tools from the van.

Slowly the doors swung open and sunlight filled the dark interior. Gerry blocked the first door open then went to do the same for the other. Cole casually approached the barn, stopping suddenly as he realized what he was looking at.

"WOW!" Cole was suddenly animated. "I don't believe it! Sonofabitch! You've got a Chris-Craft Express Commuter! This thing is beautiful! I never thought I'd find one. I'll be damned."

"This is good huh?"

"Good? Gerry this is a piece of art!"

Gerry went to the side doors and propped them open, allowing more light into the building. He couldn't help but grin. The boat was indeed a beautiful thing.

Cole simply stared. After a few moments he gushed, "This is amazing. There aren't many of these left. Only a handful in fact."

Entering the building Gerry showed Cole the damaged bow. Cole walked around the boat twice, each time pausing at the damaged bow.

"This can be fixed Gerry. I'll tell you that right now. And you'd be foolish not to do it. This is an amazing boat."

Cole went to the rear of the craft, mounted the ladder, and climbed to the command console. He strolled about the deck, moving from level to level, touching and caressing the different parts of the boat.

Cole had changed somehow. He was many things, most of them a bit slimy, but Cole did know Chris-Crafts. His voice took on extra confidence. He pointed out brass fixtures and fine joinery. To Gerry, Cole's running commentary certainly sounded like it came from a man that knew what he was talking about.

"These Chris-Crafts are the Cadillacs of the boat world. The company was started by a kid; can you believe that? Seems this kid, Chris Smith built a boat when he was thirteen, a couple of years later he was building full size duck boats. Apparently he could make a duck boat better than anyone else in southern Michigan and he got a reputation."

"You're kidding me, a thirteen year old kid?" Gerry wasn't sure if he was hearing a tall tale or not.

"Yeah, no joke. Christopher Columbus Smith, now there's a name I could never forget."

Cole climbed down the ladder, decided he didn't have all the tools he needed and went to his van. A few minutes later he returned holding a large toolbox and talking as if he had not stopped.

"So anyway, by the 1880s his brother Hank and ol' Chris Columbus had formed a little boat building business and made duck boats and small work boats for the Detroit waterfront."

"Detroit waterfront? What waterfront?" Gerry asked.

Cole climbed the ladder and had found the engine access panels. "Well, Detroit was a big waterfront town in those days. Remember, all the goods on the east side of the United States went up and down Lake Erie, then along the Erie Canal through upstate New York. If something was going to or from Chicago or New York it went through Detroit."

Cole had taken the cover off the motor compartment and was inspecting the boat's engine. Several minutes, a screwdriver, two different sized wrenches and one pair of pliers later he said, "I'll be damned." Then called, "Gerry, come look at this."

Gerry climbed the ladder and looked over Cole's shoulder. "What am I looking at?" Gerry asked.

Cole pointed. "See that?"

"What?"

"A restrictor plate! Someone slowed this boat down. This plate keeps air from getting into the carburetor and won't let the engine develop full power. Pretty odd thing to do with these boats."

"What? I don't get it, what do you mean?" Gerry's strong suit was not large engines.

Cole looked at Gerry as if he were a child. "Okay, a motor needs three things to run. Gas, air and fire. Right?"

Gerry nodded. Cole continued. "Except, you've got to get the gas and the air in the right proportions to burn properly, right? That's what a carburetor does. Most cars use fuel injection nowadays, but back in the day carburetors were the thing. Anyway, this is a four barrel carb. See those two big cylinders?" Cole pointed.

"Those are the first two barrels. The mixture is controlled by that butterfly looking thing right there." Again Cole pointed. "Those two slightly smaller cylinders are the second two barrels. When the throttle is opened wide, fuel shoots into those two barrels and that flap there opens to let more air in."

Gerry nodded. "Okay, got all that. But, what's a restrictor plate?"

"Well, if you block the barrels…if you restrict the amount of air going into the barrels the fuel can't all burn. You slow the boat down," Cole explained.

"Ah, now I see. Why would someone do that?" Gerry

asked.

"Damned if I know! They used to race these big Chris-Crafts all the time. It was a point of pride for the high rollers to see whose boat was the fastest. Goin' slow didn't cut it. Maybe somebody was messin' with this boat." He pulled himself off the top of the engine and began to crawl behind it. Soon Cole's voice came from the rear of the boat.

"Anyway, by 1920 the brothers were doing pretty good. They won a couple of races, and were pretty well known for high powered speedboats. They made boats from the best mahogany money could buy. The boats were easy to operate. Rich people loved 'em and they were reliable, at least for their day."

Cole paused to shift his position. "Hey Gerry, in my tool box there's an inspection mirror. Hand that to me would ya?" Gerry opened the box and soon found the little mirror on an extendable rod. "Got it." Cole's hand appeared above the engine and he returned to his story.

"Thanks. Yeah, so anyway, they sold boats to all the high rollers. Even Henry Ford owned one. So did the newspaper guy they made the movie about. What the hell was his name?"

"You mean Citizen Kane and William Randolph Hearst?" Gerry asked.

"Yeah, yeah yeah! That's it. How'd you know that? Anyway, in those days a Chris-Craft boat was considered a must have if you were rich. A boat like this one was what all the rich people were after. If you restore this she'll be the talk of the town that's for sure."

Cole was now laying across the top of the engine, dangling between the rear of the boat and the transmission. "If you ask me these are the prettiest wooden power boats ever manufactured. So, that's about it. The company lasted into the sixties; then somebody bought them out. It's always the same story ya know. A classic American icon, the kids take over and sell out. It's a damn shame. Somebody makes boats now and they call 'em Chris-Craft but...I don't know, not quite the same." A small lament showed itself in Cole's voice.

He pulled himself up from behind the engine with a series of grunts. "Let's take a look forward. Ya know, I really love these boats."

They climbed down the ladder and walked to the bow. The two men spent several minutes examining the damage. The boat rested some two feet off the floor. Cole lay on his back and slid under the keel. "She's hogging a little but that's because this cradle isn't quite right, might come out once she's set up right or in the water. And, even if it doesn't it's not a lot. Actually, it's pretty small considering her age," he said as he crawled from under the boat.

"Hogging?" Gerry asked.

"Yeah, she's got a little sway back goin', but don't worry, not much."

Cole stood and walked right past Gerry, his running commentary not missing a beat. Gerry found the whole experience odd. Anyone watching would get the sense that Cole was talking only to himself. He had left himself; his troubles were far behind, totally forgotten. Cole was doing the only thing that really, honestly made him happy. He was playing with a Chris-Craft.

Reaching the battered front of the hull Cole grabbed a piece of splintered planking, broke it off and peaked inside the hull.

"I'm going to pull some of these damaged planks off

so I can get to the frame. If the frame sections are cracked that's a big deal. If they're not, and they're not dry-rotted, then it's a lot better deal." Cole pulled a crow bar and hand saw from his toolbox. "You got any power out here for a work light?"

"No, sorry."

Working quickly Cole pulled several pieces of splintered wood from the front of the craft. Eventually he had removed most of the damaged wood and had made a large hole in the side of the boat. Setting the tools on the floor he said, "That should do it, I'll be right back." Cole jogged out to his truck. In a moment he had returned with a large battery powered spotlight. "Well, let's take a look."

He began to squeeze his right arm and head inside the hole. Carefully Cole inspected the framework of the boat. He noted with satisfaction the absence of water or obvious rotten wood. Then he began a careful examination of each individual rib. Apart from the hole in the exterior planking he didn't see any obvious damage from the grounding years ago.

Rolling to his right the jagged edge dug into his ribs. Cole ignored the pain and inspected the ribs near the cabin. They were intact, but the false bottom to the bilge made Cole's work difficult. Despite his discomfort Cole smiled, these smugglers were clever. From where he was Cole could see at least one other false compartment. He ran his flashlight along the false bilge. It extended several feet to the rear.

The light swept along the frame then passed a strange wad of dark gray material. At first, Cole thought the object to be a mouse nest but a small green protrusion piqued his curiosity. Cole began to wiggle forward in an attempt to gain a better view. The effort bought him only a few more inches. He grunted as the wood dug deeper into his side.

"Find something?" Gerry called.

After a bit more wiggling and pushing Cole had gained another four or five inches. He refocused the light on the mouse nest. A face stared back at him; the face of Benjamin Franklin. Cole's eyes widened. Surprised, he snapped his head up, hitting the overhanging wooden frame. "Ouch, damn!" he cursed.

"You all right? What happened? What are you seeing?" Gerry was trying unsuccessfully to look past Cole into the body of the boat.

Cole lay there for a moment, his head and shoulders buried deep inside the boat. A hundred dollar bill was right there! Recovering from his surprise Cole yelled back, "Just trying to see this frame a bit better. I think it's okay, but I'll have to get some tools." He tried to put the light down and stretched toward the mouse nest. It was out of reach by at least two feet.

Cole began to wiggle back out of the boat. Once free he turned to Gerry and said, "Everything looks good. No dry rot. The framing doesn't look cracked or rotten. There's a false bottom to the bilge that's sort of blocking my view. I'll need to grab some more tools. I'll be right back."

Cole was excited as he walked to his truck. It would be nice to pocket an extra hundred bucks on this job. He could certainly use the cash. He popped open the truck's toolbox and began pulling out various tools. Reaching the bottom of the box he found what he was looking for, a tool-grabber.

The tool was a long tube with a pistol grip at one end and a three-pronged claw at the other. Squeezing the handle of the grip opened the claw. Releasing pressure on the handle closed the claw. Cole used the tool for picking up small objects like nuts and bolts dropped in engine wells, bilges and other areas with limited access.

Gerry watched Cole walk back from the truck. "So what do you think? Should we restore this or not?" Before Cole could answer Gerry noticed the tool-grabber. "What do you need that for?"

Cole was caught off guard but thought quickly, "I'm trying to get a wood sample from the lower frame. This might work."

Returning to the boat Cole wedged himself back in the hole. There he propped the flashlight against a cross member so its light would shine on the wad. Squeezing the grabber he opened the claw and extended his arm. The claw just brushed the hundred-dollar bill. Cole did his best to push his body forward. Finally, he was able to get the claw on the bill. Smiling Cole pulled the tool back, the bill resisted, the wad moved toward him just an inch and then the bill slid out. He put the tool grabber down on the inside of the hull, picked up the bill and stuffed it into his shirt. "Any luck?" Gerry yelled.

"Oh yeah, we're good. Got all I need," Cole shouted back with a grin.

Chapter 30

The two men stood in the doorway. The day was still, cicadas buzzed in the trees. The sun washed into the barn and up to the boat's stern. Cole was explaining what damage he had found when Gerry's cell phone began to chime. Glancing at the faceplate he recognized the number of his mortgage broker.

"I've got to take this call," he said and then walked toward his pickup truck. Cole leaned against the boat and removed the bill from inside his shirt. He examined it briefly, grinned broadly then folded the cash and shoved it back in his pocket. Glancing around the corner of the building he saw Gerry sitting on the lowered tailgate of his truck, phone held to his ear.

Gradually Cole began to wonder if there were any more bills in the boat. Grabbing the heavy-duty flashlight he walked back into the barn and again wedged himself in the boat. Shining his light around the interior he finally rested the beam on the mouse nest. Now, his attention focused on what made up the wad. He thought he saw some sort of fabric and what looked like newspaper. As he studied the object he began to realize that it was larger than he'd initially thought. "Hell, this looks like something rolled up," Cole thought.

Outside he could hear Gerry laugh and begin saying his good-byes to whomever was on the other end of the line. Gerry snapped his phone shut and turned to reenter the barn when a distant buzz could be heard. He paused and looked in the direction of the noise to see a blue ATV approaching.

Eve stopped the vehicle next to Gerry and got off.

She said something while she removed her helmet. "Fine so far." Cole heard Gerry reply.

Cole didn't waste any more time. He finished his review of the craft and began packing his tools. After a short while Eve restarted the ATV and disappeared back in the direction of the house. Gerry walked back into the barn. "All done?" Gerry asked as he reentered the barn.

Cole wasn't. He wanted to get a good idea of the material he'd spotted earlier. Maybe there was more cash there. Unfortunately, he couldn't think of any good reason to delay.

"That should do it," Cole said. His mind was racing, trying to find an excuse to return to the bowels of this Chris-Craft. Unable to do so he loaded the last of his tools in his truck and followed Gerry back to the orchard's office.

Jim was standing in the office doorway as Cole took a seat on one of the office chairs. Gerry took his seat behind the desk.

"Gerry, she's in pretty good shape for her age. She's probably worth a hundred, maybe two hundred but to be honest, I don't know, I could be way off. She's a rare boat, but pretty well banged up. The smuggler's holes might give it some extra value, you know, collector's item or something like that. I'll have to do some research and look some things up."

Jim felt his shoulders sag, "Two hundred bucks? I thought sure it would be ten or eleven thousand."

"What's two hundred bucks? Cole asked.

"The boat, you just said it was worth one or two hundred bucks."

Cole began to laugh. "No, oh no, I wish, geeez, I'd have a dozen. No, this boat is worth one or two hundred thousand dollars."

Gerry couldn't believe what he'd just heard. Jim felt his pulse quicken. "You're kidding," Jim gasped.

"Oh no, these models just aren't that common anyway. Could be they're only worth one hundred, could be well north of that. I'll just have to spend some time in the books. I'll have a report to you by, let's say next Friday? Is that okay?

Gerry agreed and began to stand.

"Ah Gerry, one more thing. I'll need to get my fee today. I'll be going by my accountant's office in Traverse City on the way back home, and it would save me a hassle."

"Sure...sure thing." Gerry was a little surprised, expecting the bill at the end of the month. Cole pulled a tinted pad from his backpack and began to scribble. A moment later he then handed Gerry a blue form with a carbon copy. Gerry looked over the document, gulped and wrote the check.

"Sherrie and Eve are never going to believe this," Jim said as they watched Cole's truck leaving the orchard.

Gerry grinned and turned to Jim, "Looks like this land is paying off already."

The drive back to Charlevoix and the office took Cole east through Traverse City then north along the shore line of east bay. Cole made the drive frequently and often detoured to the topless bar just outside city limits near the intersection of state route 72. Not today.

Today the money in his pocket was all that occupied his mind. Gerry and that woman had sort of rushed him out of the barn. If they had just left him alone. He needed more time to search that boat. He was dealing with a smuggler's boat. That was obvious. He'd seen something deep in the hull of the thing. Maybe it was more cash, maybe not, but he was damn well going to find out.

Cole drove past the garish "Cherry Top Bar – All the cherries, none of the clothes" without a thought of the girls inside.

Chapter 31

The decision to repair the boat was really not a decision at all. After hearing the estimate of the boat's worth it was simply assumed the Chris-Craft would be brought back to its original condition. Jim was the most skilled woodworker and was happily planning his repairs before Eve could say, "Wait a minute."

A few minutes discussion later and the decision to move the boat to Jim and Eve's barn had been made. A decision which took some getting used to as Eve had visions of another horse stall in the exact same location Jim was intending to put the boat.

Moving the boat was not going to be an easy task. It sat on a wooden cradle inside a long narrow building. A crane could not be used to lift the boat without removing the building's roof.

The fit looked so tight that Sherrie and Eve were certain the building had been built around the boat. They loaded a ladder in the back of the truck and soon were measuring and drawing diagrams of the barn and its doors.

Sure enough, the building's doors were just high enough to allow the boat to slide in and out. The bigger question remained. How were they going to move the boat, in its cradle, out of the barn and then into Jim's barn?

Jim had moved a large combine from Michigan's Thumb area to his farm the past year. He had used a firm located in the city of Saginaw that presented itself as the best in moving out sized and odd shaped items. It was to this firm that Jim now turned.

Harris Trucking had been in the business of moving odd, large and delicate cargo for fifteen years. Don Harris stood over six feet tall and weighed over two hundred fifty pounds; he was a big man in a big man's industry. He'd built his company on an astonishing skill at loading, hauling and delivering cargo that others would not or could not move.

The Harris Trucking terminal building was located in the apex of the curve of State Street as the five lane road exited the manufacturing city. Jim parked his pickup in the front, climbed the five concrete steps and entered a functional outer office that no one would ever call plush. Two orange vinyl and chrome chairs and a matching couch surrounded a small, badly scarred wooden coffee table.

Trucking industry magazines, along with a smattering of old hunting magazines and a Bible lay on the table. A heavy, middle aged woman sat behind a sliding glass window.

"Can I help you?" she asked as she lifted a large file from a box and sat it squarely in the middle of her desktop.

"I'm looking for Don Harris. I've worked with him before. My name is Jim Crenshaw."

The woman smiled, asked Jim to take a seat, offered him coffee and then went to find Don Harris. In a moment the big man entered the foyer.

"Mr. Crenshaw, it's good to see you. Come on back to my office, how are you?" Harris was a genuinely nice man and Jim had liked him from the first time they'd met. They reached Don's office and took seats on each side of a small Formica table. Harris asked about Jim's farm and his new combine, which proved to Jim that Harris really did remember him and this wasn't just show.

Several minutes later Jim began to describe the boat, the building and the need to move the vessel into his barn.

Don listened intently, examined Jim's drawing and made several sketches of his own. Then he began asking detailed questions about both barns, the soil and access to the sites. Jim provided all the information he could but felt he wasn't doing an adequate job.

Finally Jim said, "Don, I know I sound rather thick here. I didn't even think of a soil compaction test or the slope of the ground around the barn."

"That's alright, nobody ever does. But, when you think about it I'm sure it will make sense. I've got to be sure my equipment can get in and out, the ground has to support the weight of the truck, the crane, the boat, the cradle, the boat when we put it on wheels and anything else we use to move the thing. I can't get stuck in mud or, more worrisome there in Leelanau County, the sand. And, I've got to have a good look at the route in and out. Can't get hung up on wires, can't have the trailer sliding on any hills. People always forget about a tree or a big bush. I'll need to measure the tractor doors at your barn and Gerry's barn, gotta have enough room there. And by the way, just getting that boat out of the barn is going to be a challenge."

Don paused, looked at Jim and said. "Ahh...Jim, you know this isn't going to be cheap."

"Yeah, we figured that. But we've decided to restore it to showroom quality. I figure it will take me a year or so and I can't work on it there. Besides my sister needs that barn for their orchard."

"Sure thing Jim, I'm just preparing you. How about if I drive up there next week, take some measurements and look over the ground."

"Sounds good Don. I'll meet you there and show you the building."

Chapter 32

Elaine's car, a two year old Cadillac CTS, cornered well. The complicated, challenging road running south past Long Lake, along the East Bay shoreline and into Traverse City was one of her favorite drives. Normally she pushed the car through the curving waterfront road at top speed. Today she didn't. Today her driving was methodical, reflecting her mood.

In Elaine's purse were two checks for seven thousand dollars. She had written one to the Traverse Savings and Investment Bank. She even had Cole sign it and pass the envelope through the postage meter. She had not mailed the envelope. Instead, Elaine had debited the account and transferred the money to her own checking account. Now, she was putting that same seven thousand dollars into the hands of David McFain.

The red Cadillac parked in the public lot just across the street from Clinch Park. The blue waters of Traverse Bay sparkled, sailors shook out their sails and fishing boats began to troll the debts. Already people were tossing Frisbees and preparing for a day at the beach. Elaine popped the trunk, lifted the dark gray carpeted hatch cover hiding the spare tire and removed a small locked metal box from the cavity thus exposed.

Returning to the driver's seat she placed the box on the arm rest and opened her purse. She pulled down the lining and removed a small key taped to the inside leather wall. Then, she unlocked the box. Elaine removed a small, flip phone and dialed from memory. A moment later she said,

"I'm here. Meet me at the cafe'." She pressed the disconnect key, then erased the call log, put the phone back in the box, reassembled her purse then popped the trunk and returned the box to its place.

She quickly surveyed the parking lot and sidewalk. This wasn't a day to meet old friends. Then Elaine fed the meter and walked the three blocks to the professional building and a small cafe' next to the offices of Growth Financial Management. She took a seat at one of the four outdoor tables in the back. A waiter soon appeared, lit the scented candle meant to add ambiance to the Ikea table and took her order. Moments later he returned with a chai latte.

Elaine didn't wait long. David McFain intercepted the waiter and soon appeared latte in hand.

"Thank you David," Elaine smiled, "...very dashing." He returned the smile and took the chair opposite her.

"I'm at your service Elaine. You...ah," he carefully selected his words. "You sounded a bit worked up on the phone, I'm curious."

Without small talk Elaine removed three envelopes from her purse. She carefully laid them on the table, aligning the edges in a perfect row. The fist envelope contained a check for seven thousand dollars, made payable to her investment account. The money pushed the account total over her goal of five million, five hundred fifty-five thousand, five hundred fifty-five dollars. A number she thought sounded lucky. Elaine had never diverted a complete payment before, but she knew Cole's business was failing and there wasn't much left to take. Besides, she would be gone very soon; this would be her last chance.

She slid the envelope across the table to McFain. "That should push me over the top David." He glanced at the envelope then Elaine. She smiled.

"You've done well," he returned her smile.

"And so have you." She slid the second envelope to him. It contained a large check, made out to McFain. The money represented his monthly fee plus a substantial bonus. This amount was in addition to the standard fees and commissions Elaine paid on all transactions in her accounts. This fee represented the price she paid for McFain's silence concerning the source of all the money he was handling, and for his profitable, albeit questionable, access to information. Information which had generated substantial returns.

"I think you ought to open that one David," she said.

He picked the envelope up and studied it. Seconds ticked by in silence. Then, he said, "No, I think I'll save this."

"I was hoping to see your reaction, but, I should have known. You've always kept things..." she paused. He was an attractive man, a bit older, but clearly well muscled. He'd be fun. "I don't even know where you live." She observed.

McFain's gaze shifted from her eyes to her hair. He lingered there a moment. Several years ago, when she had first approached him, he'd thought about trying to seduce her. But the first checks had been fairly large, and he quickly realized that Elaine was going to be a steady fountain of unreported cash. It would be better to keep the relationship strictly business. "I honor our friendship." McFain replied and shifted his gaze back to her eyes.

She returned the stare for a long moment, then held up the last envelope. This held the check which Cole had signed and was made payable to the Traverse bank. She removed the check from the envelope and held it over the candle. As the check flared she fixed McFain's eyes, "It's been a pleasure working with you David." she said and smiled.

McFain smiled back. "And with you."

"I need you to do one more thing." Elaine studied his face, hesitated, then opened her purse and removed a small teal green envelope. "I want you to sell everything. Transfer all the money into the Cayman account."

"What's this?" McFain didn't move.

"It's time for me to leave David. The business is going under, and I can't get blood from a stone. I'm out." She smiled thinly, "I'll need access to those funds in about a week. Can you do it?"

"Of course I can do it." He fell silent for a moment. "Then I guess this will be our last meeting."

"I think so," Elaine said as she stood. She walked several paces in the direction of her car, stopped, turned and walked back. He didn't get up. She stood there a moment, then took David's chin in her hand. She bent and kissed him long and hard.

David watched her as she walked away, she didn't look back. Finally she was out of sight. He stood, shook his head and smiled.

Chapter 33

Donna's chest entered the room before she did. An ability that always fascinated Cole. A woman had to walk with her shoulders way back to do that, yet she made it look natural, like a girl from a fifties sweater movie. "Cole baby, Alan Wisecup is on the phone." He had called five minutes ago. Donna had let him stew before she connected him to Cole. Not smart this time Cole thought. It only served to make Wisecup mad. Or maybe he enjoyed being a low life bill collector. He certainly acted like he did.

Cole had been waiting for the call. He had given some thought to taking the check to Wisecup in person just to see his face when Cole handed him seven thousand dollars. He could make the payments. Wisecup was wrong. But then Cole decided it was better if it all appeared routine.

Cole eyed the phone and smiled. "Let's see how Wisecup eats crow," he thought. He was sure Wisecup was going to thank him for the payment.

Wisecup didn't even say hello. "Mr. Prestcott, we haven't received a single payment since my visit. Nor have you made any attempt to contact myself or members of the bank. Sir, we are very concerned about this loan."

Cole's smile disappeared. This wasn't possible. His hands began to shake. "What'd ya mean I haven't made a payment? That's bullshit! I sent you a check for seven thousand dollars. I sent it last week. What about that payment?"

"Mr. Prestcott, we did not receive a payment."

'Then you'd better find it buddy. Don't think you can

jerk me around."

"Are you saying you sent us one? If so, we'll search our mailroom. But, honestly Mr. Prestcott, I doubt that we received such a payment."

"Are you calling me a liar? You little sonofabitch!" Cole's composure was cracking.

Wisecup kept applying the pressure. "Your current outstanding balance is...."

"I KNOW MY OUTSTANDING DAMN BALANCE. You don't have to keep telling me." Cole was bouncing his knees up and down under his desk.

"Mr. Prestcott," Wisecup cut in. "I did not call you a liar. I simply expressed my doubts. Sir, we will be forced to begin foreclosure proceedings on your business and other assets this coming Monday. I will personally search our mailroom and all associated employee's desks. However, should I not find that check you will be hearing from our attorneys. I am sure you realize seven thousand dollars does not come close to making your loan current. As I said, we will need..."

"I KNOW, you'll need some money. I'll find it. Now go screw someone else." Cole slammed the receiver down and leaned back in his chair. The dream was fading, in a few weeks he would be the bum on the street that everyone always thought he'd become. Panic swept over him. The eyebrow over his left eye began to twitch. The urge to run, just get away was overwhelming. Cole stood and walked to his office door, decided against whatever it was that had caused him to walk there in the first place and returned to his desk. He paced the floor. His hands were in constant motion, in his pants pockets, out, back in. He wiped them with an imaginary towel.

Was Wisecup screwing with him? Of course he had a check. Cole had signed it himself. How could he not have a check?

"DONNA!" Cole screamed.

She burst into his office a moment later. "No need to yell honey, I'm right here," she purred.

"Get me the check register." Cole was nearly hysterical.

Donna scurried to the accounting room, rummaged through the file cabinet and came back with an old fashioned green ledger. Cole yanked it out of her hands and laid it on his desk. Without sitting down he quickly paged to last week's checks. There it was, a seven thousand dollar deduction, check number 8487. His balance now stood at four hundred twenty six dollars and seventy-two cents. He couldn't fill the cabin cruiser with gas for that.

Cole sat down at his desk and put his head in his hands. Wisecup was a thief. He was taking everything and there was no way to stop him. He was going to lose it all. He'd be back to working for someone else for peanuts. He'd have to sell the house, the boats, everything. He'd end up in some low rent studio apartment over some retired farmer's kitchen smelling the liver and onions every Friday night.

The day passed slowly. Cole didn't go home. Night closed in. He walked through the office into the shop behind. Carefully he examined the tools, machines and parts room. It was gone, all gone, the bank just hadn't come and taken it yet. It was just a matter of time.

Returning to the front of the building he stopped by the company kitchen, pulled open the refrigerator and grabbed a can of Coke. In his office, Cole opened the desk drawer and took out a bottle of rum and a glass.

By midnight he was drunk. The check; he'd signed the check and Wisecup had the money. Cole knew it. The thieving bastard had to pay. Wisecup was going to make Cole a laughing stock. He'd be working at some fast food joint in three months wiping up snot from the same shit teenagers he'd hired to sweep floors. Cole emptied the bottle into his glass, flavored it with Coke and poured the mixture down his throat.

Money. Money was the root of all happiness and he needed more of it. Cole had no illusions. He knew the business wasn't going to generate the money he needed. Where could he get it? In his mind Cole made a list of the businesses in town. No one had the kind of cash he needed.

Stupid, stupid idea, robbery would just be stupid. Those blood suckers were just as broke as he was now, no matter how fancy a car they drove.

He glanced at the empty bottle. There was another around here somewhere. After a quick, semi frantic search Cole remembered. He opened his wall safe and found a bottle of Johnnie Walker Red. Behind the bottle lay a snubnose .32 pistol on top of a brown accordion file.

Probably the loan or tax papers Cole thought. He picked up the pistol and studied the gun. He didn't remember having a pistol. This could end all his problems. Cole smiled and pushed the barrel against his temple, one quick squeeze would do it.

He held the pistol there for what seemed to be a long time. Gradually his hand began to shake. Suddenly Cole threw the pistol across the office. He grabbed the bottle and poured two fingers into his glass.

He sat on the office couch. He needed cash and now. Suddenly, from a head fogged with booze and despair the picture of Gerry's boat appeared. Gerry's boat had money in it. Maybe lots of it. He needed to get back inside that boat. The money he had seen began to grow, soon it filled the bilge, and was right there, just out of his reach. It would be so easy, just cut open the boat and scoop it out. How could Gerry object? There was plenty for both. He could see the money, it was...right...there. Cole collapsed on the couch.

Chapter 34

Don Harris, driving a Kenworth T660, stopped his truck in front of Gerry and Sherrie's driveway. Behind Don's empty flatbed trailer were his two sons Bert and James. Bert, the oldest, drove a smaller truck pulling a flatbed trailer loaded with an assembly of specially built axles and wheel sets. James, barely out of high school drove a three axle mobile crane. Sherrie greeted Don as he walked toward the house. The two had become friendly on Don's previous visit and they exchanged pleasantries.

"Don that's the prettiest truck I've every seen," Sherrie exclaimed. "Is it new?"

"Well, kinda, it's new to me, and it's only two years old," Don grinned. He liked a woman who liked trucks.

"Are you going to show it to me?" Sherrie was already headed for the cab. Don smiled as she climbed up the side of his truck. This woman was certainly a fireball.

"Okay, now be careful. I'll be right there, just hang on." Don hurried over to the truck and quickly gave Sherrie the grand tour.

Back on the ground Don said, "I'll need to get the crane in first, then we'll position the wheels. After that, I'll lift the boat, slide the axles under and then pull it back. Easy as pie. We'll be out of here in no time."

"So you say Don…" Sherrie laughed, "…but I'm glad it's you and not me doing this!"

Gerry heard Don's truck from the orchard's office and was soon standing next to Sherrie. "Don, I'll get the tractor and meet you back there." With that both men were headed in different directions.

Thirty minutes later Gerry watched as Don's sons laid two-inch by six-inch boards across the ground for the next phase of the move. That task completed, their attention turned to moving four sets of wheels into position at the front of the barn. Next, a set of bumpers were placed around the cradle which held the boat.

Bert then directed Gerry as he positioned his tractor's forklift arms under the bumpers. When all was ready, the signal was given to lift the cradle. Quickly James pushed a single, small axle with only ten-inch wheels under the cradle and Gerry lowered the forklift. The boat cradle now sat with one end on the ground and the other on the small axle.

Bert then attached a cable to both sides of the cradle. The other end was attached to the tractor and they pulled the entire assembly forward over the axle. The physics couldn't be denied. The front of the cradle came up and James quickly pushed another axle under the cradle. The process was repeated and soon the boat cradle was equipped with three sets of axles.

Bert quickly showed Gerry where to position the tractor and a few moments later two cables were being reattached to the tractor. Soon James gave a wave and signaled Gerry to pull the cradle forward. Carefully they worked the cradle out of the barn into the daylight.

Gerry was even more impressed with the Chris-Craft now that he could see it from a slight distance. Don and his boys took a moment to walk around the boat. "Gerry this thing is impressive!" Don shouted. Gerry couldn't agree more. It was an impressive yacht to be sure.

Bert and James then placed two sets of straps under the boat and cradle. These were attached to the hook suspended from the crane. As Gerry watched, the Harris crew gently lifted the cradle and placed it on the flatbed trailer.

Loading complete Don climbed into the truck's cabin and stepped on the accelerator. The engine woke from its idling snore and roared. Don expertly slipped the truck into gear and crept away from the barn. A sharp right turn and the behemoth slowly moved away from the barn, across the new property and out of the orchard. Gerry climbed into his pickup and followed closely behind, cringing as the truck's wide load broke off several precious tree branches on its trip to the gravel parking area in front of the processing barn.

Don stopped the truck, shifted to neutral and set the parking brake. Sherrie opened the door of the orchard's office and called, "Everything all set Don? You ready to hit the road?"

Don climbed down from the cab and held out a clip board. "Just need you to sign this bill of lading and I'm off. It'll be dark by the time I get to Clare. I'll drop it there and we'll go home for the night. We'll leave Saginaw early, shoot up to Clare, hook up then take it down to Jim's. The boat should be off loaded and in place by noon."

"Sounds great Don, thanks so much." Sherrie signed the documents, took her copy and watched as Don and his sons drove off the property and turned south.

Chapter 35

On Friday Harris Trucking Company delivered the Chris-Craft. The boat was moved into Jim's barn in essentially the reverse order of how it had been removed.

Jim was ecstatic. He had a project for the next winter, and he intended to make it a work of art. Eve wasn't quite as enthusiastic, but found the entire project to be interesting.

The obvious starting place, at least to Jim's eye, was not the repair of the bow section. Rather, Jim decided he first needed to overhaul the boat's mechanical section, the engine, transmission and propeller drive housing. While those components were out he would have access to the internal portions of the stern and could inspect, repair and refinish the area much more easily. After replacing the engine components he would begin work on the damaged bow section.

With those three major tasks complete he would move on to the boat interior and deck. Replacing, repairing or sanding the interior wood and deck planks looked to be a significant amount of effort. In addition, the devil was in the details. Things like deck hardware, cushions, curtains, and galley hardware were small but obviously time consuming.

Jim scheduled the exterior as the last major task, thus preventing the possibility of damage to an already completed work effort while moving about the boat. He intended to strip the finish from the boat's exterior, caulk and reseal the seams and refinish the beautiful mahogany.

It was a major effort and Jim had budgeted a year for the process. Eve, more understanding of the perfectionist streak and occasional loss of interest Jim displayed in these types of projects, guessed closer to three.

Both Jim and Eve agreed the entire process would be much easier if Jim had access to a complete set of plans for the boat. With that they began a detailed search of the local library for clues on where they could locate the documents.

This was the type of task that Eve reveled in. She spent hours at the home computer and called several boat dealers in Detroit, the western Michigan city of Holland, then the eastern city of St. Clair Shores and even Chicago. No one could provide copies of the original drawings for the boat.

"Jim this is nuts!" Eve cried one evening. Jim was trying to sleep in a large chair in the living room.

"What's nuts?" he asked, not opening his eyes.

Eve sat at the kitchen table, a lap top computer opened in front of her. "I've got five emails from marinas and boat yards telling me they're more than happy to work on the boat, but they don't have any drawings."

"That's not a help babe," Jim said. "I can do that. In fact, that's what we are doing." Jim still hadn't opened his eyes.

"Well, I did find out the company was bought out in 1962."

"By who? Jim now had one eye open.

"Shields and Company," Eve said, checking her notes.

"That can't be right." Jim sat up.

"Why not?" Eve asked, slightly offended that her research had been dismissed so quickly.

"Well, I've always heard it called Chris-Craft Industries. Never heard of Smith and Jones," Jim replied.

Eve walked into the living room and sat on the sofa.

"Who's Smith and Jones?"

"The company that bought Chris-Craft," Jim replied, suppressing a grin.

"Trying to get me again! Very funny, I said 'Shields and Company' not 'Smith and Jones'. Give a girl some credit." Jim just grinned. "As I was saying, Shields and Company eventually became Chris-Craft Industries. They got into radio and television stations, even owned part of a movie company. The boat division was just part of it. Eventually boats weren't important, and they sold the Chris-Craft boat division several years ago. I'm going to call them tomorrow to see if they still have the plans from boats sold in the past. Who knows, I might get lucky."

"You're kidding. Wow, I'm impressed. How'd you find all that out?" Jim asked.

"The brand name Chris-Craft is still around. I called one of their dealers today during lunch," Eve smiled.

"Who knew the boat world could get you into the movies," Jim sighed.

Eve returned to the kitchen. A moment later Jim heard her shout, "Jim take a look at this!" Eve was already back in the living room. "Listen to the email we just got!" and she began to read.

"Dear Mrs. Crenshaw, We would be more than happy to provide a quote for work on your boat. However, your note stated that you and your husband intended to restore the craft yourselves. We do not recommend a project of that proportion for the average individual as the task can quickly become overwhelming."

"Of course he doesn't recommend it..." Jim said, "It means he's not getting paid."

"Listen to the rest," Eve explained.

"However, should you elect to pursue the project, and you wish to ensure your Chris-Craft is of the highest quality, we recommend becoming a member of the Chris-Craft Owners Association and purchase a complete set of plans from the Mariners' Museum. They hold all records, plans and hull cards for boats produced by Chris-Craft prior to the company's sale in 1980."

"That's it babe!" Jim explained. "We need to visit the Mariners' Museum …wherever that is?"

Eve was sitting on the sofa and pounding the keys of her computer. After a moment she looked up and smiled, "Looks like we're going to Newport News, Virginia."

"You're kidding, that place is great!" Jim was excited. "They've got some big Civil War museums there. I love that place."

"When were you ever in Newport News?" Eve asked completely forgetting about Chris-Craft boats.

"I couldn't talk about every trip I took hon, you know that," Jim replied, referring to his active duty days in the Air Force. "I had a trip to the Norfolk one time, we finished early and everybody went to the clubs. I went to the Civil War museum."

Eve started to laugh. "Like I've always said honey, you really are a nerd."

In the morning they dropped Molly at the kennel, drove to Detroit and boarded a flight to Richmond. A delayed takeoff, one transfer and more groping hands than Jim cared for and they arrived in Newport News, Virginia.

"I can't believe it takes six hours to get from Detroit to here," Jim complained as they approached the rental car desk. "We could have driven here faster."

"I don't like all those people padding me down when

we get to the airport," Eve added.

"Oh well, the days of arriving thirty minutes before a flight are long gone I guess," Jim said, and they settled in to wait their turn in the line for a car.

After checking into their hotel they headed to the museum. The museum had closed just as they arrived at the hotel so this was just a 'recon' trip. They drove around the parking lot, ensured they knew how to get to and from the hotel to the building and then went to dinner.

The next morning Jim and Eve were walking into the Museum's main lobby ten minutes early for their appointment. As they entered the building through a double set of glass doors under a modern art depiction of a globe with a sixteenth century sailing ship at its top Jim wrinkled his forehead.

"What's the matter?" Eve asked, knowing full well what bothered her husband.

"That's a stupid statue..." Jim muttered, "...why not make a nice globe and a realistic frigate, like the Constitution?"

"Jim, no one would ever call you a progressive," Eve grinned.

"Well, does that really look like a boat to you?" Jim insisted.

"It's art babe, it's supposed to invoke your imagination."

Jim looked at her, "Maybe...but I still think..."

"I know you do. Make sure you tell them to get a different statue before we leave. I'm sure they'll get right on that. Now, where are we supposed to be going?" Eve studied her map of the building. They walked the length of the glass-enclosed entrance way and entered the main building. A long low desk with several museum staffers sat on their right and a seven-foot gold statue of an Eagle screamed from its perch on their left.

An attractive young woman was seated next to a cash register selling tickets to a retired couple. Eve waited her turn as the couple completed their purchase then approached the woman and said they were to meet a Ms. Claudia Wells, a docent with the Museum.

"That's me." The girl said, offered her hand and a smile. Eve smiled back, shook the proffered hand and introduced Jim. After a brief discussion of their trip Claudia presented them with a clip board and pen. Eve completed the necessary information and Claudia handed them two visitor badges.

Claudia then pushed her wheel chair from behind the counter and rolled to the front. Eve's eyebrows lifted a bit in surprise. Then her life as a military spouse took over. "If there's an elephant in the room say hello," she'd been told by one of her husband's first Wing Commanders.

"How did you lose your legs?" she asked.

Claudia didn't hesitate. "Shore duty in Basra with the Brits. I'm Navy, well…used to be…but was assigned to drive a truck on a road I guess I shouldn't have been driving on." Claudia said as if she were talking about the weather.

"I'm Air Force. Never got down to Basra, did see a bit more of the Green Zone than I wanted to." Jim replied.

A short discussion of the heat, camel spiders and the stray dogs that seemed to be everywhere in Iraq followed. In a few moments they had completed their trip through a display of survival gear and shipwreck stories to a locked set of doors. Using a key held to her wrist with a mariner rope bracelet she unlocked one door and led them into a small office behind the main gallery.

"I understand you folks found a boat, how exciting!" Claudia exclaimed. "We have records on just about every Chris-Craft built up until 1980. Your boat was built before then right?"

"Yes," Jim said. "We think it was build in the 1920s because it looks like bootleggers from the Prohibition Era used the boat."

"Wow, that's pretty cool. I'd love to see it," Claudia enthused.

"Really? You're not just saying that?" Eve asked.

"Of course not! Did you bring pictures?"

"Absolutely!" Jim announced, and they spent thirty minutes pouring over a set of pictures that Eve and Sherrie had assembled.

Claudia really did want to see pictures. She examined each one in detail, several times using a magnifying glass from her desk drawer to examine various areas of the boat.

"It looks great! Those smuggler's holes are the coolest thing I've ever seen!" Claudia announced. "Okay, so, we've got to do some detective work. You showed me a picture that had the manufacture's plate. Can I see that again please?"

"Yup, wait one..." Jim fell naturally into 'military speak'. "Ahhh….here it is." He produced a picture of a plate riveted to the inside of the engine hatch cover. "Are you looking for the hull number?"

"Yes, exactly," Claudia said.

"It's 5055. We figured you'd need that," Eve offered.

"Okay, great, now let's see if we can find any records on the boat. If you'll come with me we'll go back to the archives and I'll show you what we have. On the phone you talked about needing more than the research package. I think you'll want the drawings, wiring diagrams and some of the engine documents. We can provide a lot of that. We do have to charge for most of this stuff, but it's not terrible."

Jim smiled "I expected you would. But it's okay. We're just glad to find the drawings."

"Do you have the hull card for this boat? I'd really like to have that too," Eve asked, referring to the name given to a card used by the original Chris-Craft company to record all the equipment, maintenance and sales data for a specific boat hull.

"Certainly, we have hull cards on every boat. We have a standard package we sell to collectors and people interested in specific boats. It's called 'the research package.' I'm going to bet you'll want that," Claudia replied. "I'll need a little time to hunt the drawings and other items down. Why don't you tour the museum? I'll page you when I have them."

"Sounds like a plan, thank you so much," Jim answered.

An hour later their names boomed over the museum's speaker system: "Mr. and Mrs. Crenshaw please report to the docent's office."

After a few wrong turns and asking directions twice Jim and Eve found the proper office and knocked. The door quickly opened and Claudia greeted them with a wide smile. "I've found almost everything. This is really good, you're not going to believe it." She rolled her chair behind her desk and grabbed a computer mouse. A few clicks later they were looking at pages of boat drawings.

"Claudia, this is great, but how do I get a copy?" Jim's concern was evident.

She gave a slight laugh, "Oh, that's not a problem! I just wanted you to pick out which drawings you needed.

Then we'll print those out. It's a bit pricey because these are blueprint sized drawings, but this way you get only what you need."

Claudia motioned to a desk chair and moved her wheel chair to the side. "Just take my mouse, click here."

She pointed at a computer generated box on the monitor's screen. "You'll get a total at the end. Double check your order and hit print."

Jim sat at the computer and began scanning drawings.

"And Eve, here's the data that we have on the boat's outfitting." Claudia pointed to a cardboard box sitting on a table. "Let's go through that real quick and see if you want copies. We can do color copies too by the way."

Eve stopped thumbing through the box of documents. "Claudia, we really owe you on this, thank you so much."

"Maybe we can take you out to dinner tonight?" Jim asked. A few minutes later arrangements had been made and all three were back to their research.

Chapter 36

Cole Prestcott rolled to his left, let his body weight and momentum carry him off the bunk and landed on his feet. Turning, he examined the naked body of his secretary.

Donna was fairly worthless in the office, but she was something in the sack. He reached out and stroked her right breast, eliciting a moan. Without opening her eyes Donna said, "Come back to bed baby."

Cole smiled, "Wish I could, but I've got to get home tonight." Donna rolled on her back. "No you don't. You don't ever have to go home."

"Honey I can only play for so long, then I've got to get back to the ball and chain. If she finds out about us the divorce will be held up. You know I want it clean and fast."

"Oh Cole, I wish you could do it now. Why do we have to wait?" Donna whined.

Cole smiled. She still had hopes. How could any woman be this stupid? He wasn't going to divorce Elaine. She was class and he needed class on his arm. Besides, some bastard judge would make him pay alimony for the rest of his life, and it would be a shit load.

"Get movin' honey." He ignored her question. Cole searched the cabin, spotted his pants and shirt in two separate corners, and quickly retrieved them. He finished pulling his shirt over his head then climbed the steps to the cockpit of his 33 foot Morgan sailboat. The boat was anchored just outside the Boyne City Marina's designated anchorage. The city didn't allow anchoring here, but no one had motored out to bust his chops so screw 'em, he wasn't paying their fees to anchor two hundred yards closer to town.

Cole made sure the transmission was in neutral. He gave the key a quick turn and ignited the small Yanmar motor. A glance at the oil pressure, temperature and voltage meters told him all was well. Confident the boat wasn't going to move he climbed out of the cockpit and moved forward. He found the foot control for the powered windlass, pressed his toes onto the switch and watched the anchor rode as it slowly was eaten by the machine. After a minute or two the rope transitioned to anchor chain, then the anchor itself appeared. He lifted his foot, stopped the windlass then hosed mud and weeds off the chain, then the anchor. Soon the anchor was stowed and the bow squared away.

Returning to the cockpit he checked the engine temperature. Satisfied the engine oil was warm he pushed the transmission lever to "F" and the boat began to move forward, gradually picking up speed. Cole spun the wheel and the bow slowly turned to the west. He let the Morgan grow used to the gentle up and down motion over the small waves then dashed down the steps to the cabin.

Donna hadn't moved. He snatched her bikini top from the floor and threw it at her. "C'mon, we've got to get back." She threw the top back at him, rolled out of the bunk and began to put her swimming suit back on. Cole watched her slide on the bottom of her suit, then position her top and tie the straps. Satisfied she wasn't going to be naked when they arrived at the dock he returned to the ship's wheel. In forty minutes they were back at the Charlevoix marina. Donna was offloaded with the usual drama and thirty minutes later he was securing the sailboat to the dock next to his boathouse.

It was dark as Cole walked up the dock and crossed

the short yellow sand filled space to the backyard gate. The gate was open. This was unusual since Elaine's stupid dog wouldn't stay anywhere near the house if given half a chance. In fact, many times Cole had thought about leaving the gate wide open. But, it was an innocent dog and he wasn't that cruel.

He closed the gate and began walking to the house. The curtains were open in every room. That was odd too. All the lights were on, but something...something wasn't right.

"What the hell!" Cole exploded. In the glare of the porch lights and the fading daylight he could see large truck tire marks pressed into the grass. Cole dashed up the steps of his full length porch and attempted to open the back door. It was locked. It was never locked. He didn't even carry a back door key. Cole swore then ran to the front of the house. Something was very wrong here.

An official looking notice was taped to the front door. At the top, in bold red letters were the words "Notice of Eviction" and "County Sheriff."

Cole was stunned. "What the hell is this?" he shouted and ripped the paper from the door. No one had ever said anything about the house before. He thought he would have time. They didn't just throw a man out of his house with no warning. There had been no warnings, no letters from that damned bank, nothing.

He unlocked the front door. The floor was bare. A large oval rug was supposed to be right here. He walked from room to room. The house was empty. No furniture, no wife, nothing. The only things remaining were the dust balls.

Slowly the enormity of what had happened overwhelmed him. "No, no, no...awwwww shit." Cole slowly sat on the cold hallway floor.

A while later, he wasn't sure how much of a while later, Cole found himself in the kitchen. On the counter was a wicker basket. Mail spilled off the top and onto the counter. Cole pinched off a stack of a dozen or so letters and began examining them. They were from the bank, collection agencies and the mortgage company. Some of the letters were over a year old.

He grabbed an official looking letter from the top of the pile and tore it open. It was a notice of non-payment of mortgage. The letter was dated two months ago and signed by Alan Wisecup. Cole picked another letter off the pile and tore it open. It was another notice of non-payment, only this one was four months old. This letter was also signed by Alan Wisecup.

He was doing it. The little sonofabitch was doing it, he was taking his house and his furniture and...everything!

Cole began to picture Elaine. She would scream and throw her little rich side of Grand Rapids high and mighty temper tantrum. She would make a scene that Hollywood would be proud of.

He focused on the first letter. This didn't make sense. They had been making the house payments. How could these letters be so old? Why hadn't he seen them? Cole slammed a fist down on the counter top. Then he noticed a handwritten note which had fallen off the pile and lay next to the basket. He picked it up; it was in the ornate scroll of Elaine.

Slumped against the counter Cole read, "Here's your mail. I picked it up while you were out with your little girlfriends. Seems like I forgot to give it to you for the past couple of months. Screw you."

Stunned, he reread the note. Disbelief then anger swept over him. He crumpled the paper into a tight ball and threw it against the wall. The bitch! She'd kept all the notices secret. She'd never said a word. She'd just kept being her up-town-tight-ass-self and never said a word!

And Wisecup. It was Wisecup that had corrupted his wife. He could see Wisecup now, plotting with her, scheming to take everything from him.

Cole walked through the house again. Nothing.

This was Wisecup's fault. The little bastard had done it. He'd gotten everything! His business, his house, even his wife. The man was a thief, a cheat and a liar. He leaned the back of his head against the kitchen wall and slid to the floor. His chin sank to his chest. Anger washed over him. Then sorrow, desperation and finally an overwhelming sense of failure. Not about his marriage. "Screw her!" No, Cole was going to be exposed for the failure he was. His biggest fear was being found out to be a fake. Now, it was laid out for all to see. He'd lost everything. Cole looked around the empty kitchen and began to sob.

Slowly, painfully, Cole forced himself to stop. He crawled up the wall to his feet. Cole studied the kitchen for a moment, the cabinets, the refrigerator, and lastly the pile of letters on the counter. He walked through the downstairs, each room as empty as it had been thirty minutes ago. Cole walked out of the front door, leaving it open, the house lights blazing. He stood on the porch, examining the door lights, then the railing.

Finally, Cole crossed the front yard to the street. He carefully selected a stone from the shoulder of the road, turned and was about to hurl it through the front window when headlights appeared in the distance.

Cole stopped and examined the lights. Probably the cops, how would he explain breaking his own window? He studied the big picture window again. This was stupid, why hurl a stone at his own house? It was his, not the banks, he would get it back. And, he knew just the man who could fix all this.

Chapter 37

The flight back to Detroit gave Jim and Eve time to review the treasure trove of documents they had purchased from the museum. Shortly after takeoff Jim pulled his backpack from under the seat. He fished through the bundle of drawings, eventually selecting one and removed the document. Jim then unfolded the 30 x 42 inch Chris-Craft blue print. The document expanded and consumed the fold down tray in front of Jim's seat, then flowed over into Eve's seat. A quick elbow to his side convinced him that his wife wasn't THAT understanding.

Jim refolded the blueprint to a 12 x 12 square and began to study. After a moment he realized it was pointless, he couldn't tell what he was looking at. There was no perspective in such a small view. With a heavy, staged, sigh Jim refolded the blueprint and shoved it back in his backpack. He turned to look out the window. The airplane was in a cloud. Giving in to boredom he turned to Eve.

"So what are you looking at?" he whispered.

"Well, I was trying to read the "hull card." Then some goof put a big sheet of paper under my nose so I couldn't see. When the big oaf finally moved the sheet out of the way he started talking to me while I was trying to read," Eve whispered.

"The nerve of some people." Jim leaned in to examine the hull card in Eve's hand.

"This is pretty interesting," she said to Jim in a low voice. "It contains a list of all the equipment installed on the boat."

"You're kidding! That's great! Does it give a brand name or manufacturer? We can use that information to find duplicates or reproductions."

"For some of the stuff. There's the name of the boat dealer. And the original name of the boat." Eve pointed at the dealer's instructions. "Did you know the boat was originally called "Volstead Act"? That's not the name on the back of it now is it?"

Jim's eyebrows went up. "No. Now its got some funny name like Burgoo King." He thought a moment. "Volstead Act, that phrase is familiar, I just can't remember. Sounds like the name of a play or something."

They continued pouring over the treasure trove of documents, cards and drawings for the remainder of the flight. The aircraft landed at Detroit's Metro airport on time and in twenty minutes they had recovered their luggage and found the Jeep.

"Jim, we're right next to the city. Let's drive over to the Great Lakes Museum and see if they have anything on the boat."

"Why would they have anything?" Jim asked.

"Chris-Crafts are, or at least were, Michigan boats, made near Detroit. And, we know this was a smuggler's boat so put the two together, might be a reference to the boat there someplace."

"That makes a lot of sense. Good idea hon, we might get lucky," Jim agreed.

"Good, but first we'll need to get lunch and we should probably check into a hotel right away." Eve grinned at Jim.

"I should have seen that coming! How can you stay so slim and eat so much? And who said anything about staying the night?" Jim demanded.

"I'm a high energy kind of gal. Plus, I workout so I can indulge every once in a while." She smiled. "And, right now I want a good Coney Island. And, let's stay at that B&B in Grosse Pointe."

Two hours later, their rooms secured and lunch complete Jim and Eve drove to Belle Isle and the Dossin Great Lakes Museum. Walking past the two cannons mounted in front of the museum door Jim suddenly stopped. "You know, we don't have an appointment. Who should we ask for?"

"I guess the public relations guy."

"Okay, sounds good to me. Let's give it a try. Just be prepared, we might be out of luck."

After explaining the purpose of their visit to the young man at the front desk Jim and Eve were told they could visit with a Mr. Mike Meier, director of public relations.

Ten minutes later a man with a bushy black beard broken by a large smile and booming voice greeted them from across the lobby. Jim and Eve liked the man instantly. Mike escorted them to his office at the rear of the museum.

"Before we get to business can I offer you anything? We have coffee, tea, water or pop."

Eve was from Boston and not being a native Michigander always grinned at the word "pop". In Boston, where she was from, it was called "soda."

"I'll take a Pepsi if you have one please." Eve said.

Mike grabbed a can and glass of ice from the kitchen area across from his office, gave it to Eve, then said; "I understand you have a fascinating story to tell."

"Well, I don't know if it's fascinating, but it is a little odd and we could use your help." With that, Jim began to tell

Mike about the recently discovered boat. After ten minutes Jim concluded by saying, "So, we know the original name of the boat was Volstead Act and we are fairly certain it was a smuggling boat. We're guessing it was used in the Detroit area because that's where most of the smuggling was conducted. Now, we are sort of hoping your museum would have more information."

"Chris-Crafts are a sort of institution around here, but I don't know that we would have any information on a specific boat. We don't keep records on every boat used along the Detroit waterfront. That simply would be too many and, really, most were not that remarkable. We have limited space you know. Why do you think we'd have any information on this one?"

"I, well, we, really don't have any specific reason. Just that this boat was converted to smuggle booze and maybe you would have some police record or Coast Guard record which mentions it," Jim answered.

"We don't have any police records, but we do have some Coast Guard records. They aren't all digitized; some are still on microfilm. It will take several hours to look through everything. Look, it's pretty slow this week. I wouldn't normally do this, but I can set you up in a research office. You could use that for a few days if that would be of help."

Jim was disappointed. He certainly didn't want to drive from their house in the middle part of the state to Detroit more than he needed to, but this seemed as good an offer as they could hope for. He glanced at Eve, she nodded her head and Jim extended his hand. "Deal," he said.

Mike walked them through several hallways, then behind and between exhibits until they came to a set of four small offices, each with a plain desk and two chairs. He slid a cardboard card into a nameplate holder on the third door and handed Jim the key. "This is it. Yours for one week."

Jim and Eve peeked in the office, took in the Spartan walls and total lack of pictures or decorations then glanced at each other. Eve deadpanned, "I don't know, a little paint, a few flowers, couple of throw pillows..." quoting one of her favorite movies.

Finished inspecting their new office they accompanied Mike to a room with several rows of five drawer file cabinets. There they met Mrs. Irene Bell, a small gray haired woman who Mike introduced as the museum's librarian. Irene quickly instructed Jim and Eve on the filing system used at the museum and ensured they understood that she and she alone would access and handle documents.

Jim wondered if this arrangement would work, but decided not to say anything, having already received far more cooperation than he expected. Irene then gave Eve a pamphlet which described how to access the museum's computerized records from the Internet. Irene then assigned a temporary password and user ID for them to use.

Eve quickly reviewed the pamphlet, asked a few questions and pronounced herself ready. By now the museum was approaching its closing time, and they noticed several of the museum employees tidying up their desks and eyeing the clock. Jim and Eve made arrangements to return and exited the building.

Chapter 38

Alan Wisecup was a prompt man. His father had retired after thirty-two years in the Army and had beaten, sometimes with his hand other times with his belt, a few bits of Army wisdom into young Alan. Most of which Alan had managed to forget during his six years in college.

But for some reason, which he never understood, Alan had never been able to shake his father's emphatic obsession with being on time. His father's scream sounded in Alan's head louder than an alarm clock, "If you're on time you're by definition late." That obsession with being on time had been so ingrained in young Alan that once, while still in middle school, his old man had told him to be home on time to receive a whipping. Alan knew what was coming, was scared to death, but still had hurried home ensuring he was ten minutes early. So now, twenty-three years after he'd left home, Alan still arrived for work ten minutes early.

The parking lot was filling. Cars were beginning to cruise the length of the lot like sharks circling chum. Alan parked in the far corner of the lot in hopes no one would park next to his six-year-old Toyota. Someone always did.

Cole Prestcott sat in his work van and watched Alan lock the door of his car. He'd selected his spot well. The van was partially hidden by a red Ford F250 pickup truck and, more importantly, Alan had to pass the van to exit the lot. Cole slipped out of the vehicle and stood next to the bumper.

A moment later, head down, shoulders slumped, Alan ambled past. Cole stepped out, took two hurried steps and was within inches of his prey. Before Wisecup could react Cole leaned forward and whispered, "Good morning Alan."

Wisecup recoiled at the booze soaked plume of bad breath that enveloped him. Stopping abruptly he fought down an odd wave of panic, straightened his back and said in a voice filled with strength that he didn't really feel, "Good morning Mr. Prestcott."

"We need to talk about my payment…and my house."

"Sir, the bank opens to the public in an hour. I'm sure we can discuss business then." Wisecup's reply was crisp. He looked Cole over then added, "Maybe you could get some coffee and then make an appointment to visit with me later today…"

"No, no…I've thought of that and frankly I just don't think that's a viable alternative you little shit." Cole could feel his throat tightening.

"Mr. Prestcott! I think…."

Cole cut him off, "Alan I want you to turn around now and get in my van."

"I will not. I certainly do not appreciate…" Cole shoved the short nose of his .32 caliber snubnosed revolver into Wisecup's lower back.

"I don't really care what you appreciate. I said get into the truck." Cole's voice was tight.

"I don't think that's wise Cole." Wisecup struggled to sound normal, formal and regain control of the situation. "I think we should probably talk at the café just up there." He raised his arm and pointed.

"No, no Alan, I think not." Cole's calm had returned. "Turn around Alan." Wisecup did as he was told and now saw, rather than just felt, the little pistol. "Now, I'm going to blow your head off if you don't walk back to that van and get in. I don't give a shit if it's right here in the middle of the damned parking lot. Understand?"

Wisecup glanced down at his waist. Cole held a pistol the size of Lake Michigan. He was sure he could look down the barrel and see a huge bullet pointed at him. His stomach tightened. In a low whisper he managed to say, "I understand Cole."

They headed back to the truck. Alan frantically searched the parking lot. No one paid attention, they all hurried on their way to work or breakfast or the beach or something, but not to help him! "Self-centered bastards! HELP ME," his brain screamed, but Alan didn't make a sound. Standing next to the passenger door Alan's knees began to shake.

Cole directed Wisecup to get in. "Make sure you put your seat belt on, I wouldn't want to see you get hurt." Cole smiled.

"Where are we going?" Wisecup's voice was quivering.

"We need to look for that seven thousand dollar check. Don't we?"

Alan Wisecup was not a brave man. He didn't think about the people walking past the truck. He didn't think about running. He only thought about the pistol in Cole's hand. He was sure it was a fifty or sixty or seventy inches or calibers or millimeters, whatever they used to measure guns with, it was just big! He did as he was told, even putting on the seat belt.

Cole ran around the front of the vehicle, got in and turned the key. "We're going for a short ride Alan. I hope you don't mind, but this is business. I'm sure your boss won't mind you being late to work, after all...well, like I said this is business."

Cole's van backed out of the parking lot, swung onto Grandview Parkway and joined the morning traffic. They headed east and were soon out of the city. Cole accelerated as the road opened and in a few minutes they were passing a large Indian owned casino. Glancing at his passenger Cole asked, "Ever play there?"

Wisecup began to relax. "No, no...I'm not much for the casinos." Maybe this was going to be alright. "Why would he ask me about playing in a casino if he intended to do something bad?" Alan thought.

"Too bad, you might have had fun," Cole observed. The van crested a small hill and the countryside opened up in front of them. In the distance the sun poked through some low stratus clouds and Wisecup squinted. After a mile or so Cole slowed the truck and turned south. This road was paved, but not often used. The van bounced over frost heaves and through potholes. Not more than a mile later they came to a wrought iron fence. Cole leaned forward in his seat until he spotted the driveway. A second later they turned into the Circle Hill Cemetery.

"What are we doing here?" Wisecup's voice was high, almost squeaky.

"Like I said Alan, we need to talk business." The drive extended straight back from the road and ended at what looked like a "T" in the road, but was actually the connection with a circular drive. Cole turned right around the circle and parked the van at the opposite side. "Get out."

Wisecup opened the door, swung his leg out, then fell back into his seat. "Calm down Alan." Cole said and pointed at the seat belt locking Alan in place. Alan unhooked the belt, got out and stood next to the van. Cole hurried around the front of the vehicle then grabbed Alan's arm and pushed him away from the van.

Alan began talking in one long sentence, his words spilling over each other without pause. "Cole maybe we could work an extension of the loans you know I've been thinking about those loans and the economy is surely going to turn around in fact I see hiring is picking up I think (wheeze) you'll be selling boats again in a few months I just think..."

Cole cut him off. "Stop right there Alan."

Wisecup nearly stumbled. His legs were jello. Cole removed a bottle from his jacket pocket and took a long pull. Then he walked to the back of the van. Opening the truck's doors he glanced in Alan's direction. "I always keep cleaning supplies in the back of the truck. Never know when they're going to be handy," he called.

Cole took another drink from the bottle. Standing in front of the open van doors his eyes scanned the interior. Finally, he picked up the bucket and dumped the contents on the floor of the van, then took a handful of rags from the resulting pile. He walked to Wisecup's side. "Alan, look over there." Cole pointed with the pistol. "See that bush with the headstone right next to it?" Wisecup glanced in the direction Cole indicated and didn't see anything. He nodded his head yes. "Let's walk over there." Cole announced.

They walked to the bush and stopped. "Take a seat." Cole pointed at the headstone. Alan began to sit on the ground. "No dumb ass. Sit on the headstone. Christ."

Cole shook his head. Alan sat.

Cole began to pace; he took another drink and stumbled. "I sent that check. You know I did don't you?" He didn't wait for Alan to answer. "Did you cash it? Did you really think you could hide that check and take my home and my boats and my business and my life from me?" Cole stopped and watched a pair of crows land next to a dead squirrel on the road. The birds picked at the carcass, squabbled and called. A blue jay's shrill voice pierced the air. Wisecup began to hope Cole would pass out or fall dead from the booze. "Did you think I was going to go back to living in some freezing little shit-fornothing attic again? You're trying to fu..."

"We never got a check!" Alan shouted. "I looked." Tears began to blur Wisecup's vision, his voice cracked. "Really Cole, I looked."

Cole didn't listen, he'd stopped listening months ago. "Did you know my wife left me? She packed up the house and moved out. Did you know that?"

Wisecup didn't know that. What the hell was she doing? They were going to leave the state together. They had talked about New York or Boston or Los Angles. The cold reality hit him like a winter storm. She had played him. She had never intended to take him with her. Alan began to shake.

"I didn't know that Cole, I'm sorry, I, I didn't..."

"I think you meant to take it all. I think you thought you were going to take it all away and..." Cole was wrapping the rags around the barrel of the pistol.   "...you were going to live in my house."

"I've never seen your house Cole. I don't want your house. I have my own house." Wisecup's voice had taken on the sound of a man pleading. "I didn't take anything. It was her, it was Elaine that took it. She's been stealing from you!" He could see what was going to happen and couldn't think of a way to stop this oncoming train. "Even if I'm dead the bank will want its money, you can't get away from that. I don't make the rules; I'm just a bureaucrat."

Alan decided to run. He tried to run, he commanded his legs to move, but they didn't. Alan watched as Cole walked behind him and the headstone.

"Alan, you shouldn't talk about Elaine like that. She didn't take the money Alan, you did." Cole's eyes were focused on the pistol.

"Cole, I didn't... Look, we've got programs, refinancing programs that you can use. Please Cole..."

"Alan, you know the truth."

"Cole, it's not me. It's the bank. No matter what you do to me they'll take the house and business anyway."

Cole thought about that for a moment. The crows had returned to the fight over the dead squirrel. He raised the pistol to the back of Wisecup's head and fired.

"That maybe so Alan. I just don't want you there when they come to get it." Cole said to the body.

He walked back to the van and got in. After a moment he adjusted the rear view mirror so he could look at himself. A strange set of eyes met his. "You shouldn't have done that," he said to the man in the mirror. For several seconds Cole stared at his reflection. "But he deserved it," the image replied.

Chapter 39

East Bay shimmered under a waning moon as the night fell away. It would be daylight in a short time and Cole had another twenty miles to drive. Gradually the sun climbed above the white cedar trees and found the water in a dazzling display. Cole didn't care; he had important things to do today. The cool morning air blasted through the open window of his truck and stung his face. He welcomed the chill, it kept him sharp, his thoughts clear. He sped south past Elk Lake and into the outskirts of Traverse City. Quickly passing through the still sleeping town he soon entered orchard country to the west.

Minutes later he passed the Cherry Nation Orchard's welcoming road sign. He drove past the sign until he came to the next orchard. This acreage was not tended well, it was clearly going fallow, no one had harvested here in several years. A short distance later he found the gravel road he knew was there. Turning onto the rutted side road he slowed and drove several hundred yards. Cherry trees lined the road on the north, woods and low wetlands to the south. It didn't take long, in minutes he found an equipment gate.

He opened the gate where tractors, harvesters, wagons, and other equipment entered the large orchard and drove some thirty yards off the road. He put the van in park, killed the engine and stepped down from the van's high seat. The orchard was quiet, only a few doves cooed someplace in the distance. Cole went to the back of the vehicle and examined the two-track path he had just driven.

He was certain the van was now hidden by rows of

cherry trees. Cole opened the back of the van and, after a quick search, decided to take a heavy duty bolt cutter, a crosscut saw, a crowbar, his tool grabber and two flashlights. These he stuffed into a nylon backpack.

Another quick check of the van and he set off between the trees. Fifteen minutes later he came to a broken down fence. He paralleled the fence for ten yards, came to a place where it was completely gone and simply walked onto Gerry's newly acquired property. A short walk further and Cole was face to face with Gerry's new barn.

The door was padlocked shut. This wasn't going to be a problem. Cole set the backpack on the ground and took out his bolt cutters. A grunt or two later and the chain hung loosely from the door handles. Cole's hands began to shake. Slowly he smiled, relief flooded over him. His problems were over.

He wouldn't need long, Cole guessed ten minutes to get inside the boat, retrieve the pile of hundred dollar bills he was certain lay hidden there, and be gone. A sharp yank and the chain fell away from the door. Cole then pulled the right door open and slipped inside. Finally he could see...nothing!

"NO! Ohhh no, no, no!" In sheer frustration he turned and ran several steps away from the building. Cole stopped and walked back to the building. He paced, he walked back inside the barn, it was still empty. "What the hell? WHERE DID IT GO?" he screamed. He banged his fist on the wall. He swore and kicked the door. Finally, he slumped to the ground, his back against the now closed door of the building.

Cole stared at the far end of the empty building. Cheated. He'd been cheated again. Gerry had taken his money. He had found it, it was his, not Gerry's. Without him

Gerry would have never known there was thousands of dollars, maybe millions, just sitting there. Gerry was a thief. What else could you call him? He'd taken Cole's money hadn't he? He was helping Elaine take the business from him. Gerry had to pay.

Then Cole had another idea. Maybe the money wasn't gone. Gerry had just moved the boat to the barn nearer the house. That was the only sensible thing. Gerry had said he needed that barn. The boat was just up near the house.

The money was deep inside the hull. And he hadn't told anyone, not even Donna. Maybe Gerry didn't know, maybe it was still there. Maybe he could still get it.

Cole felt better. The boat was near the house. He'd just go up there and get it, no need to hang around here. Cole stood up. He had to find that boat before anyone began a restoration. It couldn't be that hard. It was probably up front at Gerry's original barn. Cole brushed the dirt from his pants. He had a plan. This could work, it had to work.

Cole retraced his steps to the van and soon backed out of the orchard. Moments later he approached the Cherry Nation Orchard LLC sign and turned into the driveway. He couldn't see the boat in the yard. It had to be in the old barn in back. He slammed the van's door shut a bit too hard and sprinted up the steps of Gerry and Sherrie's porch.

Pausing only a moment to catch his breath, Cole mashed the doorbell. Just finished with breakfast Gerry was surprised by the early visitor, but greeted Cole warmly. "Wow, Cole, you're out early this morning."

Cole hadn't thought this through, but lying gets easier with practice and Cole was well practiced. "Yeah, well I needed some more information for that report you asked for."

"Ah, I thought you'd forgotten about the report. I know I had!" Gerry said.

Cole winced at the unintended dig. "I knew you wanted this information, but we've been pretty busy. Finally I just had to let everything go and focus on this." He patted the pad of paper in his hand. "I need some a few numbers, that sort of thing. I'll be done tomorrow but, like I said, just need a little bit more."

"Sure, what do you need?"

"I need to check which engine it has, there were more than one available, some other things like serial numbers, that kinda stuff." Unconsciously, Cole's hand brushed his jacket pocket. He could feel the hardness caused by the snubnose. He wasn't sure why he had the gun. He wasn't even sure who had put it in his pocket, but it made him feel better.

Cole had to find out where the boat was. He'd thought about coming right out and asking, but that would make Gerry suspicious. So he came up with, what he considered to be a perfect plan. He would be totally innocent. It sounded good, but try as he might Cole couldn't fight down a nervous stutter and he began to repeat himself. "Well, all I really need is the engine and transmission model numbers. If we could drive out to the boat I won't be very long."

"Sorry Cole, can't do that. The boat isn't here anymore," Gerry said.

"But...what, well...where did it go?" Cole fancied himself a decent actor, and sometimes he was right.

Gerry smiled at Cole's apparent confusion. "It's a lot easier for everyone to have it out of there. I'm going to use that barn for equipment and some storage."

Cole's mind was racing. "Tell me where the damned

boat is!" he thought. He needed to search the boat...the money was in the damned boat! Cole slipped his hand inside his pocket and found his gun. He squeezed the grip, clenching his fingers hard around the metal and plastic checkered surface, so hard his hand hurt.

"Okay, yeah, sure," he said. Gerry noticed an odd detachment on Cole's face. Cole's mind wandered. He thought about the boathouse, the lifts; he loved that boathouse. He pictured the early days, the truck he towed the two Sea-Doos with all those years ago. He could feel the loneliness, the claustrophobia of the attic room he'd rented from a farmer outside Petoskey. The room was drafty. Cold air blew through the single window like shit through a goose. He was headed back there and there was no getting out of it.

"Where did you take it? I need to see that boat." Cole's evident frustration was putting Gerry off.

"I'll have Jim give you a call, he's in charge of the restoration. He'll get all the info you need. Sound good?"

"Yeah, that's a good idea." Cole's mind was racing. He turned, then turned back to Gerry. "Ya know, just thinking about it, well it gives me sort of a problem." Cole's voice trailed off.

"How's that?" Gerry asked

"I might need to ask a few other questions. I think it would be better if I just examined the boat in-person. I might need to look at a particular part of the boat. You know, to find part numbers and stuff."

"How much more info do you need Cole?" Gerry was becoming a little suspicious; something was odd here, but he couldn't put his finger on it. "I think they're out of town, but will be back in a day or two, I'm not sure. Like I said, I'll have Jim give you a call when they get home. I'm sure he'll invite you down and you can get everything done at one time."

Cole studied Gerry. He knew; Cole could see it all over that sanctimonious face. He knew what was in that boat and he was going to keep Cole from getting what was his.

"Yeah...sure...yeah that's fine. Thanks." Cole turned and walked back to his truck without saying goodbye.

Gerry watched Cole's truck leave the orchard then went back in the house.

"Everything alright?" Sherrie asked.

"Yeah, just talked to Cole. He's an odd guy ya know?" Gerry said as he poured a cup of coffee.

"Something about him that's for sure," Sherrie replied.

A mile south Cole pulled off the road. He'd lost, he'd lost his nerve when he needed it the most. They had found the money. It was gone now. He'd never get it, he would lose everything. People would point at him and call him a total failure. They found it and then hid the boat so no one would know. Gerry was smart, he'd keep the money and screw Cole. He sat there thinking. He remembered how bad it was when he was just starting. He didn't want to be broke again. He hated being cold, hated being hungry, and most of all hated not being able to do anything. He loved having all the money he needed to do whatever he wanted. That was gone. Boredom was the real killer.

The pistol was in his hand. It felt comfortable, balanced, like it belonged. He hadn't put it there, just like he hadn't put it in his pocket in the first place. The gun was shiny, and beautiful, in a deadly sort of way. He could smell the Hoppes gun oil. He put the muzzle in his mouth. The taste of spent gunpowder and oil wasn't so bad. It would all be over in a flash.

Then it came to him. He heard the voice.

Chapter 40

Jim and Eve were back at the museum as the doors were unlocked and the building opened for the day. They checked in with Mike Meier and presented him with a dozen paczkis.

"Wow! Where did you get punch-keys this time of year?" Mike exclaimed, putting the full Michigan accent on the Polish word. Unless they were of Polish decent most people only associated the heavy donuts with Fat Tuesday. This was a real treat.

'Well Mike, ya gotta do the reconnaissance if you intend to hit your target," Jim grinned. 'Dutch Girl Donuts makes 'em year round. Rough neighborhood, but all right."

Eve grinned, "It's just a little weird seeing the cashier behind a thick bullet proof glass!"

"You can bet I'll take advantage of this little tidbit of knowledge in the future," Mike said as he lifted one of the treasures from the box. Jim and Eve took one, cut it in half and carried the paczki and two cups of coffee to their new "office." Soon they were deeply buried in their research.

Eve poured over the museum's electronic files while Jim researched Coast Guard records from the early thirties. Just before lunch, Jim's efforts paid off.

"I've got something." Eve could hear Jim's excitement.

"Look at this! In August 1931 the Coast Guard intercepted and boarded our boat." Jim was reading an official looking report with a scrawling, looping handwriting filling in several blanks on the preprinted form.

181

"The boat's owner is listed as Ray Bernstein. They thought the boat was running booze. Bernstein was a suspected bootlegger." Jim's finger traced down the form. "This says the boat was searched and nothing found. What's interesting is that the boat they stopped was, '...the famous racer Volstead Act.' How cool is that!"

Eve sat back in her chair and stretched. "Yeah, that's cool, but also a little weird."

"What? Why? It's a smuggler's boat, you'd sort of expect it to be stopped every once in a while. I'm sure even the boats that weren't smuggling were stopped all the time."

"Well, I'm sure a lot of boats were stopped. But why would they call this boat famous?"

"What?"

"You said the article called the boat famous. That's weird. Why call it famous?"

"You're right! That is odd." Jim thought for a moment. "But...I've got an idea of how we can find out. Let's go." Jim stood up and began searching for his keys.

"Go? Go where?" Eve was surprised by the sudden action. Jim was already opening the door to the little of office.

"First to the copy machine, then I think we need to review some newspapers."

They made a copy of the report, returned the original to its binder and were soon crossing the parking lot to their Jeep.

"So where are we going to review newspapers from the 1930s?" Eve asked as she buckled her seat belt.

"To the public library, of course. They have copies of all the newspapers from the 1930s on microfiche. We need to know more about the "Volstead Act".

They crossed Douglas MacArthur Bridge and turned

182

left on East Jefferson. Jim, as usual bemoaned the fact that people drove too slow, wouldn't move to the right for faster traffic or were busy texting while driving. It was the same speech Eve heard every time they drove through any village, town or city; and after many years of marriage she'd learned to tune it out.

"Jim, the library has a copy of every newspaper right?" Eve asked.

"Yeah, the Detroit Times, the Free Press, the Detroit News and a couple of others that I've never heard of."

"Okay, so we're supposed to read every paper printed for the years we think the boat was in business?"

Eve was beginning to see a long day ahead of them.

"That's about it. A microfiche isn't a digital record. The only way to search it is by date, then read that day's paper," Jim answered.

"Are you nuts? That's going to take forever!" Eve thought about the prospects of sitting on a wooden library chair for the next several hours.

"Well, I guess we can hope they've digitized many of the past newspapers, but I'm thinking that's a long shot."

"C'mon now hon, don't you want to know the history of our boat?" Jim asked.

"All I wanted was the plans so you could get this little project done and out of my barn. I'm putting two stalls right where that boat is sitting. I've already got names picked out for the horses," Eve said.

"Yeah but Eve, this could increase the value of the boat, and I'm sure this won't take too long." Jim was scrambling.

She studied him for a moment then smiled, "Alright, but at six-thirty we're heading out for dinner."

Jim looked sideways at her and grinned.

"I'm just sayin'," Eve announced and folded her hands in her lap.

They exited the Chrysler Freeway and in a few moments were nearing the public library. A few minutes later they were climbing the stairs of the ornate Italian Renaissance building.

The reference librarian did not fit the image. Jim expected an older woman with gray hair in a bun, a high collar and shoes that resembled clogs. Instead, a young man wearing a dark blue tie introduced himself as the assistant head reference librarian. Mark Lewis listened to their story, asked several questions, and then showed Jim and Eve to two small cubicles, each with a microfiche reader. Satisfied they knew how to operate the machines Mark glanced at his notes, then to Jim's horror disappeared.

"Now what?" Jim whispered to Eve.

"I don't know. He didn't say anything. Where are the rolls of film? How do we check them out?" Eve asked, not expecting an answer from her equally confused husband.

Their confusion didn't last long. Less than two minutes later Mark appeared carrying a small wooden box. "Here are the Detroit Times microfiche rolls. I pulled all the copies from 1928 through 1935. Each roll is labeled with the month and year. I've got one other item for you. I'll be right back."

Jim opened the box to find several rows of what looked like old, large metal Kodak film containers. Selecting January 1931 he handed the case to Eve who immediately began loading it into her microfiche reader. Then he removed the February 1931 can and began loading the film into his own.

As Jim began to scan the first image Mark reappeared and laid a large book on a table. "I happened across this book a few weeks ago. While pulling the microfiche I remembered it. Hope this helps."

Jim picked up the book. He studied the faded pressed words on the cover, gave up and opened to the title page, "A History of Detroit's Notorious Rum Runners."

The book was an exploration of the bootlegging trade during the Prohibition Years and it focused on the river traffic between Windsor Canada and Detroit.

"Mark, you are an amazing man!" Jim exclaimed.

Mark grinned. "Thought you might like that."

Several hours later Jim, hunched over the book, decided to take a break. He stood and rolled his shoulders then glanced at Eve. She sat slumped in her chair, slowly her head slipped off her hand causing Eve to snap her head up with a cry. Confused, she stared wide-eyed around the room.

"You fell asleep babe," Jim said. Eve looked at her palm, noticed it was wet with drool and searched for a tissue. Not finding one she wiped her hand on her knee.

Jim started to laugh. "I saw that."

"Ohhhh...you weren't supposed to be looking." Eve stretched then checked her watch. "How long did I sleep?"

"About twenty minutes. I think I've found something pretty interesting. The boat showed up a lot in 1931. Check this out." Jim flipped the book open to a page he had marked with a yellow sticky note. "Look at this."

He pushed the book across the table to Eve. "It seems the River Club used to hold boat races on Sunday afternoons. They broke the boats into divisions based on length, age, horsepower and stock or modified. One division included the large cruisers. A boat known as the "Volstead

Act" was the fastest cruiser on the river. But in August and September of '31 it lost the race on the second Sunday in each month to a boat it had beaten several times previously." Jim leaned over and placed his finger on the page. She read the rest of the article.

"Sort of explains the restrictor plate that the boat guy found doesn't it," Eve observed.

"Yeah it does. But it gets better. People used to bet on the races. Big money bets. Check out this article." Jim swiveled the monitor of his microfilm reader toward Eve.

"It seems a couple of guys bet on the "Volstead Act" and lost."

"All that's interesting but Jim, really, we're just trying to fix up a boat. We can do all this research next winter when we've got the time." Eve was thoroughly bored with the library.

"I know, I know. But, take a look at this next article." Jim pushed a button. The film sped through the machine until he lifted his finger. A few taps of the button later he pointed. "This! Take a look at this." He was pointing at an article entitled 'Collingwood Murder Trial Begins.' "Eve, this was a big deal and sort of the end of the Purple Gang in Detroit."

"The Purple Gang?" Eve glanced up at Jim.

"Yeah, you know, Jailhouse Rock, "The whole rhythm section was the Purple Gang. Lets rock, everybody, lets rock," Jim sang in his best Elvis imitation.

"Oh brother! American Idol is safe." Eve laughed.

"Anyway, the Purple Gang was the Al Capones of Detroit during Prohibition. Mean, nasty guys that weren't afraid to gun down their enemies."

"Okay, got it." Eve read the next article for several

minutes. "So these guys were murdered because of a pair of rigged boat races?"

"No, they were murdered because they were stupid. The races were just the start of their troubles, the newspapers claimed they were running booze for the Purple Gang and keeping some of each shipment for themselves. Double crossing the Purples was bad business."

"Sucked to be them wouldn't you say?" Eve grinned.

"Now go to the next sticky." Jim returned to the book and flipped to an excerpt from the Detroit Times newspaper article detailing the trial of Bernstein, Milberg and Keywell.

Eve read for a moment then said, "Jim, who's this guy?" She pointed to a picture of Sol Levine as he prepared to testify against members of the Purple Gang.

"That's Sol Levine. He double crossed the Purples somehow. I've got to read more about it, but anyway he received state protection when the gang members threatened, in court, to kill him."

"Threatened him in court? Pretty stupid thing to do," Eve said.

"It was, but apparently the guy doing the threatening thought Levine took four hundred thousand dollars from him or the gang, I'm not sure."

"Well this is all interesting, but why do we really care?" Eve asked.

"Because...." Jim flipped a page and jabbed his finger at the page. "Levine and the gang members had been rounded up at a boathouse. Look at this picture of the boat house. See the name on the boat?"

"Jim, it's The Volstead Act!" Eve exclaimed.

"Now check this out." Jim flipped to a third yellow

sticky. "The police didn't clue into the money until after the trial. They were too busy handling a murder case. Anyway, when someone read the transcripts and thought about the threat on Levine they decided to go search the boathouse. That didn't happen until....umm. Wait a minute...." Jim searched the page, "Look, the murders were in October and they didn't search the boathouse until May, see here...." Jim pointed further down the page.

Eve eyed a picture of trucks and men in front of the boathouse.

"They never found the money, and the boat was gone." Jim sat back in his chair with a satisfied look.

"So, what difference does all that make?" Eve asked.

"Well, maybe the money..." Eve's eye's lit up, she turned to Jim and exclaimed, "You think the money was on our boat?"

"Yeah, only makes sense right? Someone made off with all that cash and used our boat to do it, pretty cool huh?"

"Well, we've got a good story to tell boat guests that's for sure." Eve smiled, then added, "Okay Mr. Detective, good work, I'm impressed, but now let's get out of here."

Jim stood up, leaned across the table and took the heavy volume from Eve. "I'll make copies of these pages, and we'll be gone in a minute."

"Sounds like a deal." Eve began putting the various films and books they had been studying back in their appropriate spaces.

Several minutes later Eve grabbed Jim's arm, "By the way Jim…"

"Yeah?"

"I'm thinking Sweet Lorraine's in Southfield for

dinner. Just so you know."

"You're really making me pay for this boat aren't you!" Jim laughed as they walked down the steps toward their Jeep.

Chapter 41

The voice was soft. Almost a woman's but not. It was something like, he couldn't put his finger on it, it was like nothing he'd ever heard. Maybe like a white-tailed deer would sound like if a deer could talk. He couldn't make out the words. It was more of a whisper.

Cole whirled around in the seat; he was alone in the van. He eyed the orchard, searching for the amorphous voice. Seeing nothing and no one he shifted his gaze to the van's mirrors; no one crouched next to the vehicle. Outside the van's windows the world looked the same, but he knew.

He knew exactly what had happened. The cherry trees stood still, no bird flew, no grass waved. Not even a bee buzzed. The world had stopped.

Cole tried to slow the piston chugging in his chest. He tilted his head and listened. Now he was sure, it wasn't a whisper. More of a feeling. It was as if someone had spoken to him but directly to his brain, bypassing his ears. It was half way between words and thought. Certain that he was alone Cole forced his shoulders to drop, the muscles to sag. Slowly his back conformed to the seat. He wasn't relaxed, he was, well, he was just not tense.

It was gone, not exactly gone, not gone totally, it was in the background. He tried to stop his breathing; tried to stop the blood pounding in his ears. Then, like an explosion inside his head he heard the words: "They know where the boat is, make them tell you."

Cole studied the inside of the van. It was moving. He didn't know how or when it started, but he recognized the direction. He was holding the .32 and he was sure it had just told him that Gerry and Sherrie had taken his money.

"Kill them." The pistol seemed to be talking. He held the pistol in his lap; it was warm, it vibrated and pulsed.

Cole's van passed the orchard sign and continued another hundred yards to a tractor access that crossed over a drainage ditch fronting the orchard. He turned off the road, ghosted twenty or thirty yards into the orchard and parked.

Without knowing how or when it had happened Cole found himself out of the vehicle and walking through Gerry and Sherrie's orchard. As he approached the back of their cherry processing shed his hand went into his pocket. It was still there. The gun seemed to have a mind of its own. It wasn't saying a word, it didn't have to. Cole had his instructions, he knew what had to be done.

He withdrew the pistol from his pocket and pushed it under his belt. It was bigger now and it certainly wasn't comfortable stuffed in the top of his jeans like that but, that's how people did it in the movies. The pistol was warm.

Carefully he peered around the corner of the building. Gerry had gone back inside. Leaving the shed, Cole hurried across the shaded backyard to the rear corner of the house. He stood next to the wall and watched a crow fly over the orchard. It circled and landed on the cross tee of a power pole. The crow turned and stared at him. He thought about the bird for a moment. It seemed free and easy. He wondered what it would be like to be a crow, no worries about someone stealing your home. The crow shook its head. "Just worry about your money," the bird said. Cole nodded to the bird then forced his mind back to the task at hand.

Carefully he crept up the five steps to the backdoor. It was open and only a light screen door stood between him and enough money to solve his problems. Stepping around the corner he silently peered through the open door. Gerry stood next to the sink pulling dishes from the dishwasher and putting them in their appropriate places. Sherrie called a question to her husband. Cole couldn't hear what she asked. It sounded like she was in a distant room in the house.

Gerry's shouted answer exploded in Cole's ears. The voice grew angry. Cole stood there unable to move. Nothing moved. The crow watched. He watched himself; he was stuck there motionless. The voice demanded he move.

Straining against the glue that kept his legs from moving Cole suddenly burst free, crashed against the door and simultaneously yanked the pistol from his belt, scraping his 'muffin top' belly and stumbled into the kitchen. "Hands up!" he yelled and then thought how stupid that sounded.

Sherrie had just entered the room. She spotted the gun even before Cole's primordial yell reached her and immediately screamed. Cole was so shocked at the reaction he didn't pay any attention to Gerry who immediately palmed a carving knife from the open dishwasher. No one moved. A silent, gray cloud settled over the room. Doubt, fear, and anger flavored the cloud.

They stared at each other. No one knew what to do next. Gerry was first. "Cole what the hell are you doing? Put that gun down."

Like glass shattering, Cole's mind and will returned in an explosion. "I need the money. Give it to me now." He was into it now. He was in deep and this had better work.

"Cole, I already paid your bill," Gerry assured the crazed man in his kitchen.

"No, not that. I want the money you found in the boat. I need it now." Cole was breathing harder now.

"Cole, what are you talking about? I didn't find any money in the boat." Gerry was genuinely confused.

"Give me that money now or I'll kill both of you." Cole's throat was tightening, sweat beaded on his forehead. "Go on, get it. I found it first and I need it. G-E-T I-T N-O-W!!"

Gerry tried to be as calming as he could. "We didn't find any money in that boat Cole. I can't get you anything."

The voice came back. It shouted, "He's a liar!" Cole was amazed they couldn't hear it. "You're lying, where is it?" he screamed. Cole was becoming hysterical. He started to wave the gun around like a fire hose.

"Okay...Okay, look Cole, here's what we'll do..." Gerry began. "I'll tell you what we'll do, not you!" Cole was screaming now. "SIT DOWN," he yelled and pointed at the kitchen table. He started to laugh. "I need that money and you're going to give it to me."

"Cole, I'm not sure what money you're talking about. I paid your bill. We don't keep cash here." Gerry was doing his best to reason with their intruder.

Cole locked eyes with Gerry. "The money in the boat, give it to me. Give it to me or..." Cole looked around the room, finally his eyes settled on Sherrie. "...or, or she gets shot."

Sherrie let out a gasp. "Mister, we don't have any money. There wasn't any money in that boat."

"You're lying! You took it out. Now give it to me," Cole cried.

Silence filled the kitchen. Finally Gerry said, "We can give you the money, just let us go."

"The money is in the cherry shed," Sherrie announced. "I'll go get it."

"DO YOU THINK I'M STUPID?" Cole shouted. "GET UP! Both of you get up." His wild eyes swept the room.

They did as they were told. Gerry quickly slipped the knife under his shirt. Cole marched his hostages out of the house, across the yard and to the cherry shed. Gerry glanced over his shoulder and saw the pistol shaking violently.

Sherrie entered the building first. Next Gerry climbed the two steps and pushed through the door. Thinking this was his chance Gerry began to remove the knife from under his shirt. Cole caught the odd movement and immediately pistol whipped Gerry on top of his head.

The blow sounded loud in the morning air. Sherrie screamed. Gerry's hand let go of the knife as his body fell to its knees, his vision swirled and circled. Blood flowed from a cut under his thick hair.

The suddenness of the action surprised Cole. He hadn't meant for this to turn violent. This was wrong, it was going wrong. He was losing control; he was becoming someone else. "It's alright," the voice said, "he deserved it."

Cole picked up the knife and put it against Gerry's nose. "I should kill you for screwing with me." Then Cole began to laugh. "A knife? Are you kidding me? A knife! You brought a knife to a gunfight? You idiot. You complete idiot." He couldn't stop laughing.

Cole shoved Gerry the rest of the way into the building then stumbled in after him. A large room with processing tables and shelves of equipment greeted them.

Pointing to a spool of heavy gauge bailing twine used to bind up tree limbs Cole ordered Sherrie to tie Gerry's hands behind his back and then tie his feet together.

Sherrie finished the knots and began to stand up.

Cole reached out, grabbed her arm and flung her toward a tool bench. Sherrie's hip hit the bench with a loud 'thunk' and she cried out, more in surprise than pain. "You son-of-a…"

Cole didn't let her finish the curse. "HEY lady, shut up and turn around." Cole put the gun on the bench and picked up a baggie with long cable wraps visible inside. "Perfect," he said. Working quickly Cole soon had her hands and feet bound.

Finished with his chore Cole leaned his face close to Sherrie's. With a sick, sour breath, Cole hissed, "Now tell me where the money is." Sherrie noted the new hardness creeping into his otherwise singsong voice.

Gerry shook his head and sat back on his haunches. "Let us go and I'll…I'll get the money for you." Gerry's voice was weak. Cole pushed Sherrie to the floor and immediately smashed the pistol down on Gerry's head.

Gerry's body sagged and Cole laughed as Gerry collapsed, rolled to his side and threw up. Sherrie screamed, "We don't have it. We never found anything."

"You lied to me!"

"Yes, yes, we did. Look we don't have any money." Sherrie was begging now.

"Then where's the boat?" Cole screamed.

Sherrie rolled to Gerry's side. He was breathing but not moving. She sobbed uncontrollably. "It's gone, they took it yesterday. I don't remember the address." Sherrie was in a panic now. This insane man was going to kill her, Gerry, Eve and her brother if she told him where the boat went.

"You're lying, he told me this morning." Cole pushed Gerry with the toe of his boot then went to the office door and found it locked. "Where's the key?" he demanded.

Sherrie shook her head, she couldn't remember right

now.

"I need the key or this time I blow his head off."

"All right, all right…it's in the house, in the kitchen I think." Sherrie screamed, she was nearing total panic collapse now.

"In the kitchen. Are you screwing with me lady! Do you expect me to go back there and leave you here?" Cole only spoke in shouts now.

"No, no, please…look there's a spare. There's a spare key in here." Sherrie stammered.

"WHERE? WHERE'S THE DAMN KEY?" Cole was hysterical now.

"I don't know. I don't remember. I don't use it." Her throat tightened and her body succumbed to a pair of deep sobs.

"BULLSHIT!" Cole shouted, "You know where the key is, it's your damned business!" He fought to regain control of himself.

"Behind the calendar I think, I don't remember." Sherrie's sobs continued and her voice cracked, she could barely speak.

"Think Sherrie, think damn-it," she told herself. She wanted to find a weakness, a way to escape. She needed to stay calm, it wasn't working, but slowly she was stopping the panic.

Cole walked to the calendar and ripped it from the wall. A key hung on the nail. He unlocked the office door and went to the desk inside. Don Harris' invoice and shipping papers lay on the desk pad, exactly where Sherrie had put them. It took only a moment before Cole had what he wanted.

Sherrie was on her knees, hands tied behind her back,

her head next to Gerry's. Her tears running over his cheek. "Gerry, I love you Gerry," she whispered as she gasped for air.

Cole came out of the office carrying the papers. He was laughing. A high pitched child's laugh. He continued to laugh for several minutes, then sat down on a stool.

Carefully, thoughtfully, Cole examined the calendar on the floor. Then he stopped laughing. After a few moments of silence his attention wandered to the pistol. Slowly he began turning it over and over in his hands. Once, twice, five, six times. Finally he said, "That bitch thinks I'm going to lose my house." He fell silent.

Cole spun the cylinder, saw that only five bullets were loaded and laughed. "Safety first!" he shouted, then spun the cylinder and placed the barrel against his temple.

He stared at the calendar for a moment. Only the sound of the birds outside could be heard. Cole grinned, pulled the pistol down and placed the hammer on the empty cylinder.

Sherrie watched the madman's dance. God help her, but she was hoping he'd pull the trigger. Cole's stare met hers. It seemed to unnerve him. Cole looked down at the pistol, then up at Sherrie. He examined his two victims as if he'd never seen them before. He began to twirl the pistol on his finger, a revolution later it fell to the floor.

Cole's gaze shifted to the pistol. His laugh turned to a snicker.

Chapter 42

Jim enjoyed the drive into their farm. The fields on both sides of the long driveway were a beautiful shade of green in the spring, bursting with life in the summer, shielded the house with a golden yellow corn in the fall and gave a sense of hope for the future in winter. Their house contrasted sharply with the traditional two story, Sear's catalog circa 1925, farm house. This was a cozy two-story cottage style log home with a large porch. Right now, its soft reddish brown hue seemed to glow in the last hour of the setting sun.

Jim parked the Jeep in the garage and they began to take their suitcases and other debris from the trip into the house. Molly immediately began pushing her bowl around the floor and looking plaintively at her masters. Eve opened the pantry door, picked up a scoop of dog food, told the dog to sit and poured it in the bowl. Molly's eyes begged for the release command as Eve filled the water dish. With the word "Okay," Molly's feet scrambled on the tile as she rushed to her dinner. Jim carried the last suitcase to the bedroom, closed the garage door and went to the living room. Soon the TV was on and Jim was searching for the evening's news.

Eve poured herself a glass of wine from the bottle in the refrigerator, slipped on her heavy sweater jacket and opened the back door to let Molly run. Following the dog onto the large back porch Eve spent a moment looking over the fields. Several corn stalks shuttered unnaturally in the still air. Eve smiled; deer were in the field again.

She watched Molly racing toward the pasture, then took a seat in one of the two overly large, white wicker chairs.

The screen door slammed back against the door jamb making a homey 'BAND-bang' sound. By now the western sky was filled with reds, oranges and purples as the night captured the day. Soon the clear cool evening would burst with stars pinpricking the sky. Once comfortably curled onto the overstuffed cushion she opened her cell phone and called Sherrie anxious to tell about what they had learned at the library.

Cole's foot caught in the grassy weeds growing between the corn stalks. His arms flew out to his sides and gripped the nearest stalk for support. The leaf's sharp edge quickly slicing his skin. "Damn this..." He quickly choked down the remainder of his curse, afraid someone would hear. He had fallen to his knees so he stayed there, knees cushioned in the soft earth and rested. After a moment Cole stood, picked up his backpack and stumbled forward.

A short while later, light fading Cole faced two buildings. He selected the one on his left and slipped inside. It was an equipment shed, a tractor and some other equipment, but no boat. Cole found a garden rake and began a quick tour of the building, breaking the bare light bulbs hanging from the ceiling as he went. There was no boat here. Disappointed, Cole slipped out the way he'd come in.

A few minutes later he stood at the back of the larger building. Carefully he slid the door open, just a foot. Just enough to squeeze through. He could smell hay. The barn's interior was darker than he expected. There were only small windows set high in the walls and they were covered with a layer of dirt and dust which allowed only a minimal amount of light into the building at high noon.

Carefully Cole groped his way along a wide hallway. It was dark now. A small room, with door half open stood on his right. He stepped past the door. Bits of barnyard light found their way through dirt covered windows, cracks and holes in the barn's wooden walls. In the dim light he could just make it out. He had found it. The Chris-Craft stood tall in her cradle.

Cole swallowed a cheer, took off his back pack and began removing his tools. He placed a saw, crowbar, hammer, his tool-grabber and a knife on the ground. Then he pulled a small flashlight from the bag and settled into the task of expanding the hole into the boat. In twenty minutes he'd be rich, save his house and business and never, never worry about living in some broken down farmer's pathetic attic again.

Several minutes later Cole had nearly finished widening the hole into the boat. All he needed to do was cut one more board and he could wedge himself into the hull far enough to reach the pile of cash he knew was there and....

A noise. Not a sound of the night. Not a raccoon or opossum but man made. He didn't know where it came from. He turned off the flashlight and put down the handsaw.

Silence pounded in his ears. He wanted to turn on the flashlight and find the intruder, whomever or whatever it was. He stood, turned and faced the window ten feet away. Unconsciously Cole tilted his head and listened.

Nothing.... Maybe it was some animal, a rat or fox, something that belongs in a barn. Rationality fought to intrude on his delusional brain. It wasn't an animal, he knew it wasn't. The backyard light came on, filtering into the barn through the windows and around the building's tractor doors.

This was turning out to be a bad idea. He'd driven three hours to find the boat. Now he was going to be caught. Bullshit! It wasn't going to happen. Cole studied the barn's double doors. They didn't move. Good, whomever came through those doors was going to get...he looked around. "Where is that damned gun?" he asked himself. He groped in the dark, found his tool bag and hefted a hammer. It would have to do. This was his find.

He knew there was more money in that boat and he was going to get it. The hammer wasn't right, it wasn't enough; he needed the pistol. Whoever came in that barn door was going to be blown away. He would do it. He would blast the first person that came through those doors. No one was going to take his money again.

Cole's hand slid to his pocket. Not there. The pistol wasn't there. He spun, eyes searching the floor. The light didn't penetrate this deep into the barn; he couldn't find the damn pistol. Cole fell to his knees, he needed the pistol; where was the pistol? Sweat began to bead on his forehead. A flick of the thumb and the flashlight flared.

Cole swept the light across the floor, his tool bag, the inside of the boat, then spotted the weapon laying on a beam of the boat's cradle. He grabbed the gun and extinguished the light.

From the darkness he heard someone; the breathing was loud, fast, excited. Cole raised the gun and tried to find the sound. The breathing moved quickly from one side of the room to another. Cole struggled to find it, if he turned on the light they'd know he was here. But the sound. It was to his right, no left. It was behind him. Then the angry, excited bark of a dog filled in the darkness.

He flipped on the flashlight. A beagle stood just ten feet away, its bark constant, its howl loud. The dog bayed like it had treed a raccoon. Cole rushed at it, the dog dodged and barked again. He kicked at the noise, slipped, and fell. The flashlight crashed hard to the concrete floor and without so much as a flare it went out. He rushed at the animal, it ran. Cole stumbled forward, found a door and slammed it shut.

Eve closed her phone in disgust. Sherrie had her phone off. Eve had big news and she couldn't share it. She finished her wine and was about to call for Molly when a chorus of howls erupted from the inside of the barn.

"Ahhhh…that stupid dog…." Eve thought, "getting her back is going to take a half hour." Opening the door to the house Eve shouted, "Your stupid dog is on a rabbit again, I'm going to get her." Walking across the yard Eve smiled. The dog was Jim's when not coming when called and her's the rest of the time.

Eve had just reached the barn when she noticed Molly's bark wasn't the howl of a beagle happily running the trail of some cottontail. These were the sharp barks of a dog that was angry. "Oh no, she's cornered something. God I hope it's not a skunk," she thought. She pushed open the barn door and called, "Molly, c'mer girl."

She waited. Nothing. Normally, she would hear the gentle jingle of the tags on the dog's collar. The barn was silent. She tried again but nothing returned from the dark void of the barn's deep interior. Stepping inside she felt for the light switch, finally found it and flipped it on.

Nothing happened.

"Oh crap, I hate this damned barn in the dark," Eve muttered. Then she heard a soft whine from deep inside the dark building. Molly had somehow gotten inside the tool room and couldn't get out.

"Molly you stupid dog," Eve said as she began to feel her way along the isle to the far side of the building. Without much difficulty she found the tool room door and began to fumble with the door catch. Suddenly a flashlight illuminated just to her left. She turned in that direction. A loud bang exploded in her head. She sagged, then felt herself hit the floor. Her cheek hurt. Unable to move she watched the beam of light pass over the toes of a pair of mud caked work boots. She could hear Molly whining...then nothing.

Chapter 43

The Sports Network Scoreboard was rolling credits as Jim walked into the kitchen, took a bottle of beer from the refrigerator and went to the porch to join Eve. Her nearly full wineglass sat on the table next to her cell phone. Curious that she was not there Jim placed his bottle next to the wineglass and called into the dark backyard. Not receiving an answer he reached inside the backdoor, found the light switch and flipped on a large florescent light attached to the roof of the house. Immediately the yard and pasture beyond were bathed in light. Odd, long octopus shadows filled the gaps, but no Eve.

He called to her again, and again no answer. A nagging sense of unease began to creep up the back of Jim's neck. He walked to the equipment shed, opened the door and turned on the light. Nothing happened.

"Odd," Jim thought. He'd been working in this building just a few nights ago and the lights had all worked fine. Moving to the workbench Jim found the flashlight hanging at its end. Taking the light he quickly searched the shed. No sign of Eve. As he moved around the tractor his light moved over the light fixture screwed into an overhead beam. The light bulb was broken.

Jim hurried to the barn. Reaching for the light switch he noticed it was already in the 'on' position. He swept the beam of his flashlight across the ceiling until he found the metal conduit. Tracing the pipe with his light he came to the first light socket. The bare bulb had been broken here too. Jim called Eve's name again and again only silence answered.

Then he heard a small whine. It was Molly, she sounded far off, deep in the interior of the barn. Something was definitely wrong here. He retreated a few steps. A rack of yard tools was mounted to the wall next to the barn door. Jim scanned the tools hanging there, selected a small hand sickle and resumed his search.

Extending the flashlight outward in his left hand and holding the long curved blade in his right at the ready Jim slowly advanced. Carefully he made his way to the back of the barn, checking light fixtures as he went. The light bulbs were all broken. Eventually, he reached the tool room. Molly's insistent whine was plainly coming from inside the small room. He opened the door and Molly ran out, barking and running circles around him.

"Molly how the heck did you get in there?" Jim asked as he shined his light into the room. Molly, of course didn't answer, and Jim continued his search of the barn. He called Eve's name several times with no answer.

Cole gripped the pistol tightly. Just a few more steps and this guy, whatever the hell his name was, would be dead. Cole thought about that; maybe he'd better use the hammer. It was quieter. No, no, he'd stick with the gun. But the pistol was...

There was a better chance for a quick kill with the gun, no muss, no fuss. Over, just like that. Bang and it was done. But, it was murder. Was he really a murderer? Cole wondered. Conflicting, disjointed thoughts raced across his brain like the scenery outside a trucker's window. Jim, that was it. The guy's name was Jimmy-boy. It was the gun, definitely the...maybe the hammer.

He'd done some bad things, was doing a bad thing now. But was he a murderer? Alan's death had been justified.

Was it murder to kill someone that was killing you? Alan had been killing him. Sure it was slow, but Cole could see what was happening. The bastard had been methodically sucking away Cole's life. Any judge that really thought about it would know Cole had been justified in what he did.

The light stopped. Cole focused on the light.

Jim was now very concerned. The broken lights were odd. But, maybe Eve had chased Molly into the woods or into the field and was lost in the dark. That didn't make sense, she could see the lights of the house. Besides, even in the dark she would just walk toward the noise of the road. Something was very wrong here.

For the first time since childhood a fear of the dark crept up his back. He could feel a stranger's eyes and he began to feel very much like a trophy whitetail on opening day.

Slowly Jim backed down the hallway. He reached the door and quickly slipped around the corner and into the shadows between the tool shed and barn. The police were too far away to be of much help. It would be thirty minutes or more before they were here. He needed help now.

Maybe Eve was just lost in the field or the woods. He decided to call his neighbor, Dave Frederickson. Dave and his three boys could be here in minutes.

Cole stood silently behind a stack of equipment watching the light come closer. His prisoner rested against the wall, unconscious. He could just shoot Jim now and be done with it; no, wait, that was too much noise. Cole's mind raced, this was exciting, dangerous and the best damned adventure he'd ever had. Which was better? The gun, definitely the gun. But the hammer would be quieter.

Wait, what if Jim over there had already found the

money and hidden it? Cole would never find it then. Or, what if he'd found the money and had already put it in a bank? Then he'd need to be alive to get it out. No, better to take the wife and have Jimmy-boy over there deliver the money to him. That was it! That was a great plan. Cole smiled; he'd done it again. God, he was freakin' brilliant.

The light stopped. Slowly it retreated. Cole watched it slide further away and suddenly it was gone. Finally, he was able to leave. He opened the rear door then lifted Eve over his shoulder in a fireman's carry. Cole faced a small patch of grass and then a large field of corn. He couldn't remember the little pasture, but he was sure this was the field he'd crossed on the way to the barn. His van was parked on the side of the road a few hundred yards away.

Cole began to hurry across the pasture, but it wasn't easy carrying even a small woman.

"Hey! Who the hell are you?" A shout came from behind. Cole dropped his prisoner, whirled, pointed the pistol and fired twice.

Jim heard two loud bangs. A loud SMACK exploded from the barn wall a few feet from him. He ducked behind the building. Several minutes passed. Jim peeked around the corner again. The pasture stood empty in the cool starlight, his antagonist was gone.

Jim ran to the house. If this guy wanted a war he'd get one. Jim took the porch steps two at a time. About to enter the house he was stopped by the sound of Eve's cell phone. Knowing he should ignore the phone he headed to the basement for one of his guns; but this wasn't right. No one would be calling right now. Not exactly at this instant.

He listened. The phone went to voice mail. Then it rang again. This was a call Jim knew he needed to answer.

Picking up the phone he pushed the answer icon. A voice said, "I have your wife."

Jim's hands began to shake. The voice said something, Jim didn't hear. "I have your wife." What did that mean? How did this voice get this phone number? Jim's heart pounded in his chest. His breathing became shallow.

"HEY, I'm talkin' to you idiot! Get the money and bring it to…"

"What money? What are you talking about?" Jim was recovering fast. "I don't have any money. I did, but I bought a farm. Farmers don't have money."

"The money in the damn boat!"

"What money? Are you insane? What are you talking…"

The voice cut him off. "Don't screw with me. If you want to see your wife again. Get it and drive to the fisherman's shrine."

"The what?" Jim couldn't understand what was happening. "What fisherman's shrine?" Jim couldn't believe what he'd just heard. Fisherman's shrine? What was that? His wife was being held by the damned Riddler?

The voice on the phone began to laugh. "Think Jimmy boy, think…"

Jim's mind raced. He'd been to the statue in Glouster Massachusetts called the fisherman's shrine or statue or something like that. That didn't make sense, it had to be… In vacation country! It had to be up north. "The fish statue? In Kalkaska?" Jim asked

"Yeah, you know another one?"

"But, I don't…"

"Shut up dumb ass. Look, you get there and we'll call you. Got it? If you're not at the trout in five hours, she's history. And one more thing. We're watching. We'll watch every place you go, everything you touch and every phone you talk on. If we see a cop, if we smell a cop or even think a cop might be in the same county, she's dead. You understand? You got that?"

The phone went dead in Jim's hand. He sunk into the porch chair. This was bad. This was real bad. He had five hours to find some money he didn't know about and drive three hours north. This was as bad as it got.

Jim sat forward and began to rub his temples...money, boat, "fisherman's shrine"? What the hell? Just say the town's name, "Kalkaska."

The man said "we". That meant there were more than one of these creeps. Okay, Jim thought. He could deal with that. The caller said he would call when Jim got to the fisherman's shrine in downtown Kalkaska. The shrine was a statue of a big brook trout. Some people called it Kalkaska's elk because an elk diner raised the money to buy the statue. Jim knew exactly where that was.

Jim had watched as many shoot'em up movies as the next guy. He knew the cops would swarm all over the farm. There would be a command post and a yard full of cop cars and State Police troopers and FBI agents and none of them would act fast enough. He'd lose her, he'd lose the only thing that made life worth living. "Okay Jim, get ahold of yourself. Think, think." His mind raced. He knew all that but what was "the money" thing? What the hell was that all about? What money? He hadn't been asked for a sum, an amount, just "the money". Jim pushed the heels of his hands into his eyes. The voice had said the money and the boat. No, it was the money IN the boat!

Jim hurried to the barn, pulled open the tractor doors

and inspected the boat. He couldn't see much.

Some tools lay on the floor. Someone had been working on the boat! He needed more light. Jim rushed to the tool room and found the box of spare light bulbs. Then he tripped the barn's fusebox, took some tools from his bench and began to remove broken light bulbs from their sockets. When he had replaced them all he flipped the circuit breaker and the interior of the barn was bathed in light.

The Chris-Craft sat in the middle of the barn on a large cradle. Next to the front of the boat a handsaw, several other tools and a tool bag lay on the floor. Someone had intended to cut their way into the boat. Eve must have surprised them before they got started. Jim began his search there.

Chapter 44

Sherrie awoke laying on her side. Her hands were tied behind her back and her shoulders screamed in pain. Her ankles were tied together and her legs were beginning to spasm. She tried to open her eyes, no luck; the left eyelid stuck shut. She squinted hard and tried again. Her eyelid popped open like a stuck garage door. Now her eyes were open, but it didn't make any difference. There was no light in the room where she lay. Carefully she rolled to her back and stretched her legs. Slowly the spasms stopped and Sherrie let out a low "Ahh…"

Laying there she surveyed the place where she lay. The floor was carpeted. It seemed like a nice carpet too. Thick pile, nice cushion. A window was on one wall, its edges defined by a bit of light seeping around the blind. Okay, must be a room in a house someplace.

She tried to move her arms. It was nearly impossible, the bindings holding her wrists were tight. There was no give there. The cramps were becoming unbearable. Sherrie wanted to scream, she wasn't sure if it was from the pain, the frustration or the fear. She didn't.

There was a noise, just over in the corner to the right of the window…it…didn't…sound…quite…right.

Sherrie froze and listened. It was breathing. Slow, irregular, labored. Instantly every horror movie she'd ever seen flooded back into her consciousness. It was that man, the boat guy. He was going to kill her. No, he had other plans worse then death. She listened. The sound didn't change. Finally Sherrie asked, "Who's there?" Seconds went by with only the sound of the breathing.

She stared in the direction of the labored sound. She decided to scream. She sucked in a lung full of air, then thought, "Get ahold of yourself girl. Think, think, think, damn-it!" Her eyes were becoming adjusted to the darkness. She could see a shape on the floor. It was the source of the breathing. She rolled in the direction of the sound. It was a body, laying face to the wall.

"Gerry! Oh my God, Gerry. Say something honey, say something." She pleaded with the inert figure on the floor but it didn't do any good. Gerry lay in a pool of vomit. His head bloodied, left eye swollen shut. She knew she had to get him out of the vomit, he could choke on it or drown or something.

Sherrie rolled on her back. Then, like a worm she worked her way backwards until her hands found the collar of Gerry's shirt. Reversing the process she moved his torso a few inches so that his face rested on dry carpet. She fought down tears. "Sherrie, now is not the time! Keep focused." She scolded herself.

She needed to see more of where she was. Sherrie wormed her way to the wall then worked her way to a sitting position. She took a moment to rest then began scooting toward the window. It took several minutes but eventually her groping fingers felt the long draw cord of the blind. Now the problem was raising the blind.

After a moment she took the cord in her teeth, leaned back and tried to pull the blind up. It worked; the blind came up two inches. A bit more light crept into the room. Sherrie was elated. She let the cord go, expecting to be able to grab it at a higher point and pull the blind up another two inches. The blind fell back to its original length. Tears filled Sherrie's eyes. This wasn't going to work. This was the type of blind that required an offset on the direction of the pull to lock the sting.

She sat and stared at the just barely visible draw cord. "Don't quit," she said. Then she gripped the string in her teeth again, pulled back and holding tightly to the cord, fell to her right. It worked! The blind stayed up two inches. Working feverishly Sherrie was finally able to raise the blind six inches above the windowsill.

The added light allowed Sherrie to see the interior of her prison. There was no furniture; the room was totally empty except for Gerry. On one wall a double door with a full length mirror. She was in a bedroom; it had to be a bedroom in an empty house. The walls were painted, it must be a light color, but in the faint light she could only see shades of gray. The ceiling was interesting. It seemed to be made of wood, no it was beams of wood, with a texture between. That meant something. What? A cabin? Was she in a log cabin?

She wiggled to the window, then rolled to her knees. Bending her head she could look beneath the blind. There were no lights on in the yard but there were a few porch lights on at neighboring homes. She could make out an ordinary yard with a walkway leading to a building. Beyond the building was pure blackness. In the middle of the blackness floated a row of evenly spaced balls of light.

"What the hell is that?" Sherrie muttered. Then it came to her. The lights in the blackness were from cabins on the far side of a lake. She was looking out over water.

Chapter 45

Ten minutes later Jim had a circular saw plugged into an outlet. The saw screamed and he began cutting around the broken planks at the front of the boat. Finished with the cut he put the saw on the floor and gripped two planks. A quick pull and they were free.

Having widened the hole he crawled into the bow. Even with the enlarged hole this was a difficult maneuver. The hull sloped steeply downward, sharp edges cut into his side and he had to hold himself up with his left hand.

Carefully he began his examination of the framed interior of the hull. Jim wasn't sure what he was looking for, the caller had said money, but it could be something that was worth money. He checked behind every frame and bulkhead. Then his light hit what appeared to be a newspaper.

Just out of reach and behind the framing of a smuggler's compartment what appeared to be a clump of newspaper with...what was that? A picture of, no...a face! Jim stared at a hundred dollar bill! Pushing with his feet, Jim was able to shove his body forward another foot.

Reaching over his head he was able to just get his fingers on the newspaper. It nearly disintegrated at his touch. But as it crumbled a canvas bag was revealed. Gradually Jim pulled the bag out of its hiding place. Seconds later the bag was free and Jim was able to back out of the boat's interior.

He quickly cleared a few tools from his bench and lay the bag on the oil and sweat stained surface. Then he began to remove the contents. Out came a candy tin which Jim laid to the side, then stacks and stacks of hundred dollar bills.

There was a fortune here.

Jim swore to himself then shoved the money back into the bag. This was unfair, he was going to lose his wife to some nut over a pile of green paper. Jim knew life had its unfair moments but this wasn't part of the deal. In Baghdad his executive officer, a young Captain who was engaged to a cute little girl, had been killed when a rocket had crashed into his office window. It was the only rocket fired that week, it landed in the wrong spot. Jim understood those bits of unfairness. So did his exec, they all did, it was part of the deal. But here; at home, on a little farm in southern Michigan? Jim's fear and dread began to turn to something more.

Entering the house Jim went to the bedroom and removed a 9mm Berretta he kept in his bedside stand. Then he went to the basement and opened his gun safe. Jim owned a deer rifle and three shotguns for small game hunting. He selected one of the shotguns then grabbed a box of shotgun shells loaded with large lead balls. Used for hunting deer in thick brush and swamp "buckshot" was deadly at short range.

He began to hurry, faster and faster, his mind made up. Jim went to the garage, opened the back door of the Jeep and placed the gun on the vehicle's floor. He opened the driver's door and was about to get in when he heard Molly's whine at the kitchen door. Automatically he turned to the dog and said, "I'm busy now Molly, you're on your own for a while." Then, like a light from an angel, an idea hit. Jim laid the bag of money and pistol on the Jeep's front seat and ran back into the house.

One of Jim's favorite pastimes was rabbit hunting. The great fear of any rabbit hunter is the loss of his dog. Beagles are bred to find a rabbit then trail the bunny as it attempts to flee. Most cottontail rabbits will run in a large circle, sometimes a hundred yards or more in diameter. The beagles' role in the hunt is to pursue the rabbit until it comes back to the starting point. But, sometimes a beagle will run into a smart rabbit. The smart ones will double back on their trail or make a feign one way then go another; all in an effort to shake off the trailing dog. If the rabbit is successful, the dog sometimes becomes lost and the hunter now must find the dog. In days gone by this was a very difficult proposition. Inevitably the dog was lost at the far side of swamp or patch of briars so thick the hunter couldn't pass. Many dogs have been lost for good in this fashion. It was a problem that vexed many hunters and cost a great number of family pets.

Modern technology came to the rescue with the advent of the global positioning satellite system. Now, rabbit hunters equip their dogs with a GPS locator on a collar. A small receiver, no larger than a cell phone is carried by the hunter and the dog's position is shown relative to the hunter. It was this collar and receiver that Jim sprinted down the stairs to the gun cabinet to retrieve.

Returning to the Jeep Jim pushed the collar into the newspaper bag. Its bright, hunter orange color jumped out at Jim even in the dim light of the nighttime garage.

"Damn" Jim moaned. He slumped against the seat and thought a moment. Then he had it. He ran to the barn, and hurried to his workbench. A short search and he had what he'd come for. A filthy rag hung on a nail pounded into the end of the bench. It was gray, oil stained and perfect. Returning to the Jeep Jim emptied the newspaper bag. Then, he turned on the collar, wrapped it in the rag and positioned it at the bottom of the bag. A quick glance and the rag appeared to be part of the bag itself. Satisfied, Jim piled the money bundles back in and set the bag on the floor of the garage. Now the test.

Jim climbed into the Jeep and backed down his driveway to the road; here he checked the unit. Direction was shown accurately, distance was correct and the signal meter showed five bars. The unit was working perfectly.

Chapter 46

Sherrie lay perfectly still on the carpeted floor. Her attention was divided between the sounds of her husband and the sounds of the house, or cabin, or prison, whatever she was in. She had spent the last several hours trying to break free of the binding that cut into her hands and feet. She'd ended up with bloodied wrists and sore shoulders but hadn't made any progress in loosening her restraints. The night was quiet, the only sound an occasional owl's hoot or Canadian goose's honk.

Without warning a moan could be heard in the far, far distance. She listened, straining for some clue as to what caused the noise. Then she recognized the sound of a garage door opener. Panic gripped her as she lay on the floor; he was coming. She was going to meet her fate and there wasn't a damned thing she could do. She glanced over at Gerry. He lay where she had left him. His breathing was steady now, regular, deep, and healthy, but he was still unconscious.

In the cool night air she heard a door slam. Then she heard a woman cursing. Someone was in the backyard. Sherrie wiggled to the window, rolled onto her knees and peered into the darkness. She didn't know if the ambient light was better, or her eyes had fully adjusted to the darkness, but things were clearer now. A man was dragging, pushing and kicking at a woman as he forced her to walk the length of the sidewalk to the large building at the end of the walk. At the door the two stopped, the man appeared to be trying to find the key for the door.

Suddenly, the woman turned and kicked him. The toe

of her shoe connected squarely with his knee. A small cry of pain, then a shove. The woman bounced off the building, lost her balance and fell to her knees. He grabbed her by the hair and hauled her to her feet. An instant later the door opened and they disappeared inside.

Several minutes passed, then Sherrie watched the man walk back across the yard in the direction of the house. It was Cole. Panic gripped her. Instinctively she began crawling, rolling, moving anyway she could think of toward the darkest corner of the room. Then she stopped and without conscious thought reversed direction and placed herself between the door and her husband.

Eve had lain on the floor of the van for the past several hours. She was sore, stiff, angry and scared. During the long ride she had managed to lift the blindfold an inch allowing her to see below the edge. It hadn't been easy; her hands were bound together behind her back using a plastic cable wrap. In the darkness Cole hadn't noticed her efforts.

He pulled her out of the van and hurried her through a door. Then she was pushed and dragged across a grassy yard to a sidewalk. She cursed, screamed and struggled to get some separation from this monster. Finally, they stopped at some sort of door. She could hear him fumble with a key. She tilted her head back and spotted his leg below the blindfold. Eve's right leg flew out in a vicious kick, catching Cole squarely on the knee. He swore and slapped her hard on the side of her face. She fell back against a wooden door, recoiled forward and fell to the wooden walkway.

Suddenly he had her by the hair and was pulling her up. She stomped downward with her foot, managing to land a glancing blow on her antagonist's foot. The kicks hadn't helped her situation but Eve was determined to fight.

Cole opened the door and violently pushed her inside. She landed hard. Her head bounced off the building's wooden deck and her blindfold flew across the floor. Dazed, she lay on her stomach for a moment then rolled to her knees. Cole smirked then reached to the side of the door and turned on the lights.

Even terrified, Eve had room for amazement. Two rows of boats floated on either side of a wide waterway. Each boat rode at a small dock and the entire structure had a golden glow under soft light reflecting off the cedar log paneling. The whole thing was majestic.

Cole hooked one hand under her arm and lifted Eve to her feet. "No more! Stop fighting me." She glared at him. He leaned forward, nearly touching his forehead to hers. "Stop kicking or I will hurt you and I will hurt you bad," he said it as if it were routine.

"Your breath stinks," she said. He smiled, opened his mouth and exhaled in her face. Then, pushing and pulling, she was marched around the left set of docks.

They walked past two ski boats, a fishing boat and what looked like some sort of paddle boat. She spotted a door at the end of the walkway, just past the last boat. There, Cole opened a door and, with a violent shove, flung Eve inside.

The boat house janitor closet smelled of cleaners, was small, dark and a prison. Her wrists screamed in pain. The thin plastic wrap cut into her skin and she could feel the sticky blood on her right hand.

She lay where she had landed for several minutes. She tried vainly to see in the darkness of the storage closet. Finally conceding defeat she wiggled to her knees, then stood. Relief washed over her. She had been terrified that Cole had intended to load her on a boat and dump her in the middle of the lake.

Now she set about exploring her new prison. Carefully, Eve pushed her right foot forward until she bumped into a solid object, then she stepped to her left and repeated the process. After a moment she found the side of a metal shelving unit. This might hold something that she could use. She would return to the shelves later.

She worked her way around the closet, finding some wooden handles, mops, brooms and the like. Finished with her initial exploration she returned to the metal shelves. She wanted to know what was on the shelves but couldn't see anything in the dark room.

Slowly an idea formed. Awkwardly she fell to her knees, then to her side. Carefully she wiggled backward until her finger tips touched the lowest shelf. A bit more effort and she could reach the back of the shelf. Now she began feeling the items on the lowest shelf. She found what she thought was a bucket, a plastic bottle and several spray cans. Nothing that could help.

She got to her feet, did her best to stretch her shoulders then turned and faced away from the shelves. She bent her knees and squatted so that her hands were level with the second shelf. This was much harder. Her legs cramped, but she stayed in the awkward position. Her fingers identified objects; several spray cans, a plastic jug of some sort and some gloves.

By standing at her full height she was able to back up to the third shelf and explore it. Another jug of cleaner or something similar, a package of sponges, a small pile of rags and more cleaning supplies.

Frustrated that her search had found nothing useful

she leaned backward on the far edge of the shelving unit. Something jabbed her back. It took only a moment for her hands to find the offending protrusion. A bolt extended from the far leg of the unit. The nut was loose. For a moment the loose nut didn't mean anything to her and she decided to experiment with the mop and broom handles. But as she began searching for the wooden poles an idea began to grow.

Carefully Eve made her way back to the shelf and began to run her hands along the third shelf until she located the bolt. Slowly, painfully, she began to twist the nut. It resisted at first, but then turned easily. After several minutes it fell to the floor with a gentle tap-tap, leaving an inch of threads exposed. Positioning her hands on both sides of the exposed threads Eve began to rock back and forth, scraping the plastic tie wrap on the bolt.

Cole was satisfied with his work. He finally had the woman safely locked in the boat house storage room and his two prisoners in the house were equally restrained. He returned to the house and went to the bathroom in search of Band-Aids; she'd bit him once and scratched his face twice before he'd gotten the cable wraps secured. Nothing grievously hurt, in fact, Cole started to laugh. She was kinda fun, he'd have to get her and Donna together.

Finished bandaging his cuts and scrapes Cole ascended the stairs to what had once been the guest bedroom. He opened the door and peered around the room. The woman lay on her side. He could see the whites of her eyes; big, round and staring at him. She didn't say a word.

Cole studied her. He walked across the room and nudged her leg with the toe of his boot. "Get away from me you bastard," she spat.

"Yup, you're alive and kicking," Cole replied. He turned to Gerry and kicked him in his back. Gerry didn't move. Odd that he was still out. Oh well. Cole recrossed the room and closed the door.

Leaving the empty house he stood at the foot of the large boathouse. His sailboat was tied to the dock running the length of the outside wall. To be honest, it was a pain in the ass to put the large sailboat inside, but Cole liked it there when he showed guests the boathouse. A big boat like that totally inside a boathouse was impressive as hell. Cole smiled at the thought. The sloop rocked gently on the small waves.

He was exhausted. That wouldn't do. He had his ol' buddy Jimmy bringing him some money. He needed to be alert, on top of his game. The morning promised to be exciting, and profitable. Cole thought for a minute, smiled, then checked his watch. He was a little late. Jimmy must be in a panic. Fishing around in his pocket he came up with the burner cell phone he'd purchased the day before.

He turned the phone on, waited for it to find the network, then dialed Eve's cell phone.

Chapter 47

Kalkaska is a small town living on welfare, Social Security and the tourist trade. Moderately famous for being the home of Trout Unlimited, a conservation club devoted to preservation of wild rivers and the fish that inhabit them, the town has long attempted to style itself as the inland fishing capital of northern Michigan. An attempt which has not met with great success. The town fathers most noted effort is the the annual "Trout Festival".

The festival begins with a ceremony in the town square at the fountain, known locally as the "Fisherman's Shrine". The fountain, topped with a statute of a leaping brook trout, is in need of some touch-up paint, and stands in front of the community center and historical museum. To say that the town mothers were unimpressed with the festival, or the fish, puts it lightly.

Jim sat on the concrete bench to one side of the giant fish. The cool, early morning air did nothing to ease the pounding in his head. Jim decided he had the first migraine headache of his life.

He checked his watch. The caller was late. Another ten minutes slipped past. Now, worried that Eve's phone would not ring, having checked the cell phone signal strength at least twenty times, the phone finally erupted to life.

"Okay asshole, you got the money?" the voice on the phone asked.

"I got it, let me speak to my wife?" Jim replied.

"Not till next time. Now, listen up. Go to the ticket booth at Fort Michilimackinac, got it?

Jim had never heard the word the caller had just used before. Was that someplace or something? Did this guy work for some obscure tourist board or travel company?

Fighting down a wave of pure fury Jim did his best to stay calm, "What? Are you fu..." He stopped, told himself to be calm, took a breath...and lost the battle. "Are you insane?" Jim exploded. "What the hell...where the hell is that?" Staying calm hadn't worked out.

"Whoa there Jimmy. You'd better relax. What's the problem, you've never heard of Mackinaw City? It's the fort at the foot of the Bridge stupid."

"That's a long way from Kalkaska." Jim said, not bothering to hide his anger.

"Yeah, sucks to be you. You've got an hour forty-five to get there." The voice shot back. Then the line went dead.

Cole chuckled. He needed some sleep and having Jim drive back and forth across northern Michigan seemed a good way to get it and with the price of gasoline it seemed extra funny. He'd thought about having Jim take the ferry to Mackinaw Island, but didn't do it. Hell, he'd given Jim a break, what was he so upset about?

Cole walked the length of the dock next to the boathouse. He thought about the woman he'd locked into the storage room. Deciding he was too tired to torment her Cole climbed into the aft cabin of the Morgan sailboat, set the alarm clock and fell asleep.

Jim ran to his Jeep cursing the man, the phone, the boat and the money. It was almost a hundred miles to Mackinaw City, then where would this jerk send him? Two hours later Jim stood at the ticket booth of the old French trading fort. Above him towered the southern end of the "Mighty Mac", third largest suspension bridge in the world. It didn't impress. Jim paced, he sat, he worried.

Finally, an hour after he arrived the phone rang. "How's the view?" the voice asked.

"I'm not playing this game much longer. Let me talk to my wife." Jim spat.

"You'll talk to her when I decide you'll talk to her. Now, listen carefully ass hole. Drive to Boyne Mountain Ski Resort. Buy a ticket for the 10 A.M. ride on the Twin Zip. Take the money to the top of the zip line. Get off the lift; walk under the chair lift to the top. When you reach the brown machinery building I want to see the money so hold it up. We'll be watching. If we don't see the money, or think you're playing a trick, it's all over, got that?" The man didn't wait for Jim's answer. "Then walk down the mountain and take the zip line back to the lodge. I want to see your style as you ride the line down." The voice started its odd laughter again. "Then I want to see you driving out of the resort thirty minutes after you drive in, got it?"

"No deal, I want my wife before I drop off the money."

"You're not in a position to be making demands asshole." The phone went dead in Jim's hand.

Jim sprinted to his Jeep, started the engine and began the long drive back to the resort that he'd passed on his way to Mackinaw City. As he drove Jim reviewed his plan. It might work, he figured his chances were less than fifty-fifty, but he didn't see any other choice. Right now he didn't have enough information. Events were driving him instead of the other way round. He couldn't get inside his opponent's head. Try as he might Jim couldn't come up with an idea better than get the collar into their hands, track them down and kill them. It was a small chance. But he and Eve had plans, he wasn't going to lose her now; a small chance was better than nothing.

Chapter 48

The Boyne Mountain Ski Resort is open year round. Located on a ridge running north and south it's one of the Midwest's largest ski resorts. For skiers familiar with miles long ski runs of the the Rocky Mountains or even the runs of New England, it is merely a bump on an otherwise flat landscape. However, the resort owners have done the best they can with what they have. Short but challenging ski runs on the front of the hill keep the resort full during the winter. During the short Northern Michigan summers two world class golf courses, cut into the trees on the top and back of the ridge, ensure the resort stays relatively full.

While Dad golfs the kids spend the family money on the resort's various adventure park attractions. The most popular being the zip lines. Each ride is scheduled on the hour, exactly one trip per ticket. Tickets are sold for the specific times. Using the ski lifts, patrons are carried to the top of the euphemistically named 'mountain' and deposited at a small building where they are given a final demonstration and safety check. Then the kids, and nongolfing parents, are strapped into a harness, suspended from one of two cables and sent on a high-speed thrill ride.

One ride, known as the Twin Zip simply returns the rider to the bottom of the hill. Its attraction is that it is placed parallel with a second zip line. The arrangement allows riders to race each other down the hill.

The other zip line is known as the Adventure Tour. Its start is approximately two hundred yards further up the hill from the Twin Zip. Once deposited at the Adventure

Tour start, the rider is given the final safety check then sent on a tour of the ski hill and resort grounds using seven different zip lines.

Jim's Jeep skidded to a stop in the resort parking lot at exactly nine-thirty. He grabbed the newspaper bag, lifted the rag and turned on the collar. Then Jim stuffed the bag into his backpack and sprinted into the large, rough oak log cabin style hotel lobby. Several people were milling about the lobby, three men carried golf bags past Jim and out to the parking lot.

A small line had formed near a kiosk on the opposite wall. Jim studied the scene then decided the kiosk hid the zip line ticket counter and hurried in that direction. He rounded the kiosk just as a group of six teenagers and two adults were finishing their purchase. The excited group slowly made their way from the counter. A grandmotherly type with two youngsters were next. The attendant made one of the children stand next to a candy stripped pole, "See Grandma, I told you I was high enough," the little boy shrieked.

This was taking too long! He'd miss the ten o'clock ride, then what? A flash of panic swept over Jim, what if there were no tickets left? What if the ten o'clock had sold out?

The Grandmother finished her purchase and the three headed to the lift line. Jim was next. The young cashier looked at him, "For the ten o'clock? How many please?"

"Yeah, the ten o'clock, just one," Jim handed over his credit card.

The young man paused, glanced up at Jim, then continued with the transaction. After a moment he asked, "You a fan of zip lines?" and handed the credit card back.

"No," Jim replied taking the card and his ticket and

trotting out of the building.

A small, fenced in area had been set up where skiers normally queued up for the lift line. Several benches had been placed inside and faced an opening blocked with a small white vinyl coated chain. Several teenagers, the parents, the grandmother and her two charges were spread about the benches.

Jim placed the backpack on the bench and sat down next to it. Carefully he examined the resort. Hundreds of windows from the hotel, shops, lobby and stairwells stared back. He began at the top floor, sweeping his gaze along that floor then the next. He held little hope that this exercise would lead to his wife, but it kept his mind busy.

"Beautiful day isn't it?" the grandmother asked.

"Yes, I'm sure it is," Jim replied and began to examine the shops lying directly across from the zip line waiting area.

"Are you here with your family?" the woman was looking at him intently, expecting a friendly reply. Jim looked at the woman, a long steady glare, he couldn't afford a friendly conversation, not now.

"No," was all Jim said, then picked up his bag and moved to the other end of the bench. The woman sat straight up, said "Well...." in her most judgmental tone and pulled a novel from her purse.

A young woman, about nineteen or twenty, exited a small building at the end of the lift line and approached. Her shirt said "ZIP TO FUN" and she wore a Michigan State Spartan baseball cap, her blond ponytail was pulled through the back and danced as she walked. She asked for everyone's attention then went through a short safety lecture. Harnesses and helmets would be fitted at the top and additional instructions would be provided. She then began the traditional "move to the right, then join the line" speech.

Jim checked his watch. It was nine fifty-eight. Jim was at the back of the line; in front of him stood the grandmother and her two grandchildren. The lift seats were wide, normally seating three skiers across. The teenagers each sat three to a seat. The parents sat by themselves, then came the grandmother and her two charges. The children were excited and began pushing and shoving each other. The attendant winked at the grandmother, then said "Would you two big kids like to sit by yourselves?" This delighted the pair and soon they were seated at opposite ends of a lift chair. The attendant buckled each child's safety belt around their waist, then lowered the chair's standard safety bar. With a call of, "Get ready, here ya go!" the lift moved the chair forward, the children squealed and a new seat rolled into place.

The attendant directed the grandmother to the seat, then indicated to Jim that he was to take a seat as well. Jim sat down. The woman glared at him, said nothing and looked off into the distance.

The attendant gave a shout and waved her arm. The lift began moving steadily up the mountain. Jim began to study both sides of the wooded chairlift path as the seat climbed.

The mountain, in reality the hill, was fairly low and this lift only went to the half way point. As a result the ride only lasted a few minutes. An attendant at the top stood on a temporary wooden deck where the winter snow normally allowed skiers to glide off a moving chair. The attendant lifted the each chair's safety bar, unbuckled the children and directed traffic to a set of benches arranged similarly to those below and located next to a small shed which held the harnesses and helmets.

Attached to the equipment shed was a deck which served as the launching point for the zip line. Jim's seat stopped and started as each chair discharged its passengers. The delay infuriated him, but there was nothing he could do. Soon enough Jim's chair stopped at the deck. A pretty college student, her hair in a braid, wearing shorts and a Northern Michigan University tee shirt, quickly raised the seat's safety bar. Without a word Jim was on his feet and climbing toward the top of the hill.

The girl, surprised but familiar with the jerks who abused her system, immediately yelled that he couldn't do that. Jim ignored the calls and continued to climb.

Frustrated, the girl shook her head, muttered something about crazy old men and began her duties with the remaining zip line patrons.

After ten minutes of climbing Jim arrived at a brown concrete block building with a wooden sign over the door. The sign, painted light blue with gold old English lettering said, "Mechanical Building No. 3". Jim scanned the woods in all directions. He was out there, the man who had his wife. Jim grit his teeth and steeled himself for the events to come. Would they take the bait? Would he be able to keep the tracking device in range? Would his Eve be freed? It all depended on what they decided to do now, they were entirely in control. He slipped the backpack off his shoulder.

From the woods two hundred yards away Cole had Jim centered in his binoculars. There it was! All that money just waiting for him to come and pick it up. He watched as Jim put the backpack on the ground and removed the ancient newspaper delivery boy's bag. Jim tossed the backpack on the ground and held the old bag over his head. Then, exactly as he'd been told, Jim disappeared behind the building.

A moment later he returned; slowly he picked up the backpack, then turned it inside out. He held the backpack in an outstretched hand and turned a complete circle to show he no longer had the newspaper bag. Cole began to grin, he thought Jim looked like an idiot trying to do some native dance. This was really beginning to be fun.

Carefully Jim began the return hike to the zip line. Unfortunately, he forgot the power of the hill. Quickly he gained speed as the slope of the mountain pulled him down. Involuntarily, Jim began to run, then his legs couldn't keep up and he fell, rolled several times and stopped. Cole erupted. Unable to stop laughing Cole put his binoculars down and wiped his eyes.

Jim stood and began zig-zagging down and across the face of the hill. It worked and he was able to stay on his feet all the way to the Twin Zip tower. A furious Jim Crenshaw found the girl from Northern Michigan University reading a book and sitting on a lawn chair in front of the shed. All the riders had been dispatched and her job was done until the next batch arrived. Not saying a word, Jim opened the door to the shed, took a harness from a peg on the wall and begun putting it on before the girl noticed him. She was immediately on her feet.

"You can't do that sir. I'm sorry but you can't ride until the next scheduled run at 11 o'clock."

"Miss, I've got to get back down that mountain." Jim shot back.

"I'm sorry. It's a safety thing." Jim could feel the eyes of his antagonists on him. He had been told to take the zip line back down and he wasn't about to risk disobeying that instruction.

"I'm sorry too. But, I'm going and I'm going right

now." Jim finished clipping into the harness and walked to the zip line.

"SIR!" The girl yelled. "You've got to stop or I'm going to have to call security."

"Call 'em." Jim growled. Then he hooked on to the cable and ran off the edge of the platform.

Cole was nearly hysterical. Jim's legs and arms flew out to his sides as he missed his grip. His body twisted uncontrollably as he dangled from the zip line. A quick moment later Cole calmed a bit as Jim found his form and completed the ride, but the whole scene was still funny and Cole continued to chuckle. Using his binoculars Cole watched Jim land at the bottom. Two security guards were running toward him. This would be fun.

Jim extended his feet, hit the platform, took three steps to stop his momentum and stood. Immediately the two, in what appeared to be police uniforms, were grabbing him by the arms.

Jim quickly examined the men, no side arms only what appeared to be tasers and medal expandable batons in leather cases. Security guards. The mad man's warning to keep the police away or he'd kill Eve swirled in Jim's head. Then Jim could feel the seeds of a plan begin to grow. Maybe this could be turned to his advantage.

Cole watched as Jim slipped out of the harness. The security guards had a firm grip and it was clear they were not happy with poor Jimmy-boy. Cole struggled to keep the scene centered as his body shook with each new hysterical laugh. Finally, one on each side, Jim's arms firmly in their grip, the two security guards led him into the main lodge.

The doors swung shut behind Jim and the guards. The interior of the Grand Lodge was rustic, with a stone floor and massive timber framing. Jim didn't see any of it. The three men faced each other. Before the guards could say a word Jim announced, "Gentlemen, I know this looks bad. But I had to do what I did. There's a madman up there watching me and he has my wife. I need your help."

The guards studied him. The younger man rolled his eyes and glanced at his partner. The older man, apparently the more senior, looked Jim over, glanced at his gray hair and finally said, "Tell me about it."

Jim quickly described what had happened at the house then his fruitless travels around northern Michigan. The guards still appeared skeptical. Frantically, Jim went through the thing again, still he could tell they didn't believe him. Then Jim remembered the GPS receiver. He pulled the unit from his jacket pocket and turned it on.

Jim's farm was displayed squarely in the center of the screen. A moment later the screen dissolved then reappeared in a pale green road map. The map was centered on their exact location. On the screen, at what appeared to be the half mile circle, a blue dot was slowly moving from left to right. Jim glanced at the strength meter, it was weak, one bar.

"There he is," Jim said pointing to the dot. "He's moving to watch the parking lot. He's waiting to see me drive out the driveway."

The older guard studied Jim. "I'm telling you the truth," Jim said firmly.

After a short pause the man nodded his head slightly. "Dave, I believe him," he said, not taking his eyes off of Jim or the GPS screen. It took a second or two but the younger man fell in line. "I do too Bill," he said.

"Good," Jim said. "Now, please, I've got to call the police."

"No good. Nearest police post is in Petoskey, at least forty minutes away," Dave said.

"You're right, okay…" Jim thought about this new problem for a second or two. Then, turning to face Bill he said, "Will you two help me?"

The security guard didn't hesitate. "Any way we can. What's your plan?"

'Dave," Jim said, picking up on their names. "You're my height and build. Put my coat on; then go out to my truck. Drive out of the parking lot, turn south and stop when you're out of sight," Jim instructed.

"Don't get out of radio range," Bill advised his partner and held up his radio.

Jim looked at Bill, "When one of them comes down from the mountain, you and I nab him.'

Bill stood silent, going over the upcoming action. Then asked, "How many ya think there are?"

"Not sure. I've only talked to one man on the phone. He said 'they' a few times, but I've only talked to him. Could be only one, could be more," Jim began to see his plan falling apart.

Bill thought this over, then turned and looked up the mountain. "Bullshit. I don't believe it, there's only one."

Jim eyed his new ally, "I like your optimism, but I can't take the chance."

'Look buddy…say, what's your name anyway?"

"Jim"

Bill nodded, "Okay, Jim, think about this. If there were more than one, they woulda picked a different spot, they wouldn't have been so afraid of having you get close to 'em. The perp picked the side of a mountain because he's a little shit and wanted to be able to see you from a mile away.

And I'll bet ya he doesn't have the woman, ahhh..."

"Eve"

"Yeah, Eve isn't with him. He's jerked you around about talkin' to her hasn't he?" Bill didn't wait for an answer. "See, he couldn't bring her here, too difficult. He couldn't control her and watch you. I'm telling ya, there's only one."

"He's never wrong about this stuff," Dave chimed in. "I've worked with him for three years now. He's got the gift."

Jim thought this over. "Okay, I'll buy the logic. Only one madman out there." Jim didn't like the situation, but maybe it was just a little bit better than he thought.

Chapter 49

Cole sat with his back against a large aspen, elbows on his knees, binoculars focused on the resort parking lot. After a short wait he watched Jim exit the lodge, parking lot side and walk to his truck. A moment later Jim's Jeep sped out of the resort's parking area, turned onto the long entrance road and exited south on the two lane highway.

Cole watched the vehicle until it was out of sight. Then, still chuckling at the scene with the guards Cole stood and began the next phase of his plan.

Jim and the security guard sat on the bench outside the security office. Jim held the unit between them, each studied the small GPS screen intently. The green dot wasn't moving. Jim began to worry that his scheme had been discovered. He had gambled and lost, now this madman, or madmen would take their revenge on Eve. The bile came up in his throat and he could feel his eyes begin to burn.

Suddenly Bill's radio emitted a loud piercing beep, then a voice erupted from the little box, "Security, there's a fight in the bar. Bartender says a man with a knife. Be careful Bill, get there quick!"

The guard's face paled. "I have to get this. I'm sorry Jim, I've gotta go."

There was nothing else to say. "Go. I'm alright."

Jim was feeling many things at the moment, "alright" was not one of them. "And thank you," he said.

Bill stood, looked in the direction of the bar, then back to Jim. "I have to stop that, I'll be back as soon as I can. I'm so, so sorry." Jim could see the conflict in the man's face.

"GO!" Jim said, not wanting the man to see his failure any longer. Bill turned and ran down the hall.

Remembering his truck Jim jumped to his feet and yelled, "Radio Dave! I need the Jeep back." Bill waved an arm and rounded the corner.

"Can things get any worse?" Jim muttered and he returned to staring at the GPS. Slowly the dot began to move. A momentary wave of relief swept over him. His hand slipped under his shirt and felt the handle of the Berretta. This was going to end soon.

He began reviewing options, could he just charge up the mountain and track these thugs down? He quickly dismissed that as a losing idea. He had to track them back to where Eve was being held, then take them on his terms, not theirs. He needed the Jeep. If these people got to the parking lot and onto the highway while he waited for the return of his vehicle it was all over.

Slowly the dot began to creep across the little screen. Minutes dragged by. The dot faded, disappeared, then reappeared. The strength bars flickered, first three bars, the bars faded to two, one, then disappeared. Fear, and doubt bordering on panic, turned Jim's stomach sour. He couldn't afford to lose that signal. Eve was in trouble and here he sat on a bench, doing absolutely nothing.

His frustration mounted. The signal began to improve, one bar, then two. The dot reappeared, still moving to his right. Then it stopped.

The security office door banged open. "DUDE! Bill is in a fight! I gotta go." Dave ran past Jim, threw the Jeep keys in the air as he passed and sprinted toward the resort's bar. Jim caught the keys, shouted, "Good luck" and glanced back at the GPS. The dot was gone.

He knew what was happening, the signal was being interfered with; he'd nearly lost Molly last winter because of the same thing. He turned the unit off, then back on, hoping to reset the computer. After a maddeningly long time the screen glowed again. Still no signal.

Fighting down panic Jim ran to the Jeep, pulling his jackknife from his pocket as he ran. Finding two indentations on the vehicle's radio face he inserted the blade and pried the cover off. Folding the knife's blade in and unfolding the screwdriver tool he found the radio's setscrews and quickly removed them. Then, Jim slid the radio out of the dash.

Turning the unit over he unplugged the vehicle's coaxial antenna cable and put the radio on the floor. Carefully, Jim removed the GPS's rear cover exposing an antenna plug. He quickly shoved the Jeep's antenna connection into the unit, flipped it over and pushed the "on" button. The unit began its set-up process. Jim turned the key in the ignition, the antenna amplifier was now powered.

The GPS flashed, then a road map appeared. A frighteningly long moment later the machine located the GPS satellites orbiting overhead, then self-cleared the memory. The map began sliding to the bottom of the screen, then dissolved, and reappeared with his current location at the center. Jim glanced at the top right corner of the screen. Five bars were displayed, all of them bright green. He had a good signal. Jim pushed the blue "Locate" button just above the keypad. A small green ball appeared on the screen. Using the distance scale on the lower left of the screen Jim estimated the dot to be over a mile away.

Suddenly the dot began to move rapidly, straight across the screen. This confused and worried Jim. He'd never seen Molly run this fast, even in her younger days on the fastest rabbit. He was certain an all-terrain vehicle could not be moving in such a straight line across this terrain. The only explanation was that the unit was having a difficult time keeping the signal or maybe the unit had malfunctioned. That could be a disaster. Just as suddenly the dot stopped moving.

Jim quickly flipped the GPS receiver over, opened the back and pulled the batteries out. Inspecting each battery he decided none had leaked or appeared to be defective, nevertheless he pulled a pack of double A's from the glove box and replaced them all, then returned the cover to its place. He turned the receiver back on and watched the display go through the same familiar process.

The signal hadn't moved. After a minute or two Jim stared in amazement as the dot again shot across the screen. Jim was now thoroughly confused. The dot again stopped for several minutes then, again shot across the screen.

How was this happening? Jim looked in the direction of the mountain. He could see the Twin Zip chairlift above the roofline of the resort. It was slowly taking riders to the zip line's launch pad. Another lift to the right moved to the very top of the resort, people in shorts and tee shirts dangled twenty feet above the earth. That was it, the Adventure Tour! Who ever had the backpack was taking zip line runs to move from one side of the resort to the other.

Again, Jim studied the screen, as before the dot shot across the screen then stopped. This time it didn't stop long. It began to drift toward the west. Switching the machine's view to a wider scale it immediately became clear. The signal was moving over the top of the hill to the golf course on the backside of the resort. His tormentor had left the zip lines and was on a golf cart or ATV or similar vehicle and heading across the course to the roads on the west side of the resort.

Jim started the Jeep, popped the clutch, did a U turn, and raced out of the resort. He'd expected the man to come down to the resort parking lot, he'd been fooled, now he was paying the price. A half mile north Jim turned west and floored the Jeep. The signal disappeared momentarily, then flashed nearly two miles away; one bar appeared then disappeared. He was almost out of range.

Cole's pickup truck bounced along the road behind the resort. He descended the small mountain, turned south and accelerated on Powder Ridge Road. Passing the cabins on both sides of the road Cole cleared the mountain, turned back north and accelerated.

Jim's Jeep leaned heavily to the outside of the curve as he raced around the north side of the resort. His only chance now was to head-off his prey on some back road.

Approaching the area where the dot had accelerated Jim found a golf course. His enemy had exited the back of the ski area onto a golf course, then driven away. The dot was at the extreme edge of the map and moving south. Jim accelerated and raced after it. By his estimation he was nearly three miles behind. The unit was performing beyond its advertised range only because it was plugged into the Jeep's antenna and it had a clear view of the sky. As soon as Cole put one of these ridges between himself, the southern horizon and those satellites the signal would be lost.

The signal was now moving directly across Jim's front, parallel with him, not away. This was his chance. Jim stepped hard on the accelerator and the Jeep shot forward. At the same time he pulled the pistol from his belt and sat it on the passenger seat.

Just as quickly as he had accelerated Jim was forced to slow, the road had become a twisting, back and forth slalom course with trees tight up against the shoulders. Jim accelerated through a shallow curve in the road, cleared the far corner and found himself just yards behind a group of bicyclists in brightly colored uniforms. The group filled the road. Jim's left foot smashed the clutch at the same moment his right hit the break. The tires screeched as he downshifted the Jeep and let the engine help slow the vehicle. Honking his horn Jim swerved in between two riders, slowed, then accelerated around two more. He shifted again, accelerated and passed the leader of the pack.

Glancing at the rear view mirror Jim found several of the riders were flipping their middle fingers up at him. It didn't matter.

Jim careened around the next corner and nearly screamed. Laid out before him was the reason the signal had moved parallel to him rather than away. There sat Deer Lake, and while it was only a few hundred yards wide it was three miles to go around. Helplessly he watched the green dot slide off the map and disappear.

Chapter 50

Eve's shoulders, neck and arms screamed as the muscles cramped and spasmed. She'd been working the plastic cable tie back and forth over the exposed threads of the bolt for what seemed like days. The thick, heavy-duty plastic wasn't giving at all. She couldn't tell if she'd made any progress, she couldn't see her hands nor could she see the bolt or the cable tie. Several times she'd slipped and gouged her wrists. Her 'saw' seemed to be cutting her more than the plastic tie. More than once she'd thought about giving up, sitting down and just letting her fate come to her.

But she'd never quit at anything and she told herself this was not going to be the first time. She needed to keep her anger up, not give in to despair. She cursed, she kicked and one time, after a particularly painful slip she stomped one foot on the other and let the pain increase her anger. Then, with her jaw set she went back to the cable tie and began to saw again.

Suddenly, the tie separated. The restraining force being instantly released caused her hands to fly out. Her left hand crashed into the wall, her right flew awkwardly outward. Her wrists, and now knuckles were bleeding, but she was free.

Rubbing her wrists and rolling her shoulders Eve slid to the floor. She rested a moment, then put her scrapped wrists to her mouth and washed the wounds with her saliva. It seemed to help and she sucked the pain away.

It was daylight; light crept under the door. The silver pool extended several inches into her cell and spread, not far but enough for her to make out the bottom of the wall opposite where she sat. That was it, simply the bottom of the wall. No help there.

Eve got on her hands and knees and moved to the opposite wall. There she sat looking at the wall recently vacated. In the corner she thought she could make out the wooden handles she'd identified God-only-knew how long ago. She stood up and went to the corner. A broom, a snow shovel and a metal shepherd's hook for holding a lantern or bird feeder were all that was there.

Next Eve began examining the walls of her cell. The wood was made of pine and, much to her irritation, she loved the smell. On the wall opposite there appeared to be a pinhole of light. A knot hole in the wood. She got up, and hands outstretched, she slowly made her way to the wall. There she positioned her right eye at the hole and peered at the morning light.

"What the hell?" Eve gasped. Water. All she saw was water. Her mind raced. "How'd I get onto a boat? Am I in the middle of friggin' Lake Michigan?" she said to the knothole.

Trying to remain calm Eve stood very still and tried to feel any motion. There was none. She listened for a motor. Nothing. She returned to the hole and looked out again. She couldn't tell if the water was moving past her or if the waves were merely creating the illusion of motion.

Now, totally confused Eve sat back down on the floor, knocking a bottle of window cleaning solution over as she did. The plastic bottle bounced, shed its cap and rolled to the foot of the door. Blue fluid began to pour from the open top. It seemed to glow in the small light from under the door. Instead of spreading in a pool the liquid gathered between the boards and dripped away. Eve stared at the wet spot for a moment. There was something to this, but she couldn't decide what it was. On her hands and knees she crossed to where the fluid had run out and examined the floor. It was made of wood planks. Each plank seemed to be ten inches wide and was butted against the plank next to it. But the planks were of a lesser quality than she expected, many had knotholes and some felt like they were cracked. Searching the floor with her hands Eve finally located a good sized knothole.

She'd heard Jim complain about knotholes in wood many times over the years and knew they were weak spots. Eve sat against the wall and gazed at the dark brown flaw. Finally, thinking aloud she said, "You, Mr. Knothole, are coming out of there."

She found the corner with the metal shepherd's hook and removed it. Placing the end of the shepherd's hook in the knot she began to pound on the hook with the heaviest can she could find. In a moment the rod had pierced the wood.

Eve levered the rod to the side and popped a circle of dark wood from the plank. Dropping to her knees she examined a hole of about one and a half inches along the edge of one board. Below, not two feet away was the lake.

"Ah, okay, I'm still in the boathouse," she said, feeling a bit foolish about her confusion.

She sat back on her knees and eyed the knothole. Eve was overjoyed, freedom was just a three fourths of an inch of pine away. Her only problem was how to remove the plank. Finally she decided that if the shepherd's hook had worked once, it might work again.

The plank was stubborn, didn't move and the rod bent. Frustrated, Eve began to search for something heavier. She tried the mop handle, it wouldn't fit through the hole.

That was the limit of her tools. Cleaning supplies were all the closet held.

Eve was tired, sore, frustrated and scared. It was no good. Three quarter inch boards were going to insure she died right here. She leaned back against the wall. After a moment she took two deep breaths. "Think Eve, think damn it!" she cursed. She tried to see the entire utility closet from where she sat. Then an idea came to her. She was sure she'd felt a roll of duct tape on one of the shelves.

"Most important tool ever invented," Eve muttered, echoing her husband who frequently made "hillbilly" repairs as he called them.

A quick search and Eve located the tape. Taking the broom and the shovel from the corner she laid them on the floor. She placed the shepherd's hook between the two and extended it three inches beyond the handles. Carefully she taped the shovel handle to the shepherd's hook.

Finished with that, she laid the two next to the broom handle and taped the entire assembly together, sandwiching the metal rod between the two wooden handles. She made a quick inspection of the completed sandwich pry-bar in the light coming through the knothole.

The wooden handles supported the rod but kept it from bending only if she used the tool with the wooden handles on top and bottom. This would have to do. Eve again attacked the plank with the knothole.

Chapter 51

Five miles past Deer Lake, Cole Prestcott entered Boyne City. Ignoring speed limits he turned left at Division Street, a small shortcut he had learned many years ago and avoided the downtown area. Soon Cole joined Lake Shore Drive and was accelerating as he passed the town limits, oblivious to Jim's frantic efforts to catch up. He was soon racing past the large condo buildings and summer homes of down staters who spent their summer weekend days on the lake and their nights in the bars of the vacation towns of northern Michigan.

Several miles and ten minutes later Cole approached the tiny village of Ironton. Here, the south arm of Lake Charlevoix pushes through the village and extends twelve miles south along an ancient valley cut during the last ice age to the metal working village of East Jordan.

Ironton is noteworthy for two things. Earnest Hemingway's uncle lived here and the surrounding area became the setting for several of the famous author's Nick Adams short stories. And, Ironton is the home of the Ironton Ferry. Famous for its many appearances in the work of both professional and amateur painters and photographers. It was this ferry that now stood between Cole and his beloved home and boathouse.

Jim, driving blindly as he was a full mile out of range of the dog collar entered Boyne City just as Cole had. Unfortunately, Jim was unaware of Cole's side street short cut and was soon crawling through the tourist crowd at the center of the small town. Several minutes later Jim found himself facing the lake and a choice. He could turn left and follow the south shore or he could turn right and follow the lake on its north shore. Jim checked his GPS receiver again, and again, found it empty of the little green ball.

Frustrated, he slammed his hand onto the steering wheel, cursed and took a chance. Jim turned right, was into high gear as he passed the grocery store and sped out of the village.

A long, agonizing five minutes later Jim came to the entrance of what had been Cole's favorite golf club. Without warning the little green dot appeared on the GPS display. Jim's frustration again exploded, the dot was shown on the opposite side of the lake. Jim was just short of two miles from his target, unfortunately there was a large lake in-between.

A primordial scream of frustration filled the inside of the Jeep as Jim raced off on the ten mile circle around the lake. A short distance later he intercepted the highway. An angry blare of horns erupted as Jim ignored the stop sign and turned south. Several miles later he was racing through the village of Cherlovoix, not paying any attention to the picture perfect marina, storefronts or waterway.

Here he could go straight south, to Traverse City, or circle the lake back toward Boyne City. A quick glance at the GPS and he turned back to the east. Leaving town he raced past the airport, a small strip mall and then several houses. Less than five minutes later he slowed and pulled his Jeep to the side of the road. The dot had stopped moving just a quarter mile ahead.

Cole stopped his truck in front of the house, pushed the garage door opener and waited for the door to withdraw. As he waited Cole planned his next move. He would load the two women and Gerry onto his boat, sail into the middle of Lake Michigan and dump them overboard. Then, it would be time to head to Canada.

There he would find a lake side cottage for the rest of the summer. By the time winter came he figured he'd be long forgotten, then he'd come back, pay off the house and the business loans and he'd be back in business. Or maybe, maybe he would forget it all. He could move to Mexico or the Caribbean or maybe South America someplace. Cole smiled, he was back on top.

Sherrie heard the moan of the motor as the garage door opener engaged. Panic swept over her. Her legs began to shake. She was sure her hands would be shaking if they weren't so tightly tied behind her. Desperately she tried to be calm, to think, to figure some way to fight back.

She couldn't, her knees quaked. "Stop it! Damn-it just stop." Sherrie had just begun to calm herself when the bedroom door opened and Cole walked in.

She sat on her knees facing the door. "Okay lady, time for you two to go for a ride." Cole stopped, thought about that phrase and started to laugh. "That's good, 'Go for a ride', sounds like in the movies, doesn't it?" Cole laughed again.

"What are you doing? Why did you take me?" Sherrie demanded.

"'Why did I take you?' Lady are you really that stupid? Because you've got my money. You were going to keep it and I found it. And I need that money to keep my house." Cole's eyes bore into Sherrie.

"What money? What are you talking about? WE DON'T HAVE ANY MONEY." Sherrie screamed at Cole. Cole smiled, "Yes you do. No, I should say, 'you did' because

I've got it now." Then Cole crossed the room and stood over Sherrie. "And you're not going to tell anyone about it."

Before she could react Cole's arm flashed from his side. His fist landed just above her ear canal and it seemed as if the entire world exploded with a loud bang. Stars filled the room and a mountain of pain erupted in her head. Then a gray curtain settled over her eyes. She slumped to the carpet, felt the fabric on her nose and watched the room spin. A moment later the floor fell away.

Gerry's unconscious body got smaller and she felt something pushing on her stomach and ribs. Carpeted stairs appeared in the distance, and she felt herself being carried on Cole's shoulder like a sack of potatoes. She was outside for a moment. She could see the sunlight and trees and water. Then she was dumped to the ground and dragged into a building.

Eve heard the door of the boathouse open. Quickly she hid the shepherd's hook pry-bar in the rear of the closet. Turning back to the closet door she noticed the light coming from the hole she'd been making. Searching frantically for something to cover the hole she grabbed a bucket, turned it over, placed it on the hole and hoped.

Pausing to listen she could hear a voice several yards away. She had one more, small, moment. Eve scanned the room for something to use as a weapon. The darkness limited her choices to what she could feel. Previously she'd identified a glass jar and a metal spray can. The footsteps were only feet away; they would have to do.

She grabbed her weapons and stepped to the back of the closet. There Eve sat down and put her hands behind her back. Maybe he wouldn't figure out that her hands were free. And if he did, well the jar and can had better find their mark.

The footsteps stopped. Involuntarily, Eve bent forward, listening. She heard a thump as something heavy was dropped to the floor. The doorknob rattled as someone fumbled with a key. Cole pushed the janitor's closet door open and the bright sunshine filled the room. Involuntarily Eve flinched as the light hit her dark accustomed eyes.

"I brought you a little company," Cole said, then he turned, grabbed Sherrie's hands and dragged her through the door. Scanning his catch Cole said, "We're going for a little boat ride in a bit. Hope you like boats." The door slammed and Eve heard the key turn in the lock.

"I'll be right baccckkkkk," Cole called as he walked away.

Eve quickly went to the body on the floor. "Hey, hey," she gently shook a shoulder in the darkness. "Are you all right?" Eve whispered.

Sherrie moaned, "That SOB hit me in the head. Where's Gerry?" Sherrie's head hurt but had stopped spinning. "My hands and feet, they're tied."

"Sherrie...oh Sherrie!" Eve tried to hug her.

"Gerry's not here honey. But we've got to get out of here. That monster is coming back, and he said something about a boat ride. We can't get on that boat. That would be bad, really bad."

"I can barely move. My head hurts and my hands and feet are tied."

Eve felt around in the in the darkness for Sherrie's hands. She found an elbow, then the wrist. "Oh crap! You're tied with plastic wire wraps. The damn things are nearly impossible to cut," Eve moaned. Then she found Sherries leg and traced it to the ankle.

"Same on your feet. I don't have anything to cut them

with. It's going to be hard getting you out of here, but we have to try, we can't stay here. You understand me? We've got to get out of here."

"Your hands and feet are free?" Sherrie asked.

"Yeah. It took me forever but I sawed through the wire wraps on a bolt over there. Listen, I've been trying to make a hole in the floor so I could get out. I'm nearly through…" She held the improvised pry-bar up and said, "Once I can get the wooden handles through I think I can pry up the board. I was going to drop to the water under this boathouse and…"

Sherrie rolled to her back and moaned.

"Ohhhh….ouch, my head is spinning again. Eve, listen to me. You're going to have to get help."

"I know, but I can't leave you. Maybe we can…"

"You have to Eve. I can barely move, and when I do my head spins. Get help. It's our only chance." Their eyes met. Eve reached out and hugged her sister-in-law. "Alright, I will. Remember I love you," she whispered.

Eve picked up her pry-bar and began working to remove the offending board.

Chapter 52

Cole backed down the staircase dragging the semiconscious Gerry behind him. Gerry's feet bounced off each step and with each new bounce a low moan emitted from his dry throat. Gerry tried to make sense of what was happening and, try as he might, he was failing miserably.

He remembered lunch or was it breakfast? Then a scream, after that, time stopped. It restarted a few moments ago with his feet bouncing on a carpeted staircase. From someplace far away a voice said, "Gerry I didn't think you were this damned heavy."

Whose voice was that? What was hitting his feet? Nothing made sense. Who was talking? He was tired. Maybe he'd just take a nap; he'd figure this all out later. Gerry closed his eyes, his head hurt, he couldn't sleep. What kept hitting his feet?

Cole reached the bottom of the staircase. Gerry was heavy and the effort was making Cole angry. He flung Gerry's arms to the floor. "Owwww….." Gerry moaned.

"I'd shoot you right here you thieving son of a bitch…" Cole didn't finish his sentence, he was looking for something to carry Gerry with. He had to get him out of the house and onto the boat. Cole had seen plenty of cop shows. He knew they used a spray that made blood shine with a black light, and they had other tricks that could even show who it was that was shot, or maybe it was their blood or DNA or something like that. It didn't matter, they were all going for a boat ride. But first Cole had to get Gerry onto the boat.

He thought about that for a moment. Then smiled, "What do you haul trash in Gerry?" Cole asked. "What? Can't come up with an answer? C'mon buddy, it ain't that hard. A wheelbarrow! I'll be right back, don't go anywhere!" Cole headed for the garage laughing as he walked through the empty house. "Don't go anywhere, that's a good one."

Gerry knew he had to escape. Opening one eye he watched Cole cross an empty room and disappear through a door on the opposite side. Then Gerry tried to place his left hand on the floor and push his head and shoulders up. He pushed, then pushed again. He couldn't do it, his head spun, stars swirled across his vision and a buzz filled his ears. Gerry's arm felt like it weighed five hundred pounds, he let it fall to the floor. He was so tired, all he needed was five minutes. He....just....wanted....to....sleep.

Soon Cole returned pushing an empty wheelbarrow and whistling. He loaded Gerry into the wheelbarrow and headed across the grass. In a moment he was on the dock and next to his sailboat. Lifting Gerry to his feet he pushed the semiconscious figure over the rail and to the deck of the boat. Gerry hit the floor like a laundry bag. Cole giggled.

Gerry lay there a moment, groaned, attempted to stand and fell back to the deck. Cole boarded the boat and began pulling Gerry's body into the forward cabin. Gerry gave Cole a weak half-hearted shove, received a punch in the stomach in return and laid back on the cabin floor.

The dot was barely moving. The quarry had stopped running. He wondered how much time Eve had, what would the madman do now? Jim slowly drove past the house, a large log structure straight from a magazine.

Nothing. No guards, no vehicles, no one waving a

sign that said 'help'. He wasn't sure. Was it this big house? He checked the GPS again. It had to be.

Jim parked the Jeep in a stand of blue spruce some fifty yards past the driveway. He was certain this was it.

This place held the dog collar and therefore the man, or men, he reminded himself, that he was after. Exiting the vehicle he pushed the the pistol between his belt and his jeans. He closed his eyes and whispered, "God forgive me for what I'm about to do," then went to the back of the Jeep.

Opening the back door of the Jeep Jim took an additional pistol magazine from the ammunition bag on the seat. He stuffed this into his back jean's pocket. Then he lifted the shotgun from the floor. He shook out several shells from a box of single ought buckshot and loaded four shells into the tubular magazine. Pushing a small lever next to the trigger guard he released the forestock and pumped a round into the chamber. Then Jim pushed a fifth shell into the magazine. Emptying the box on the seat Jim grabbed a handful of additional shells and stuffed them into his pants pocket. He was ready.

Glancing up and down the road Jim assured himself that he was alone, then sprinted across the two-lane road. A second look around, only this time looking for more detail, and Jim was jogging toward the pretentious log mini-mansion. Once there, Jim crouched behind a large downy serviceberry bush and removed the GPS from his pocket. Switching the unit to its highest sensitivity the screen went black then glowed bright green and settled into a display that looked like a radar screen. In a moment the dot appeared, it was just thirty yards to the north.

He studied the house for a moment, then the GPS. The dot was behind the house. There was only water behind this house. That didn't make sense. What would they be doing in the backyard? Then the reality of the situation burst over Jim, someone was getting a boat ready.

If Eve, and his sister and Gerry were put on a boat he'd loose them all before help arrived. But, what if others were in the house? He couldn't move past the house without making sure no one was inside to spring a trap. An old Air Force saying popped into his head, "Check six," he whispered to himself then glanced around and headed for the house. Jim was not going to be ambushed from behind.

A carved set of double front doors stood at the top of five stone steps. The door on the left was open just an inch or two. He pushed it fully open with the shotgun muzzle and carefully scanned the home's front room.

There wasn't a single piece of furniture. It was empty. Then, expecting bad news with each step, Jim sprinted across the room and began clearing the remaining downstairs rooms. They were all empty of people and furniture.

With the shotgun barrel leading the way, his heart pounding and hands sweaty, Jim approached the staircase. He took a deep breath, then began to carefully climb the stairs to the second floor. Three minutes later Jim was sure no one was home.

Now Jim found a window overlooking the back of the property. He removed the GPS from his pocket and got a new fix on the dot. It was still there. Only now Jim could see the building he was certain held a madman, and his wife.

A line of azalea bushes ran along the side of the property to the lake's shoreline, suggesting a borderline with both neighbors. A fieldstone sidewalk, beginning off the deck attached to the back of the house, led across the manicured backyard to the massive boathouse. Extending out from the shore, and immediately next to the boathouse was a long dock. Maybe five feet wide and made of white painted wood, the dock extended nearly the full length of the building. At its end the dock turned ninety degrees left and five feet later ended at the foot of a brown windowless door.

A large sailboat was moored to the dock; its stern flush with the end of the dock; its bowlines strung to cleats placed every twenty feet on the open waterside of the structure. The boathouse itself was made of massive logs, with what appeared to be large floor to ceiling windows on both sides.

Carefully Jim descended the stairs, crossed the empty living room, and stepped out of the wide, double front doors. He jogged to the corner of the garage, peeked around and seeing no one he walked to the waterside of the building. Here he could see the entire backyard and the boathouse.

The windows of the building were a problem, anyone inside the boathouse could see him, but he couldn't see inside the building. He studied the front of the building. A large wooden double door was centered in the glass paneled front. To reach the double doors would require Jim to cross the open backyard, once again, anyone inside the building would see Jim's approach.

Jim carefully worked his way along the line of azaleas until he was kneeling behind the last bush. Here he had an even better view of the building. The front windows were clear, but the side windows were covered with a solid sun screen. He opted for the dock and the door at its end.

Swallowing hard he checked the shotgun, flipped the safety off and hurried to the dock. Carefully he scanned the boathouse and sailboat for any movement. Nothing. Then, gun at the ready, he slowly made his way along the dock.

CHAPTER 53

Eve pushed the wooden handles into the hole she had been chiseling into the floor. The hole wasn't big enough. "Damn!" she whispered. She eyed the hole in the floor, two handles wouldn't fit, but one would. Using her fingernails and her teeth, she began tearing at the duct tape.

Soon the two handles separated. Gripping the mop handle she fit it to the hole and pushed. It almost fit. Standing the handle straight up she gripped it high and lifted her feet, hanging all of her weight on the makeshift pry bar. The edges of the hole wouldn't support the weight and the handle broke through. She nearly shouted with joy, caught herself and whispered "I'm through!" to Sherrie.

Now Eve tried to lever the board up. She pulled as hard as she could, nothing happened. She tried to sit on the mop, putting all of her weight on the prybar. The wood only groaned but didn't pull free.

"Sherrie, I'm going to stand you up. I want you to lay on this mop while I push the broom handle under the edge, got it?"

Sherrie did her best to grin. "Let's do it," she whispered.

Eve pushed hard to wedge another handle into the hole. It didn't work. "Try again," she whispered. Sherrie did her best to balance on the mop. Her head spun and nausea threatened to overwhelm her. Eve gave up on the broom and sat on the mop handle. Just as she reached out to steady her sister-in-law a loud "POP" filled the closet and the board broke out of the floor.

Sherrie grinned as Eve hugged her. "We did it kid! We did it."

"Yeah, we did!" Sherrie whispered as she slowly lowered herself to the floor. Painfully Eve pushed her hips through the hole in the floor. She looked at Sherrie and whispered, "I'll be back as soon as I can." Then, feet dangling in the lake she wiggled her shoulders through the hole and slid into the water.

The water was cold. Eve surfaced and gave an involuntary shiver. She wiped the wet hair from her eyes and looked around. She was floating two feet below the floor of the boathouse. A forest of round concrete pillars supported the structure. To her right was the west exterior wall of the building. Moving to the edge of the building she peeked around a piling and studied the shoreline.

Nothing, no houses, just brush and rocks.

Eve decided to check the opposite side of the boathouse. Moving back under the building she soon saw a patch of sunlight and a path of open water. She could see the hulls of three boats floating peacefully next to each other. Past the boats lay a small patch of water, like a driveway, then three more boats on the opposite side. Turning to her side she did her best side stoke. Slowly, carefully, as quietly as she could Eve crept to the stern of the nearest boat. Peering around the edge she studied the far end and both sides of the boathouse. She didn't see the madman, but this was no time to take chances.

Taking a deep breath she pinched her nose and kicked her way to the bottom. Once there she hurried across the open area to the far side of the boathouse. Rolling on her back she peered upward. She nearly surfaced, then realized she hadn't reached the deck on the far. Two more strong kicks and she was certain she was below it. Afraid of being seen from someone on the shore, or someone looking under the boathouse she swam to the lake side of a piling and edged her way to the surface. She wanted to let the air in her lungs explode outward, she wanted to suck in a fresh lung full of clean air and stop the terrible pounding in her ears. But the idea of that noise terrified her. She gently emptied her lungs, and gripped the piling. Hanging there she panted as if she'd run a marathon.

Expecting a clear view of the shoreline Eve was disappointed to see only a white sailboat hull blocking her view.

"Okay, now what?" she muttered. She needed to move to the other side of the boat. Carefully Eve released the piling and breast stroked to the very edge of the building. She could see an open space, then the dock just a few feet in front of her. Eve had to cross four feet of open water and get under the dock. After that, she would go under the sailboat. From there, well, she'd figure it out then. Suddenly the shadow of a man on the dock swept past her. Panicked Eve dove for the bottom.

CHAPTER 54

The sailboat sat motionless in the water. Jim stood even with the Danforth anchor suspended over the small bowsprit. He could see shadows through the darkened porthole windows but no detail. Glancing at the door, occasionally checking the shoreline behind, Jim studied the boat. Nothing moved.

As silently as he could Jim approached the door to the building. A voice exploded in the silence. "Bye-bye dumb ass."

The voice came from behind. Jim attempted to spin to his left, but it was already too late. Cole Prestcott had spotted Jim through the dark green tinted windows of the boat. He'd been hiding in the galley way of the sailboat as Jim approached. Now he stood on the boat deck with a wooden boat hook raised above his head. Jim attempted to raise the shotgun to ward off the blow, but the weight of the implement and the power with which the madman swung it was too much. The boat hook knocked the gun to the side and drove into Jim's shoulder. His collarbone exploded in pain. Jim stumbled back, dropped the shotgun in the water, lost his footing and fell between the boathouse and dock into the lake.

Cole jumped off the boat and ran to the edge of the dock. He expected to see Jim attempting to swim away or if he was lucky a body floating in the dark water. All he saw was a swirl of silt stirred up from the bottom. Frantic to find his target Cole slammed the boat hook into the cloud of silt. Each time he succeeded only in hitting the bottom stirring up more silt. Cole got to his knees and carefully looked under the dock. No body floated there.

Mystified Cole ran across the sailboat and checked the opposite side, nothing. Unable to believe his prey was laying at the bottom of the lake Cole began jabbing the boathook into the silty bottom as he worked his way to the shore. Between stabs he carefully checked under the dock and to the sides for any sign of Jim. After five minutes Cole was convinced that Jim wasn't coming back to the surface, at least breathing.

Jim had splashed into the water just two feet in front of her. Thinking fast Eve dove to the bottom and grabbed her husband. His body was limp for only a second and then he tried to fight away from her. Holding tightly to his shirt she pushed her face into his. Jim's eyes met hers and a smile spread across his face. Then Eve pulled him back between the pilings and under the building wall. They surfaced between the boats.

Hugging Jim tightly, Eve kissed him. "Jim, I was afraid I wouldn't see you again." Her words spilled out in an incoherent stream. "He was going to kill me. He was going to kill me Jim! And Sherrie's hurt. And Gerry is...I don't know where he is. I couldn't...Jim..." Eve choked back tears, took a breath, then said. "Jim, I'm scared. That madman is right outside."

"Shhhhhhiiiiiisssssshhhh....I know, I know. Okay, okay..." Jim fought to stay calm. "Be quiet hun, he's right out there. We're okay babe, we're okay," Jim whispered.

He rolled his shoulder and massaged it with his left hand.

"Okay? What do you mean 'okay'? We're not okay,"

Eve countered. "Sherrie is tied up in a closet over there." Eve pointed between the boats. "She's got plastic cable ties on her hands and feet, we need a knife or something like that. I don't know where Gerry is. Sherrie just said he was hurt bad."

"Is she alright?" Jim asked.

"She's hurt, that madman hit her on the head, she's woozy, can't stand."

Jim thought about that. "I don't think we've got time to get help. We've got to do this on our own," Jim paused. "Stay here a second." He slipped to the next piling and peeked at the dock. A moment later he was back.

"He's working his way to the house, looking for me," Jim said. "Go see if you can get Sherrie untied. I've got to come up with something for this guy."

"But..."

Jim reached for his pistol, "Oh no!'

"What? What 'oh no'? What do you mean 'oh no'?" Eve demanded.

"My gun, it fell out of my belt when I hit the water."

"Well, let's go find it!" Eve shot back.

"The bottom is all muck. We don't have time. No, that's not going to work."

"You've got to have a gun." The confidence Eve had felt a moment ago began to slip away.

"I know babe, but we don't have one. Look, swim over there, get Sherrie free and go get help. I'll stop this idiot or at least slow him down. You two get outa here as fast as you can and call the cops. Sound like a plan?"

"NO! That's a stupid plan. How are you going to slow him down? He's big and he's got a gun!"

"Okay, I'll swim over there and you slow him down."

"Jim!"

"Look he'll be coming through that door any second. It's our only choice, go get Sherrie and get out of here. I've got some ideas, don't worry." Jim was already pulling himself out of the water.

She didn't move. "What ideas?"

"They're not fully formed, but I've got 'em", he said as he stood on the deck. Eve surrendered to the inevitable and quickly swam back to the storage room. She struggled for a moment to clear the lake water and was soon back inside the closet.

Chapter 55

Cole came to the end of the dock, turned around and yelled at the water. "Hey Jim! I'm coming, I'm coming and you're not going to see that little wife of yours again. I'm coming Jim."

A plastic water bottle drifted out from under the building. Cole pulled his pistol, aimed and fired. The bullet missed the mark by several yards. Seeing how bad his aim was Cole began to laugh.

Catching his breath he shouted, "Can't even shoot a pistol...I know what you're thinking. I'm a screw up right? But I can hit yooouuuu Jimmy boy, don't worry, I can get yooouuuu."

Cole then walked to the front doors of the boathouse. Grabbing both door handles he pulled the two doors open in one motion, framing himself in the door.

"Jimmmmyyy, I'm here," he shouted. "Should I go left or right? What do you think Jimmy boy?"

Cole studied the boathouse. He turned left and walked to the end of the deck. Looking the length of the building he could see the door of the storage closet. It was closed. "Think I'll try the other side," Cole said.

Raising his voice he called, "I'm coming Jimmy." Then Cole reversed direction and walked to the right side of the building. Four docks extended from the walkway into the water. Of the four berths, three were occupied. Looking the length of the deck Cole saw a canoe paddle had been placed in front of each of the three boats resting in their slips. Next to the wall several fishing poles were spaced out along the entire length of the deck. Cole placed his left hand under his right, gripping the pistol with both hands. He didn't know why, but it was what they did on TV and he thought it looked good.

In the slip nearest the front of the building was Cole's twenty-two foot fishing boat with dual Mercury outboard engines and a small enclosed cabin. Cole came to the bow of the boat, pointed his gun and fired through the deck into the cabin. He gave a short chuckle, "Did I get ya Jimmy?" he called.

Not hearing anything Cole walked to the next boat. Here was his beloved Chris-Craft. Stopping just short of the bow of the boat Cole smiled. Someone had tied fishing line to the standpipe next to the wall. The line led across the deck to the water. If he hadn't seen the line he would have tripped.

'That's the best you've got?" Cole yelled. "A piece of fishing line to trip me? A...a...whatda ya call these? A trip wire! You set a goofy, friggin', trip wire? This ain't TV Jimmy!"

Stepping over the trip line Cole eyed the Chris-Craft. He thought about firing through the deck into the cabin, but the idea of marring the beautiful mahogany finish simply was too much for him. Cole slowly walked along the dock to the side of the boat. He kept the pistol centered on the cabin hatch.

A short gangplank went from the dock to the boat. Rubber bumpers kept the boat from rubbing against the dock and ruining the wooden finish. Cole took one step onto the gangplank, bent over and studied the interior of the Chris-Craft. The cabin door was open.

Suddenly a splash from below. Cole spun around just in time to see Jim standing in the waist deep water between the Chris-Craft and the dock. He was holding a canoe paddle like a baseball bat. Jim swung the paddle, crashing its edge into Cole's knee, buckling his leg and collapsing him into the Chris-Craft. Cole screamed in agony as his anterior cruciate ligament ripped with the sideway force of the blow.

"Sonofabitch," he moaned. Coming to his knees Cole extended his arm over the side of the Chris-Craft and fired blindly into the water.

Silence.

Carefully Cole crawled to the back of the boat. Slowly he raised his head above the boat's side. Jim was no where to be seen. Painfully Cole got to his feet. He studied the water around the boat then yelled, "That was a good one Jimmy!" He studied the water, shifted his gaze to each boat in turn, then yelled, "Wow, that hurts!" as he rubbed his shattered knee.

"But Jimmy, watch this!" Cole leveled the pistol and fired three shots at the closet where Eve and Sherrie lay. He gave a loud laugh, leaned one hand on the boat gunnel and carefully worked his way to the gangplank.

"Think I'm outa bullets Jimmy? I ain't! NO, no, no...I got more Jimmy!" Cole slumped against the wall. Reaching into his pants pocket he withdrew a handful of bullets. With a flick of his thumb the pistol's cylinder fell open. Cole dumped the empty shells onto the deck. "See Jimmy...see." He reloaded by feel, never looking at the pistol, his eyes searching for Jim.

CHAPTER 56

Wood exploded over Eve and Sherrie's heads. Splinters ripped through the small closet. Eve screamed and threw herself on the floor, landing on Sherries legs. Another loud bang and wood again exploded through the room. Sherrie screamed. A thud, not an explosion, a sort of "smack" as if from a rubber mallet as the final bullet hit a pair 2 x 4's in the wall's corner structure. Then silence.

They lay on the floor and listened. Finally Eve asked, "You alright?"

"I think so," Sherrie replied. A moment later she whispered, "Eve, my hand is sticky and wet."

Quickly Eve began running her hands over Sherrie. "It's your shoulder, you've got a piece of wood stuck in it. I don't think it's too bad."

Sherrie hugged her, "I'm scared," she whispered.

"I am too honey. We'll be all right. Gerry will be all right. We'll get through this," Eve said.

Sherrie shook herself, grabbing control back from the edge of panic she pointed at a ray of light coming from one of the bullet holes. "What's he doing now?" she asked.

Eve peered out of the hole.

"See anything?"

"He's standing in the wooden boat. I think he's hurt. I don't see Jim. Wait...yes...Jim's in the water. He's hiding behind the last boat."

"Is he hurt?"

"No, I don't think so. But he needs help. I'm going over there."

"What? You can't. Eve you don't have a gun."
Sherrie's throat tightened as she spoke.

"I can't just sit here. I'm going." Eve began to slide
her feet through the hole in the floor. Sherrie began to argue,
realized it was useless then hugged her. "Be careful,' she
whispered.

Eve nodded, unable to speak. The danger outside
seemed very real. Then Eve slipped back into the water.

Jim moved along the side of Cole's ski boat. The
water was deeper here. The cold was sinking in and his arm
was stiffening from the blow he'd received on his shoulder.
Carefully he sank below the surface and swam under the boat.
He surfaced under the deck in front of the boat.

Seconds later he heard Cole's boots moving above
him, there was a definite limp. Jim waited until the limp was
past, then moved to the side of the deck. Hooking his fingers
over the dock's edge Jim kicked and pulled as hard he could.
He launched clear of the water, his torso extending two feet
above the deck. In the instant he was clear of the dock Jim
bent forward, reached out and grabbed the pant leg of Cole's
uninjured leg. A flash later Jim's torso crashed back to the
deck squarely on his stomach. His diaphragm was thrust
upward and his lungs emptied in a painful rush. But, he
wasn't to be denied. With all his strength, Jim pulled the pant
leg toward him's chest.

Cole tried to spin and bring the pistol to bear on Jim's
body, but the physics of the thing couldn't be denied. Cole's
bad leg couldn't support his weight alone, the force and the
pain were too much. Cole's body spun and came crashing
down on the deck. His gun hand bounced off the rail of the
Chris-Craft, knocking the gun in the air. The pistol landed on

the dock and slid out of reach.

With a yell and a scrabbling kick, Jim wiggled the rest of his body onto the deck and was crawling after the pistol. He caught up to the weapon just as it came to rest on the edge of the wooden deck. His hand found the pistol grip and he began to get to his knees just as a mighty blow landed across his shoulders.

The pistol flew out of his hands, hit the side of the runabout and splashed into the water. Jim collapsed on his stomach, thought fast and rolled to his right. A canoe paddle crashed into the deck where his head had laid just a microsecond ago. He kicked his right leg out at the surprisingly quick Cole Prescott catching him in only a glancing blow.

Eve surfaced next to the Chris-Craft and spotted Cole limping away from her. Quietly she climbed out of the water. Suddenly she saw her husband vault out of the water behind the monster and bring the man down. Jim quickly got to his hands and knees and crawled after the pistol now skidding to the edge of the deck. Her heart sank as she watched Cole grab a canoe paddle and smash it down on Jim's back. Jim grunted in pain and rolled at the same time. Cole smashed the paddle down on the dock in what surely would have been a killing blow. Panicked, Eve searched for a weapon. Jim grabbed at the canoe paddle, his hands slipping off the slick surface as Cole pulled the paddle back.

Several fishing poles lay against the wall. One had a big red and white spoon with a large treble hook at the end. The lure was held to the reel by one of the three hooks. Picking the rod up she loosed the hook, wrapped her finger around the line and opened the bail on the reel.

Then, Eve reared back and cast the lure at Cole's

shoulders. She missed high and left, the spoon sailed past Cole's left ear.

Cole heard more than saw the red and white fishing lure flash past his ear. The line stretched tight as Eve closed the bail and the spoon's forward momentum stopped. For the briefest moment the lure hung motionless. As one part of his brain prepared to smash the oar down on Jim another wondered at a fishing lure materializing from nothingness just three feet in-front of his face.

The lure snapped back, hit his chest and lay there. It was only an instant. Eve gave a loud yell, turned around, and with the fishing pole gripped firmly in both hands, began to run. The lure was yanked upward, driving the hooks into his flesh with a searing pain, the line tight over his shoulder. Cole screamed as the hooks tore up and into his chest, the force pulling him upward off his feet and backward. He landed flat on his back, the hooks still digging, the force unrelenting, his body being pulled away from Jim as Eve continued trying to run. His skin ripped but didn't release the hooks. The pain seared into his brain.

His scream was truly blood curdling, combining intense pain with the ultimate surprise. Frantically Cole's fingers dug at the lure, but it was no use. The barbs and the tension on the line kept him from pulling the hooks out. His chest erupted in pain, blood quickly soaked his shirt. In a Herculean effort, he struggled to his feet. Cole wrapped one hand around the line and began pulling, trying to release the tension on the hooks ripping at his chest muscles. With his other hand, he groped for the pistol.

Suddenly the edge of a canoe paddle crashed into his good leg. More pain exploded in his overwhelmed brain. Cole screamed and collapsed on the deck, his hands not knowing whether they should grip his injured knees or the searing pain in his chest.

Eve's primordial screaming added to the terror. Again, the hooks ripped upward. Then, somewhere at the edge of his consciousness he heard, "Eve, Eve! Stop...stop, it's done. We got him." Jim was yelling over the screams of the madman.

Eve stopped and turned to see Jim standing over Cole, the canoe paddle gripped like a baseball bat.

"You got him?" she called.

"I got him hon. Good job, that was a hellofa cast." Jim grinned at her.

"I can let go of this fishing pole?" Eve asked as she angrily snapped the pole back with one more good pull.

Cole let out another scream.

"Yes! You can drop the pole," Jim grinned.

Eve threw the pole in the water, leaving a bit of tension on the line and eliciting another scream. She stood next to Jim and looked down at the bloody shirt and screaming man at her feet. Without warning she bent over and slapped Cole across the face. "That's for Sherrie and Gerry."

Chapter 57

Jim carried a large vase and a plastic water jug. Next to him, Eve held an equally large bundle of flowers. Gerry had been flown by helicopter to the University of Michigan Hospital after being stabilized in Traverse City.

They stepped out of the elevator and headed for the nurses station. Moments later a nurse was escorting them into intensive care and they were standing at the foot of Gerry's bed. Gerry snored peacefully while monitors and gauges silently reported his health for all to see. Next to Gerry's bed a second hospital bed had been rolled into the room and Sherrie lay sleeping.

Eve leaned toward Jim. "They're both asleep. We'd better just put these in water and go."

"We can wake Sherrie up," Jim whispered.

"No, we can't. Now come on, let's go," Eve murmured.

"She'd do it to me," Jim complained.

"Jim!"

"I'm just sayin'."

"I can hear you two you know," Sherrie said in a loud whisper. Then she grinned and opened her eyes. "You're right dear brother, I would!"

Eve rushed to her and wrapped her arms around Sherrie's neck. Jim picked her hand up and gave it a squeeze. "How ya doin' sis?" he asked.

Sherrie gave a full report covering everything the doctors had told her that morning. "I'm going to be fine. I'll have a little scar where the wood stuck me. And the doctors said I suffered a concussion, but given time I'll be alright. I don't have many symptoms, just some dizziness and headaches. The usual things associated with a concussion. In a couple of days they said they'll release me. They said the headaches will go away after a few weeks."

Eve grew somber. "Tell us about Gerry." Sherrie's eyes misted over and Jim squeezed his sister's hand. "They said he's suffered severe traumatic brain injury. They did an MRI on him every three hours last night. The doctor said they're worried about blood clots. He's on blood thinners now and they think he's out of the woods, but they want to keep monitoring him." Sherrie began to cry. Jim hugged her and Eve put her hand on her shoulder.

"They said he's going to have a long recovery. Maybe a year or more," Sherrie whispered. "He's going to have a lot of mood swings and some memory and speech issues. I'm not really sure what that means, but..."

Eve interrupted. "We saw it in the military Sherrie. It means he'll struggle to put thoughts to words, forget what he was going to say, where he parked the car, that sort of thing. Sometimes more important things, his name, address, your name. But he's still there, never, ever, forget that he's still there."

Jim put his hand on Sherrie's shoulder. "He may get angry over meaningless things. Our friend, Ryan, found himself pounding his mailbox with a big rock because he didn't get a magazine. Over time it should get better. Your love will be a big help, he'll need every bit of it you have." Sherrie wrapped her arms around her brother and sobbed.

Chapter 58

The last of the morning clouds had burned away and spectators slowly took their seats. Several young boys ran through the crowd supplying towels to those who asked, and many did. Half of the folding lawn chairs were in shadow and still had a coating of dew. Elaine took a towel from a young boy, handed him a blue, angle fish dollar in return, and began to wipe her seat. Esso Cricket Club had led 124 for three when play had ended the previous evening. Now, the boys from the Paramount Cricket Club were preparing for their inning.

She didn't really care for cricket, didn't understand the rules nor the scoring, but the man she'd spent the last few days with was nuts for the silly game. She checked her watch. At ten she would make her excuses and leave.

Several men stood near the three sticks. Another man bounced a ball as fast as he could at the goalie while another swung his bat like a golf club. After what felt like days Elaine had decided this game didn't make sense and had given up trying to understand.

A large jet airliner swooped overhead. The plane was landing at the only airport on the island located just a few hundred yards away. The noise was deafening, Elaine held her hands to her ears and cringed. No one else seemed to notice. When her hearing returned she checked her watch and decided the time was close enough. She leaned over to John, or Brian, or whatever his name was, and kissed him on the cheek. "I'll be right back," she whispered.

"Bring me a Caybrew, would ya luv," John or Brian

said with barely a glance. Elaine smiled, grabbed her purse and walked to the clubhouse.

Minutes later Elaine stepped from her taxi and entered the Cayman National Bank. A young woman greeted her with a friendly "Hullo" and Elaine stepped to her window. Elaine explained her intent to withdraw a significant amount of money and presented her account card. The girl noted the amount and went to find her supervisor. This would only take a few moments, would Elaine please take a seat. Elaine did as suggested. Several minutes passed.

Soon a darkly tanned woman in her late fifties approached, introduced herself as Ms. Jane Wilcox and asked Elaine if they could speak in private. Elaine followed Ms. Wilcox to an inner office and was invited to take a seat. Elaine did as she was told, an uneasy feeling beginning to creep up her back.

Wilcox stood behind her desk. After a moments hesitation she said "Ms. Prestcott, I'm sure there must be some confusion. We cannot honor your withdrawal request."

Elaine paled. "I'm sorry? Why not?"

"Well, Ms. Prestcott, your current balance is substantially less than two hundred thousand. I'm sure you've made a simple mistake in...."

"WHAT? NO! I've not made a mistake. I'm making a withdrawal of two hundred thousand dollars. There's exactly five million five hundred thousand five hundred and fifty five dollars in that account!"

"Ms. Prestcott, there is no mistake. Your account balance was..."

Elaine's voice was loud, bordering on hysteria, "I know what my balance is!"

"Again, I'm sorry, but if you'll indulge me a moment."

Ms. Wilcox sorted through several sheets of paper. "See here, your account co-holder, a Mr. David McFain, withdrew all but five hundred fifty five dollars and fifty five cents; an odd amount I'm sure, on Friday last."

Elaine took the proffered paper. She examined the document carefully. She remembered signing it. She had to sign it, it allowed David to deposit money in her account. She studied the paper carefully. Indeed, allowed him to make deposits.

She flipped the page and began to read. Her hands began to shake. She didn't remember this page. It was a two page document, not three. She continued to read. He could make deposits AND withdrawals? He could make as many withdrawals as he wanted. David McFain wasn't an advisor, he was a co-holder of the account.

Gradually, the realization that McFain had taken it all, everything she had worked so hard for. All the afternoons in some cheap hotel with Alan Wisecup had gotten her nothing. All the years and all the nights giving herself to that greedy, self-serving Cole Prestcott.

Everything she had taken from Cole had been taken from her. She'd been swindled. It was all gone. The enormity of the disaster began to overwhelm her. Where would she live? How would she eat? Failing to see the irony, Elaine began to cry.

Chapter 59

Sherrie held Gerry's arm as they stepped off the dock onto the deck of the cruiser. "I still have a balance problem, but the doctors say that will probably come 'round." Gerry said with a smile.

Eve hugged him. "You've come a long way. We're very proud of how hard you've worked."

"And we've got something for you," Jim said while reaching into a canvas bag. Out came a mahogany picture frame. "What's this?" Gerry asked smiling.

Jim smiled, "Well, it seems there was a tin full of baseball cards in the newspaper bag. I found the tin on my bench last month. This is the best of the group. You're not going to believe it, but this, my friend, is a 1914 Cracker Jacks Detroit Tiger's Ty Cobb baseball card."

Sherrie looked at Eve. "A baseball card? So what?"

Eve grinned, "Its Ty Cobb, he's very famous."

"Well, it's awful old. Is that good?" Sherrie asked.

Eve nodded her head and smiled, Sherrie had no idea. "Yeah, that's good. Very, very good."

Gerry looked at Jim. "Oh buddy, I hope there were more like this."

"Let's just say we don't have a problem paying for the gas," Jim grinned.

The large cruiser's engine rumbled to life then settled into a steady throb. Lines were cast off, bumpers pulled in and stored and seats were found. The boat gently idled out of the marina, turned to the north and the throttle was slowly pushed forward. In perfect synchronization with the throttle the throb turned to a roar and seconds later a rooster tail of white spray followed the boat's every move. She was rocketing across the Grand Traverse West Bay now and heads were turning on every vessel she passed.

Jim turned to Gerry and grinned. "Sounds good doesn't it?"

"Are you kidding me? That sounds great!' Gerry yelled over the roar.

In the back of the thirty-four foot Chris-Craft Express Commuter, Sherrie and Eve's hair flowed backward, whipped by the wind. Their eyes were bright, happy and tearing with the wind. The restoration of the boat had taken longer than expected, but not the three years Eve had silently guessed. Gerry laughed and tilted a bottle of beer in the universal sign of a toast. Jim accepted and tilted his beer back in acknowledgment.

The boat raced past the Leelanau Peninsula light house and turned its nose in the direction of Beaver Island. At this speed the run to the island would be over almost before it started. Jim was smiling so hard his cheeks hurt. This was going to be a great summer on the lake.

"Hey, do you guys want to make a run around the island first, before we dock?" Claudia Wells sat at the wheel, her wheelchair folded in the cabin below. Claudia's hair billowed behind her as well. Her smile was as bright as the sun.

"You're the skipper!" Gerry called back.

Jim turned to Eve, "Never leave anyone behind," he said. She smiled back and nodded. Yes, this was going to be a fine summer.

END

About the Author

HJ Gaudreau is a retired Air Force Colonel. Originally
from Michigan, he currently lives with his wife Eve and
beagle, Molly, in Oklahoma. They have one son, living
very near to his Uncle Gerry and Aunt Sherrie.
The house is for sale and they hope to soon move home to
northern Michigan.

SAMPLE THE CRENSHAW'S FIRST GREAT ADVENTURE

BETRAYAL IN THE LOUVRE

Amazon Readers React:

The book starts off fast and doesn't let up. I highly recommend this book and look forward to the sequel...

If you like mystery combined with the good guys coming out winners, this is for you. The characters are likable and you find yourself rooting for them to succeed in their quest to find the lost treasures.

Enjoy a longer excerpt or purchase this and other books by HJ Gaudreau at
www.hjgaudreau.com

A simple trip to an antique show leads to a fight for their life

Jim and Eve Crenshaw have found peace on a small farm. It's a peaceful life. But when they find an ivory tube containing one of the four pieces of French Royal Regalia they are propelled into a world of international conspiracy, priceless antiquities, and ruthless killers.

Marie Antoinette's heart breaks as her oldest son is ripped from her arms.

A WWI doughboy is caught in the horror of war.

Chased by Europe's most dangerous killers, only Jim's cunning and Eve's bravery can save them. Fast paced, non-stop suspense pushes this story through the French Revolution, World War One, Montreal, Paris and the French countryside.

BETRAYAL IN
THE
LOUVRE

*Enjoy a longer excerpt or purchase this
and
other books by HJ Gaudreau at*
www.hjgaudreau.com

Prologue

The notice that would forever change their lives was not found in a local, big city newspaper; rather it was in a weekly crier called the "Michigan Voice". That Eve saw it at all was a bit of a surprise. They rarely, if ever picked up the Voice. But for some reason fate intervened, and Jim had grabbed the paper as he left the town's only hardware store. Now, sitting on the back porch, drinking her coffee, waiting for Jim to finish in the barn, Eve thumbed through the only reading material available. And there it was, third page, lower left: "Antique Show and Charity Auction Returns to Detroit." Jim, more than Eve, enjoyed the show. Rarely could they afford the items for sale; this was not a "clean out the garage" kind of antique show. This show was hosted by some of the country's finest auction houses. They didn't attend as buyers. Jim was a collector of arcane bits of trivia and simply found the auction to be a treasure trove of "interesting stuff".

Suddenly, the baying of a beagle could be heard behind the equipment shed, a gray ghost raced around the building and headed for the pasture. Molly had picked up the scent and was close behind the rabbit.

Jim stepped from the barn, slid the door shut and walked to the house. "Your antique auction is next week," she said as he climbed the porch steps. Jim washed his hands at the outdoor sink then sat in a deep wicker chair next to his wife.

"Great! That thing is always so interesting. And this year I've got something I want to take."

Eve started to laugh, "You really are a nerd. You know that don't you?"

Jim just grinned.

"What do you want to sell?"

"Well, I'm not really sure. Remember that stuff my great grandfather brought back from World War One? I'm hoping someone at the show will recognize it and be able to tell me a little bit more."

"Like if we've been hauling junk around the world for the

past thirty years or not?" Eve asked in a gentle dig.

"Well, yeah," he grinned. "In any case, I thought this was a good chance to have it appraised. At least someone might be able to tell me what it is. And if not, maybe the Tigers are playing."

"I knew there was more to this than an antique auction! C'mon, call your dog and let's go in. I'm hungry."

Chapter 1

Paris

3 June 1789

General Nicolas Luckner was out of bed before the man, for a man it surely was, on the other side of the door pounded a second time. In a moment he had a brace of .60 caliber holster pistols in his hands and was standing, naked, back to the wall, next to the door. The woman in the bed felt a wave of fear wash over her. The wave crested, then, human nature what it is, she admired the view.

From outside the door a young man's voice called, "Mon General, it is urgent."

Luckner recognized the voice of his new adjutant and relaxed. The man, boy really, had been with him for only the past two weeks. This was the first time he'd been to the General's room after their morning drill. Luckner opened the door and let the man-boy in. The adjutant instinctively began a salute, saw the General was naked and attempted to look away. He turned his right shoulder to the General and found himself facing a young, naked, red-haired woman sitting cross-legged on the bed. His surprise evident he involuntarily took a step backward, whereupon he collided with the General. Shaken he spun around to meet the now angry glare of the man he feared more than anything in this life and, he was convinced, the next as well.

He stammered once, cleared his throat and before the General had finished inhaling in preparation for what surely would be one of history's great tongue-lashings he managed to stammer out the news he had been sent to deliver. "Sir, ah...Col DeAubry asked that...you have...you are supposed to ..." The Adjutant's young eyes couldn't overcome the powerful draw of the woman's naked body. Like a bee to honey his eyes, without command, turned to her. The woman caught the glance, and vixen that she was, instantly decided to toy with the man-boy. She went into an

3

exaggerated yawn, stretching her arms over her head, thrusting her bare breasts at the Adjutant. Then, like a cherry on top of a banana split, she smiled. The Adjutant's slim hold on his composure cracked.

The breach only lasted a moment as a thick hand slapped him on his left ear. The General stared down a long pointed nose, suppressed a smile and waited. The young officer regained his composure, stiffened, looked directly at the General and said, "Sir, Col DeAubry has asked that I relay a message."

"Well?" General Luckner's expression was stern, as befit a General. He was enjoying this little game. The man-boy tried again, "The King has summoned you." Luckner's brain instantly went to full attention.

"For what purpose? When and where? These things should have been said already." Luckner did not suffer fools gladly, the game was over, the humor gone. The young man was now angering the General. Had he never seen a naked woman before?

"Le château de Versailles. Immediately."

"Tell the Colonel 'thank you' and I shall be with him in five minutes," Luckner said. The Adjutant, from sheer habit, saluted; stole another glance at the naked woman and fled the room. The General closed the door behind him. "No, he probably hasn't," he thought. Then his mind snapped back to the summons.

It was time, he was sure of it. This was necessary. There had been enough of patience, negotiations, maneuvering, politics and talk, talk, talk. Now, he was going to be told to round up the rabble and stuff them into the Bastille like so much sausage. Or, better yet, he'd put them to the sword tonight. He began to assemble his uniform. In a few short minutes he was dressed; except for the boots. He could not find his boot hooks. His frustration grew as he looked under the bed, under the rug, behind the door…then he remembered. Reaching into the pile of woman's clothing on the floor he found them. The woman smiled at him. In a moment his boots had been pulled on and he was out the door.

Outside the tavern Col DeAubry sat comfortably astride his horse, his attention focused on the hard piece of bread and moldy cheese which constituted his breakfast. A tall, rather lanky man, DeAubry had been born to a shoe cobbler. He had run from his apprenticeship at the first chance. At the age of twelve he'd taken a job as an assistant to a farrier and developed considerable expertise with horses. Five years later the man who had become more a father than employer was killed when a horse with an abscessed foot kicked him in the head. DeAubry found himself without means, a great deal of expertise in horses and a perfect fit for the cavalry.

The Colonel was known as a calm, sensible officer who could make things happen. He'd been with the General his entire career. Except, of course, for the three years he'd spent, at Luckner's insistence, with Rochambeau. He had survived a fever in the West Indies and distinguished himself on more than one occasion while fighting the British in their war with the American colonialists. His study and knowledge of siege warfare had been particularly useful in the later part of that campaign.

Under Luckner's sponsorship he'd risen to an almost unheard of rank for a man so low born. He was a trusted second to the General and the men feared and respected DeAubry as much as they feared and respected the General.

A few moments after DeAubry received the message a smartly dressed, fully alert General Nicolas Luckner exploded from the tavern's front door and mounted the horse held by the Adjutant. DeAubry relayed what little information he had, took up his position on the General's left and they began the short ride to the château de Versailles. It was mid-afternoon, a light rain fell from a gray sky. The rain was welcome in Luckner's mind. It kept the rabble in their houses and it washed the sewage and animal droppings from the streets.

As they approached Le Potager du Roi the General noticed several handbills tacked to the trees outside of the royal garden's tall fence. Before he could pull one from its posting he spotted several men running across the road into the buildings and fields to his right. Instinctively his hand went to his pistol and he surveyed the doors, windows, alleys and bushes along his route. He wished he'd taken an escort; two men and a man-child would not do. He was not afraid of these traitorous fools, but he did not wish to be delayed. He would speak to DeAubry later about this.

Not knowing what the handbills were all about but feeling they may play a part in the upcoming meeting with the King he stopped, dismounted and ripped one from the trunk of a large oak tree. The Colonel did the same. DeAubry was shocked by what he read, the author accused the Queen of being a lesbian and whore. "More attacks on the Queen's reputation." DeAubry muttered as he shook his head. Luckner read the paper in his hand. It railed against the King's treasurer Monsieur de Barentin, incompetent government and the King's intelligence. He snarled, crumpled the paper and tossed it to the ground. Other bills peppered the trees and buildings for the next several hundred yards. They walked their horses for a few moments, silently reading the posters.

DeAubry examined the fields and buildings. A boy appeared from behind a cottage. He yelled something and threw a rotten apple in their direction. The apple landed well short. What were these people about? There had been a time, not so long ago when the French military had faced down the British across the globe. People had looked at him with pride. Now? Well, now things were different weren't they? DeAubry couldn't put his finger on it, something was happening. He was looked at with contempt, sometimes hate. He didn't understand it, he didn't know what it was, but he knew change was coming. And, from all he had seen, it wasn't change for the better.

Luckner was mounting his horse. The rain was thicker now; the sky seemed a darker shade of gray. Settling into the saddle the General pulled his collar up against the wind and the rain. He pulled his sword, indicated to the Adjutant to do the same, then leaning toward the still dismounted DeAubry he said, "Have as many men as possible, with good horses, at the palace in an hour. I suspect we're going to be busy tonight." Luckner then turned his horse in the direction of the château, kicked the animal with his heels and cantered away. DeAubry would do his best, but horses were becoming scarce.

Chapter 2

"The Detroit Antiques Show is the biggest in the mid-west and I'm not going to miss it. Who knows, we could have something worth bizzillions of dollars." Herman James Crenshaw, retired Air Force Colonel, now proud co-owner with his wife of a sixty acre farm called from the attic of his cottage styled log home. "Hey, do you know where that box of my great grandfather's stuff is?" The sound of boxes being moved and old furniture banging could clearly be heard above Eve Crenshaw's head. "Damn..." More thumping of boxes. "Eve could you bring up a flashlight please? I forgot to turn on the light."

She stood at the bottom of the attic ladder, face turned up to the dark void overhead and smiled. "Yes Jim, I'll get you a flashlight." Eve walked into the kitchen and retrieved one from the pantry. "Hon, here's the flashlight." She climbed the ladder, flicking on the light switch next to the attic door and pulling a cobweb from her shoulder length honey auburn hair. Light filled the room, making the flashlight superfluous. "Did you find it?" she asked, doing her best to suppress a grin and failing.

"No, but I did find that lamp you bought in North Dakota." They both laughed. It was the worst lamp they'd ever seen. They bought the lamp to use as a gift in their squadron's dirty Santa Christmas gift exchange; the object of which was to find the ugliest, funniest gift possible. Unfortunately, Jim had received orders before the party and they'd spent that Christmas moving into another house at another Air Force base. Now, here they were nearly thirty years later, retired from the Air Force and they still had it. She laughed at the absurdity of the thing. Jim smiled at his wife, he loved how her golden eyes sparkled when she laughed.

"Hey, here it is!" Jim triumphantly held up a wooden Boraxo soapbox. He sat the box on the floor, knelt beside it and opened the top. Inside was a mess kit, with his Great grandfather's name crudely etched onto the back of the pan. Jim held up the mess kit, showed it to Eve, still standing on the ladder, and then placed it on the attic floor. Next he held up a cigarette lighter with "Ardennes 1918 – Crenshaw" carved into the side. "Can you

7

believe these things were used in the mud and trenches of World War One? It's amazing." Jim was an unabashed history nut. In rapid succession the lighter was followed by a knife, a badly aged book with a faded cover, a handful of uniform decorations, none of which Jim recognized, a patch with a red arrow pierced by a small line and a dirty light coffee brown coloured tube with dirty brass ends.

"What's that?" Eve asked.

"I don't know," said Jim "but this is what I've been looking for. I've been wondering about this thing since we found it when we went through Mom's stuff. I'm betting it's a map case, maybe German. I'm hoping someone can tell me at the show. But maybe it was used to carry something like a unit flag or maybe it was a spacer of some sort."

"Let's open it and see what's inside."

"I've tried. I can't unscrew the damn thing and these lids don't pop off. I'm afraid of breaking it if I put too much pressure on it," Jim replied. Studying the tube for a moment Jim looked at Eve and said, "It just seems like it's pretty well made, it's a quality piece; but what it is I'm totally blank on. I've tried looking in museums and on-line and I've never seen anything remotely like it. So, this is my last hope at solving the great Crenshaw mystery."

"Well, let's hope the mystery is solved then," she said.

They examined the tube. It seemed fairly stained and dirty. It had some markings on the side but they couldn't make out what they were. The ends were metal and appeared as if they would polish nicely.

"This thing's filthy. I'll get a couple of rags and some soap and water." Eve started for the workbench.

"No, no, we can't do that. They say you shouldn't clean an antique; it makes it less valuable. We better wait. I want an expert to see this thing."

"Jim, that's nuts."

"No it's not, any expert will tell you that."

"Name one."

"That fat guy on TV, he says that all the time," Jim began to grin.

"You're making that up…but okay." She looked at Jim and smiled back. "Just wrap that thing up before you put it on my car's carpet."

"Okay, okay, you've got a deal," Jim said as he began putting the various items on the attic floor back in the box.

"That's all you're taking? It's a forty dollar ticket! We've got to take more than just that," she exclaimed.

"Well, I've got a couple of tools that I could get rid of. And, we could take this lamp," Jim smiled.

"The lamp? No, that's special." Eve laughed and backed down the ladder.

Chapter 3

Louis XVI studied the scene outside the rain-streaked window. The lead lined windowpanes distorted the view of the ornate gardens of the Château de Versailles. He didn't see the distortion, he didn't see the gardens. He simply stared in the direction of the Hotel des Menus Plaisiers. The afternoon was cold, gray, wet. It seemed as if a dark cloud simply grew from the horizon, centered on that damned hotel. The cloud expanded up and over him. It closed in around him, through him and squeezed his heart so that it was hard to breath; even harder to think. And now, more than ever he needed to think.

Things were going badly and he knew it. It was a slow, rumbling avalanche and it was coming right at him. Insults had been shouted. Shouted at him! Things were said in the newspapers and on handbills. Most of France had suffered poor harvests, the Treasury was empty, and his wife was making a mess of things. A raucous group of Parliaments, the councils in each region, had demanded action. That fool, François de Paule de Barentin, had encouraged a general meeting with the nobility, the clergy and the people, an Estates-General. It was a rarely used thing, it would be the first since 1619. And now, there they were, assembled in that damned hotel. Things were not calmer; they were worse. The Estates-General was a disaster. The whole thing was a mockery to his reign.

He had lost control from the beginning. His advisers had no advice of course, worthless fools. They simply made matters worse. The commoners had not understood their role. They even tried to sit in the front of the theater! These uncultured fools didn't even recognize the protocol of such a meeting. The rules for the conduct and proceedings were clearly established in L'Etiquette of 1614. The clergy and nobility were to sit in the front, dressed in the formal regalia defined by their station in the nobility. The representatives of the Third Estate; landsmen, tradesmen and minor members of the nobility were to sit at the back; far away from the throne as befit their standing. It was simply the way things were done.

That had been the first issue, harangued and argued with but finally overcome. It had been, well…uncomfortable.

Then Barentin began with a procedural process formalizing the rules for the conduct of the assembly. The fool completely misread the crowd. He talked for hours, forgot what he was about and tried to get right to the financial situation of the country and address taxes. It resulted in a near riot. They wanted to talk about procedures. Louie had already agreed to double representation for the commoners. He had made a major concession. Was that not enough? Surely that had no impact on the procedures for votes on issues before the Estates-General. Each estate would vote by orders – thus each estate had an equal voice. That was certainly fair; he did not see an issue. Individual votes would apply only insofar as how the total order voted. To do otherwise, was contrary to the rules. Besides that, well, damn-it, he was the King.

Last week these fools had formed the Communes. What the hell was that? Worse, they had invited him to participate! Participate! Of course he had refused, what choice did he have? This was an action against God! He was King and a representative of God. It could not stand!

Finally, his Councilors understood; military force would be necessary. He didn't want to do that to his own people. Yes, it might work. No, he couldn't do that. He vacillated. He couldn't decide. Now even that seemed to be slipping away. What was happening?

He could sense a growing danger. It was out there, perhaps in this black cloud of mist sweeping up from the river Somme. It pushed down on him and his Palace. It crept in, hidden on the back of that mist. He could not stop it; he didn't know how to fight it. But he knew, he knew that change, danger and, perhaps death itself was stalking him. He could feel it, sense it and it chilled him. His stomach had tightened; a taste of bile had risen in his throat and was with him day and night. He had waited long enough; he would not be irresolute about this, now was the time. Now he needed to protect the throne and his son.

And that was the purpose of this afternoon's meeting. Was he being prudent? A coward? Or, realist? He hadn't decided, and he no longer had time to think of it. The heavy clap of boots on stone echoed behind him. He glanced one more time in the

11

direction of that hateful hotel, noticed the rain had increased. An omen? He turned to face Lieutenant General Nikolaus Luckner.

Luckner was a German. And, as such he couldn't rid himself of his German accent. He was one of the few men Louis had ever heard who could make the beautiful French language sound hard and rough. He was tall and weathered having spent his life under saddle. Louis supposed he could be called a good-looking man. Those looks and the size of his purse assured him of a warm bed each night. His military expertise was without question though in a few short years he would, not for the first time, change his loyalties. He was well educated, having studied with the Jesuits of Passau. His military experience was extensive, and to say varied understated it. He had served with the Bavarian, Dutch and Hanoverian armies. He had fought as a commander of Hussars during the Seven Years War against Louis' father. Now however, he seemed to have found a home in the French army. He was a strange pick for the task at hand the King thought. But, the two had an odd closeness that seemed more a function of nature than of their personalities. Was he a friend? Louis thought not, but he was no enemy. In any case, here he stood, looking directly at the King.

Luckner hadn't yet made his obedience; no sign of acknowledgment, he simply stared at the King. It irritated Louis, but he didn't have time to make a point of it. After a moment's pause, Louis spoke, "Nikolaus, I have a most delicate task for you."

"At your command sire," Luckner said.

The king smiled in spite of himself. Luckner never used the honorarium "Sire", it sounded ironic, fake and contrived coming from him. Yet, perhaps the seriousness of the day had made itself known to him. Who could know? He looked hard at his General. What was in the man's soul? Could he be trusted? The choice had been made, he continued.

"I believe there is some danger on the horizon. The communes seem to reject the authority of the King and it will take some time to reassert that understanding."

"Have you considered simply putting them to the sword?" Luckner asked fully expecting to be sent out to do just that.

"I have. Yet the countryside would not bear it. The people would rise up against me. No, it is better to work this out. But, there are some…" He paused, his face grew dark. No, not dark. Something else, Luckner couldn't put his finger on it. "I think we will have some difficult days," the king said more to himself than to his General.

Louis turned to the window. The dusk was deepening into night. The rain had steadied and except for the pattern inlaid in the marble courtyard, the Cour de Marbre, he couldn't see anything. He thought about that, yes, the scene was blurred outside as well as in. He was quiet for a long moment. Luckner became uncomfortable. What was happening to this King? The man needed to stiffen his spine, put the leaders of this crisis to the block and be done with it. He was about to interrupt the silence when the King turned. He seemed to have found a bit of strength.

"My son, Louis-Joseph, will die tonight. An announcement will be made at dawn. His death will be attributed to tuberculosis. It will fit well with his illness of last year. You are to take the Dauphin, along with a woman of the Queen's choosing away from Paris. My suggestion is to Montmedy or Sedan Castle, but you may have better knowledge. He must not be recognized or his very existence known until the Estates-General is successfully closed."

General Luckner knew what this meant, but remained silent. Instead he nodded his head in agreement, but inwardly he wondered if it ever would be "successfully closed." Nevertheless, this was a prudent decision and a minor ruse that could be explained in due course. "Of course, it shall be done my friend," he said.

The King again turned to the window. Over his shoulder he said, "Things will never be the same…" He grew thoughtful. Luckner stood in silence.

"Sire?" The irony was gone.

Louis turned, looked directly into Luckner's eyes and said, "Take my son's Letters of Royal Patent and funds for a long stay."

The King looked past his General. Silence filled the room. Luckner knew this was not the time to interrupt the King, he focused on the man's eyes. They were heavy; he looked tired. No, not tired…they were, what? Dead?

"And, Nicklous, I need you to take some other things. Remove "La Joyeuse", the Coronation Crown, and the Holy Ampulla with my son. Ensure only your most trusted men accompany you…tell no one, save, in good time, the Dauphin."

Luckner's face hardened; his grey eyes narrowed. He knew now what was in the King's mind. "Sire, I'm sure it will not come to that. The crown is safe with the House of Bourbon."

"I'm not so sure. In any case, do this for me."

Lieutenant General Nikolaus Luckner, for the first time, took his adopted King's hand and kissed the royal ring. He bowed, walked backward for five paces, turned and with crisp military bearing, walked out of the room.

Louis the sixteenth slumped. A wave of sadness; the sadness of a parent losing a child, not a King losing a kingdom, swept over him. He turned to the window once more. He knew. He knew deep in his soul that he would never see his son again.

Chapter 4

Waco, Texas

10 August 1917

The 32nd Infantry Division under Major General James Parker had been assembled from the National Guard units of Wisconsin and Michigan. Some of its elements had deployed with General John "Black Jack" Pershing in his pursuit of the Mexican border raider, Poncho Villa. Thus, the Division was experienced in large troop movements and the issues associated with supplying a large, mobile group of men and machines.

Commanding General Parker was an experienced and intelligent soldier. Unlike many military men of his generation he paid close attention to world politics and technological innovations in addition to the more traditional study of military history. As early as 1915 he felt certain the United States would be drawn into the conflict just starting in France and spreading across the Western Hemisphere. His estimations proved prophetic. When a German diplomatic message, the 'Zimmermann note,' fell into United States hands exposing Germany's attempted alliance with Mexico against the United States the country quickly abandoned its neutral policies. The United States declared war in April 1917.

Parker had been certain his division would be one of the first sent into action. He had already set his mind to the issues of moving this huge organization from here to there and keeping it in action once assembled on foreign soil.

In his youth, Parker had been taught that an Army was dependent on hay and the feed bag. That was nearly true today, only hay and the feed bag had been replaced with gasoline and spare parts. And, now one more item had been added to the list, mechanics.

Mechanics were few and far between, so General Parker decided to teach his own. And, he knew that moving a Division

15

was difficult and slow. He wanted it fast and easy; so beginning in the summer of 1916 he had his men pack and unpack trucks, tear down and rebuild engines, change tires, overhaul weapons, move, shoot and do it all again. They marched, they exercised, and they attended classes. They could strip and reassemble their new 1903 Springfield rifles blindfolded. They could disassemble their trucks and reassemble them.

The training in the heat of west Texas was brutal. The men from Wisconsin and Michigan suffered. Most had been struck down with heat exhaustion at least once, several more than once. One man had died of heat stress. But the training never let up.

Corporal John Turner rolled over in his bunk and looked over the side. "Oushel, I'm telling you, this is the hottest summer I ever been through. I ain't never been this hot; I swear Hades itself ain't this hot, nooo, it ain't."

Turner had joined the Army after a fight with his father. "Pup" as his father had called him had accompanied his Uncle on a trip to Chicago when he was thirteen. He had seen the big city and wanted no part of being a dairy farmer after that. By the time he was sixteen he'd quit school and was planning his escape. The next year he announced he was leaving and his father had erupted. Six months later he was in Chicago, penniless and, when he could sneak past the owner, sleeping in a barn. It only took a week of Chicago winter to convince him that he could crawl back to his father and admit he was beaten or join the Army. The Army looked like the better option.

"I swear if I take apart another truck engine I'll go crazy. I'm telling you John, I've seen the insides of every motor in the division!" Oushel Crenshaw replied.

Oushel and John had become good friends over the past several months. Oushel admired John; he was older, had been in the Army six months longer and knew how everything worked. John was where someone went to find out the latest news. John was someone who knew about things, he was smart. Oushel was an only child. His mother had died of measles when he was four. His father worked as a lumberjack and they followed the tree line around northern Michigan. It couldn't last, eventually the trees were all gone and his father went to Detroit hoping to land a job with Mr. Ford. The day Oushel turned seventeen, he told his father that he didn't want to work in the factory and he was joining

16

the Army. Six weeks later he was on a train for the first time in his life, headed to Waco, Texas.

In early November John announced that they were "on the list." Oushel wasn't sure exactly what that meant, but didn't want his friend to think him stupid so he didn't ask. A day and two trips through the chow line later he had it figured out, they were going to France. Everyone wanted one last leave.

"Think the General will let us take leave before we go? I'd like to see my Dad," Oushel asked John that evening. He was a little embarrassed about asking, but he did want to see his father. They'd been close for his entire life. Now he was afraid he'd never see him again.

"Ain't no way. He can't have us trying to git home and back. Suppose orders come down for us to move right now. No, I seen this before, we ain't gettin' no leave." Turner rolled a cigarette, licked the paper and twisted the ends.

"Well, I'm asking the Captain anyway."

"Ask all you want, he ain't gonna let you go."

Oushel thought about that. John was probably right; at least what he said made sense.

"I could take the train. It would only be a week, maybe ten days."

"Oush, it ain't possible. The Captain got his orders and they say no leave for nobody. You ain't goin.'"

A day later Oushel tried anyway. John was right, no leave was granted. The 32nd Infantry Division began to move to Europe in December. In January they suffered their first casualties when a German U-boat sank a troop ship carrying elements of the transportation section. By February the Division was scattered across the ports and bases of England and southern France. It took three weeks for the Division to reform. Several of the more junior officers complained the war would be over before they saw action.

The Germans launched a major offensive, with a hundred thousand men in March. In April the Division went into action. The majority of the officers didn't live to see the summer.

BETRAYAL IN THE LOUVRE

Available in either traditional paperback or on your e-reader today!

*Enjoy a longer excerpt or purchase this and
other books by HJ Gaudreau at
www.hjgaudreau.com*

www.ingramcontent.com/pod-product-compliance
Lightning Source LLC
Chambersburg PA
CBHW022137170626
46807CB00005B/1977